Scarlet Day Walker

Christopher Galvez

Chapter One

Dark Times

Belgium, 1991

They were late reaching the port and although they had finally arrived neither Erik nor his female companion could stop running any time soon. They could feel it getting closer—too close; a shadow that moved faster than the speed of light, a predator that had every intention of brutally killing them. It had come as no surprise. He knew that he'd have to answer for his indiscretions; his willful violation of the convocation's order. His plan seemed achievable. A stretch, but within grasp.

For miles it had searched for them from the sky, its eyes far better than any human's. One of the ancients is what Erik suspected, making it the most deadly killer even for his kind. Outrunning it was impossible; outsmarting though—maybe. The best chance of surviving was hiding, but hiding and they would miss their ship and if that happened they would be stuck in Belgium and would die anyway. If that could be prevented, he wanted his best to try and stop it. After all, he had so much to live for, but everything deep inside him warned that his time was close to running out.

What had helped was the blizzard and the number of people that were on the streets. The temperature had already fallen to zero degrees, but that hadn't stopped quite a few people from getting out and running necessary errands before the storm worsened and kept them inside their homes. Now that they had reached the port, Erik hoped that their oversized fur lined coats with the hoods cinched closed to hide their identities would make them blend in with the dock workers. A fiery red lock of hair slipped out of the opening of his companion's hood.

Erik smiled when he saw it.

She was perfect. A spitting image.

Needing to get going because neither of them had a moment to spare; they searched the sky then the buildings that sat at the start of the port. When they saw no shadows, they hurried. With every step their boots sank into the snow and slowed their progress. But they had to try. They had to live, but how when the shadow had already arrived at this same location?

"Should we split up?" the woman asked.

"No," Erik answered swiftly. "We make it together or we don't make it all."

The redheaded woman gave a swift nod and sprinted ahead.

Off in the distance, cranes lifted freight containers to load several docked ships. It's there they saw the shadow again, moving swiftly through the falling snow with large wings that could become sharp enough to slice through anything like a long heated blade, much like dark clouds cloaking the port floor.

Erik studied the maze of freight containers and knew that slinking in and out between them would be the best place to hide and also keep moving. Grabbing the woman's hand to make certain they weren't separated, he moved fast, impressed that his companion could keep up because his speed matched the speed of the predator flying through the white sky.

"Kuda my idem?" the woman asked. *Where are we going?*

"Rozovyy korabl," Erik answered. A pink freighter was what they needed to find, but for now the freight containers hid a lot of their view—containers that were so closely stacked together that both of them had to walk sideways before they could reach the next stack of containers and keep going.

A horn echoed in the distance. One of the freighters would soon set sail. Erik glanced at his watch and knew it would be the ship he was trying to reach. "Pochti gotovo. Idti!" *Almost there. Go!*

They moved as quickly as they could, passing one aisle of containers after another. In no time they had only one more left turn and the ship should be visible. Erik ran faster, his and his companion's speed so rapid that dockworkers didn't have a chance of seeing them. They were close. Wind swept over and darkened everything around them as it swooped down. Erik could see pink winking at them behind several containers. He and his companion had traversed the massive yard of the docks in less than a minute. A good thing since both of them were running out of time.

They came to the end of the last aisle when Erik let out a sigh of relief. The Guru One sat a short distance off. A horn sounded again followed by a burst of boiler steam as the Guru One slowly pulled away from the dock. If they hurried, they could jump high enough to reach the main deck. But would they be safe or would it see them and follow them on board in which case every passenger and crew would lose their lives?

Erik couldn't risk it. He just couldn't.

"What are you waiting for?" his companion asked with furrowed brows, strands of red hair blowing in the wind.

Erik let out a breath and lowered his gaze. Maybe it had all been wishful thinking. That he'd even discovered that the leaders of the convocation had learned about his secret had been sheer luck on his end. He stared at the woman standing next to him. Three weeks ago she'd been human. She was carefully selected and vetted. It had been then that his world had fallen apart. Five years of wedded bliss and no one had been the wiser. He had managed to even keep the secret from his beloved wife. Not until three weeks ago did she find out. But it was for her own good.

"Maybe we can fight," he suggested.

His companion had no fear. Newborns of her kind rarely did. He knew her decision when she searched the containers and dock for their enemy. As if it had been summoned, it lowered fast from the gray sky in great speed and landed directly before them. The ground shook like an earthquake beneath their feet.

Wings flared behind the creature's back, the motion so rapid that in a millisecond his enormous wingspan was revealed; tall wings of almost gray, translucent flesh and held together by connective tissues that looked a lot like bones with sharp deadly tips. It happened swiftly.

Instinctively, they both took several rapid steps back; eyes bulging. The temperature didn't affect him; not even the slightest shiver. Like Erik had suspected, the convocation had sent one of the ancients. An enforcer. When Erik realized this, he looked at his companion and spoke softly.

"I'm sorry. Choosing to fight had been a mistake. What I should have told you to do was run and hide."

Another booming horn sounded as the Guru One pulled further away from the dock.

Erik eyed his enemy and spoke first. "Viktor, I—"

Viktor shushed Erik, then gave a shake of his head while pressing a finger against his lips. Erik cocked his head and peered past Viktor at the Guru, now half the size and continually shrinking as it picked up speed and took on the sea. The chance of escape gone.

"You know why I'm here, yes?" Viktor asked, but didn't wait for an answer.

Erik's eyes trailed to the ground. He stood brave and erect. His shoulders pressed back and his head held high. His hand gripped hers as he whispered, "I love you."

Erik closed his eyes and waited for the inevitable at the same time that a young woman on the main deck of the Guru stood between two towers of shipping containers, freezing although she had bundled in layers of winter clothing. She stared anxiously at the docks and watched the three figures get smaller with every passing second.

When one of the figures had fallen from the sky, she stared on in disbelief and fright. Some kind of fight is what she had expected; her heart raced faster and faster as she waited for it, but instead of a fight it happened very swiftly. The wings pulled in front of the creature like a pair of scissors, their sharp tips slicing the necks of Erik and his companion as easily as a searing hot knife through a thick stick of butter.

Blood sprayed the air as Erik's and his companion's heads separated from their bodies. The creature grabbed the heads with both hands as his mighty wings were hidden again inside his spine. After examining the faces he held, he dropped the heads next to their bodies. As his hand reached out, fire extended from it and lit the corpses on fire. The flames were high. The creature walked casually through the flames and disappeared.

The woman sank back to the floor of the main deck and covered her mouth with both hands. The wind sliced through her clothing as she tucked her fiery red hair beneath her hooded coat. The Guru One was 5,823 nautical miles from its destination and in twenty-four days if all went well the ship would dock in New Orleans.

Chapter Two

Darkness

New Orleans, 2020

Katalina breathed a sigh of relief as she approached her Tahoe. She scanned the empty parking lot and spied a lone vehicle in a dark corner. Her heart slammed against her chest out of nowhere. She pressed a button on her key fob that unlocked only her driver's door. Again, her head swiveled before opening the door. Once inside, she immediately tapped the lock button on the inside of the door panel and all locks electronically activated. She jammed her back into the cushioned seat and enjoyed the silence. She drew deep breaths in and out, trying to slow her heart rate.

Seconds went by before screams broke through the silence. Not piercing screams. Screams in her head. A woman's scream. Katalina's hearing was acute—always. Sometimes, all her senses seemed to explode with intensity, amplified beyond human possibility. She didn't question it. She used those to her advantage, and it served her well as a detective.

Her Tahoe shook violently; the roof seemingly about to cave in as if someone or something fell on top of it. She grabbed her gun and pointed it toward the ceiling. She squeezed the trigger, prepared to blow holes in her precious roof. The vehicle shook. Loose gravel crunched just outside of her door. The pressure of a hard gust of wind echoed through the cab of her vehicle. Solid black was all her rearview mirror offered. A quick spin threatened to reveal whatever stood behind her SUV. Katalina reached for the door handle and gently tugged with her left hand.

Her door popped open with a cold steel slide forward at the ready; the sights on her gun glowed making a target acquisition that much easier. Left foot out followed by the right foot and a quick squat beside her open door. Her arms formed a perfect isosceles triangle with her weapon of destruction prepared to destroy whatever lies before it. It was quiet outside. She closed her eyes and listened. An apartment complex towered behind Irene's restaurant and Katalina took cautious steps toward it. She drew in a deep breath through her nose. The aroma was undeniable. She smelled blood.

At the forefront of her brain, she tried to rationalize. Who enjoys the smell of blood? Whose mouth waters at the sight of it?

Focus, Kat.

She tucked her gun against her chest and picked up her pace running up the stairwell like a snake following a heat source. Halfway up the fourth floor she slowed and extended her gun ahead. She stepped lightly up the last three steps and peeked around the balcony. The front door was open. The smell of iron was strong. Her stomach groaned, threatening to give away her stealthy approach.

Off in the distance, she heard police sirens that seemed to be getting louder—they were coming to her. She felt the prickling along the back of her neck as the hair stiffened. She sensed something was off. *I'm not alone*, she thought. She smelled the blood but felt something unexplainable. Katalina looked to her left. Nobody. She looked to her right. Nobody. She knew someone was there and she felt like she was being watched—maybe even baited. Each step she took, the feeling of a presence grew stronger. She knew exactly where to go. She'd never been in that apartment before, but she knew to go directly to the bedroom at the end of the hall.

Like a magnet, she was being drawn there. Her chest pounded. Her hands fought against her willpower to keep her gun steady, but they shook anyway. She somehow knew it was in there—drawing her in. Begging to be found or preparing to attack. Katalina inhaled and briefly held her breath before kicking the bedroom door open.

The force nearly blew the door off the hinges. A scream escaped her lips when she burst in. Her vision was as sharp as an eagle's. She saw a body on the floor in her peripheral, but the moment she entered a shadow captured her attention straight ahead. Her primal instinct took over and sent her chasing the fleeting shadow. It was eye-level and disappeared behind waving drapes that cloaked an open window.

"Police!" She shouted. Katalina advanced through a pool of blood, ignoring all crime scene protocol. Tunnel vision took over. She failed to sweep the residence for any threats. Instead of checking each room, she advanced ahead. Each step sloshed in blood-saturated carpet. She reached the open window and peered down. Outside the window was a four-story drop. No balcony. No ledge. Just a forty-foot drop. The moment she peered out of the window, the presence that drew her to the room had vanished.

"Hands up!" a burly voice from behind her shouted.

She knew it was a patrol officer. She heard his radio blaring the moment the cruiser entered the parking lot.

Katalina complied. "I'm a cop," she shouted. Her hands rose and she released the grip on her Glock. Her finger remained in the trigger guard, but the gun rotated upside down.

"Don't move!" the officer shouted.

She remained steadfast and controlled. She knew better than to contest. She wasn't ready to die—not at the hands of a fellow brother in blue. More footsteps trampled up the stairway—through the living room and into the hallway. Radios blaring, patrol officers speaking tactically—giving orders.

"You, cover wall number one. Once in, I'll go right. You peel left. Chavez, you cover our flank."

Katalina recognized the voices. It was one of the shifts from her precinct. Once they entered, the groans could be heard.

"What the fuck?" one officer cried.

She could hear his heart beating from across the room.

"Get it together," barked another. "Get detectives out here!"

The first officer in, who was giving Katalina the orders, was still zeroed in on his redheaded suspect who held a gun. "Turn around slowly," he ordered.

Katalina complied again. She was halfway turned when he recognized her.

"Oh, shit. Detective Andrews!" He lowered his gun and apologized.

Katalina rose to her feet and tucked her Glock back in her waistband. Since she was a detective, she was in charge and she wasted no time. "Everyone back out. You, tape the area off—begin on the balcony." She pointed to a young patrol officer. "You—" Next, she pointed at Xavier, the officer who held her at gunpoint just moments before. "—get a crime scene log started." Moments later, her partner arrived looking haggard and still asleep.

"Hey, Duce. Welcome to the party," she joked.

"What the . . . You look like shit. Did you decide to ignore professional standards and investigate this in your pajamas?" Benoit asked.

"Haha, very funny." Katalina shot Benoit a sarcastic look. "You know how I'm a shit magnet. Well . . ."

"You walked in on this? Randomly?"

"Not so randomly," she whispered. "I was drawn here."

Benoit squinted his eyes and focused on Katalina's eyes. "Okay. What do you have?"

"I just missed him."

"Him?" Benoit asked.

"I heard a woman's screams, and I entered a short time later. When I did, I felt the killer in this room. The moment I entered, the drapes waved and . . ."

"And what?" Benoit pressed.

"And nothing. It's as if he vanished into thin air." Katalina stared out the window toward the street below. Benoit stood beside her, peering outside. He poked his head outside and glanced left then right then up and down.

"There's no way anyone could have escaped this way. A four-story drop would likely kill anyone. Or at least immobilize them. There's nothing down there. Are you sure you didn't cross him on your way up?"

Katalina shook her head, her mouth opened as if to speak, but Benoit kept pressing.

"Maybe this happened much earlier, and he escaped through the front door. Once the coroner arrives, we'll have a better timeline of her death."

"Do you have a spare pair of gloves?" Kat asked Benoit. He dug in his back pocket and produced a pair of white nitrile gloves. Katalina stretched them over her fingers. When she released, it made a slapping noise. She giggled every time she put a new pair of gloves on. "Are you ready for your exam, Mr. Doucet?" she asked Benoit.

"Um, no, ma'am. I don't have to get my oil checked until I'm at least fifty."

The victim was a petite blonde with curly hair. She was nude. The skin beneath her forearm was sliced vertically and exposed her bone. Katalina knelt beside the victim and analyzed her body while Benoit searched the bedroom for identification cards. Her stomach growled again. A trickle of saliva escaped the corner of her mouth. The smell of fresh blood consumed her thoughts. She just wanted a taste. *Get it together, Kat*, she thought.

Katalina held the victim's arm and rotated it to study the wound closer. Her previously white glove, now bright crimson. *Just a taste.* She heard Benoit shuffling behind her as she studied the consistency of the blood on her gloved fingers. She rolled her index finger against her thumb and stared at it with awe. A quick scan; left then right provided her with a brief window to seize the moment. Katalina brushed the metallic gore against her mouth. She immediately licked her lips as the blood absorbed in her body. Instantly, she felt satisfied. Her face burned red with shame despite the euphoric feeling. Her already acute senses were enhanced. A rush of adrenaline coursed through her veins. That was her first taste of human blood.

"Here we go," Benoit studied a driver's license. "Sheila Melancon. White female. Twenty-three years old. Looks like she works for Ladybugs Cleaning Service. She was a maid."

Katalina ignored Benoit. She heard him but was slipping into a trance. Her body was on the verge of convulsing with pleasure.

"Kat."

Silence.

"Kat! You okay?"

Katalina's face flushed with embarrassment. Her concentration now broken, she rose from her knees and stood erect.

Soon a uniformed officer called for a detective. "Detective! Hey! I think I found something!"

Kat and Benoit raced toward the officer who was standing in the living room holding a handwritten note.

I need you. I want you. I would hurt for you. I would leave this world for you if I can't have you. My eternal love.

"Suicide note," Benoit mumbled.

"It sure looks like a suicide. The razor blade is still in her left hand," Katalina said.

"Didn't you hear screaming, Kat?"

Katalina nodded. "I did. That's what tipped me off."

"Why did you suspect someone was in here? It sounded like you were insinuating that someone was here with Sheila."

Katalina stared out of the bedroom window that initially drew her in like a magnet. Something was gripping her attention. "Duce, could someone have—"

"Kat. There's a suicide note. She still has the razor. Didn't we just agree that it was definitely a suicide?" Benoit pled.

Katalina peered at the open window. "Yeah, but, Duce—"

Benoit gave Katalina a confused look. "Don't let Sergeant Daigle hear you say shit like that. He'll bust your ass back to working petty thefts and burglaries. I need you here with me, in homicide."

Katalina's face soured when Benoit mentioned the sergeant. She stared out the window at the black night. Little golden dots scattered through the fog, doing their best to illuminate the night. Her mind drifted to an uncomfortable time.

Katalina stared outside and said to Benoit, "I won't mention that to the Salty Sarge."

But something had drawn her to that window. Suddenly, it felt like she was being watched again. She listened. She inhaled. Nothing. No sounds to analyze. No smells to offer any hints. And nothing visibly out of the ordinary. The hair on the back of her neck stood up. Her heart skipped a beat and she felt scared. Katalina seldom felt scared. It was close—watching her. She knew it. She felt it. She recognized the anxiety and was drifting into deep thought when Benoit snapped her out of it.

"Hey, Kat. You okay? You seem checked out. I'm starting to get worried."

Katalina's trance broke as she walked into the bathroom. *Get it together.* "I'm good. Just processing everything, Duce."

Katalina's eyes met Benoit's in the mirror. He stared at the glass with a blank expression as if he was in a trance. His lips parted slightly but no words escaped. He was frozen. Kat heard his rapid heart rate.

"Duce!" She leaned into Benoit and jammed her shoulder into his enough to startle him. He gasped when she bumped him, breaking his trance, and turned to face her. His eyes told a story of sheer terror. His eyebrows arched upward, and his mouth remained slightly agape.

"Duce. What's up? Are you okay? Now *I'm* worried." Katalina grabbed his hand and pulled him out of the bathroom into the hall.

"The mirror. I—I saw . . ." Confusion painted Benoit's face, something Katalina had never seen before.

"What about the mirror? What did you see?" Katalina stepped back inside of the bathroom and studied the mirror. "I don't see anything strange, Duce. Just a kick-ass detective staring back at me."

"What are you?" Benoit asked.

Katalina's eyes furrowed. "Don't give me that shit, Duce. I'm not in the mood. I'm tired. I look like shit and I really need a diet Coke or another shot of bourbon."

Benoit pulled Kat aside and whispered, "Kat, you had no reflection in the mirror."

She looked dumbfounded and waited for a witty quip to follow or a shit-eating grin; nothing. She quickly realized Benoit wasn't joking and stepped back inside the bathroom; Benoit shoulder-to-shoulder with her peered forward at his reflection, then turned and looked at Kat beside him.

Katalina's head shook in confusion. "You need some sleep, buddy. C'mon, let's wrap this up."

A uniformed officer announced, "Hey, detectives! A neighbor said she saw a man and a woman enter the residence earlier tonight."

Benoit seemed to gather his bearings. He stared at Katalina with curiosity. Katalina said, "Hey, Duce. I'm taking lead on this one, okay? Can you just take some preliminary photos before forensics gets here? I'll start canvassing the area and talking to neighbors. I'm ready to get out of here. It's almost sunup and I need some rest before heading into the office."

Chapter Three

Hunting Grounds

An enigmatic man with a cold stare and cocky scowl on his face sat at the far end of a slick bar topped with worn wood dampened by years of spilled beer and over-poured shots. Dmitri's eyes were dark—almost black, except for when the perfect light drew out hints of burnt sienna undertones. Dmitri was a night owl who loved the party life; and the hunt. He enjoyed the quaint little bars secretly hidden within the mystical city—especially those that were considered historical. Bourbon Street was always an option for an easy night cap, but Dmitri preferred the finer things in life. The hunt. The chase. He had been told how handsome he was his entire life by both men and women, and he knew it, so he saw no need to relegate himself to trash.

"Vodka, please," he told the bartender. Dmitri tapped the bar with his index finger as he ordered his drink, much like a poker player calling a hand.

"Straight?" the bartender asked. Dmitri's eyes were cold and filled with hate when they met his. The bartender mouthed the word "okay" and reached for a bottle of Grey Goose.

Dmitri's gravelly voice admonished the bartender. "No! Stoli. The bottle." The bartender's eyes grew large. His hands trembled. Something about Dmitri seemed to frighten him.

A heavy Cajun accent interrupted Dmitri's silence. "Mais, ain't you a breath of fresh air."

Two barstools over, a middle-aged lady turned to face Dmitri and offered an inviting smile. A cigarette was dangling from the corner of her mouth. Fine creases outlined her mouth from years of pursed lips gripping cigarettes. Her lipstick was a faded red, just hours before vibrant. Her skin was leathery as if she had tanned her entire life. Dmitri flashed a dapper smile and gave her a pity wink.

"I'm Missy. I ain't seen you in here before," she said. "You don't look like you're from round here."

"Dmitri. Lived here most of my life, nice to meet you."

"Mmm where's that accent from? Europe?"

"Perhaps. I travel a lot, but I call this place my home."

"Your entire life, huh? What's that, a whopping thirty years?" A white cloud enveloped Missy's face as she exhaled.

Dmitri's palms turned up as he shrugged. "Eh, feels like a century, his eyes never leaving his bottle."

Missy laughed, then spewed a wet textured cough. Her lungs struggled to work properly and sounded like she had bronchitis. "I know whatcha mean. Every day I wake up, I feel a hundred, but you don't look a day over thirty."

"That's awfully nice. I know it's not polite to ask a woman her age, but surely you mustn't be over forty." Dmitri knew better. He knew exactly who Melissa Boudreaux was. He knew she was forty-six even though she looked fifty-six. He knew she lived a hard life and loved picking up young men who fell on hard times and wanted a night with a stranger just to forget their miserable marriages.

"Merci," Missy said. "Smoke?" She pointed a pack of Marlboro Reds to Dmitri.

"No thanks. That shit'll kill you."

"Ain't that right," Missy mumbled. "And that?" She pointed to Dmitri's drink. She tried more small talk, but Dmitri was not giving her the attention she craved. Every question she asked, he gave a short one-word answer. Melissa wasn't his target. She was an easy score, but that wasn't Dmitri's style. He stole a glance at another woman seated at the far side of the bar. Her face bitter with disgust as she shook her head in disapproval.

"Would you excuse me, Missy?" Dmitri asked.

She waved Dmitri off as if he was a waste of her time. He smiled and disappeared to a pub table tucked in a dark corner of the bar. Dull yellow light painted half of the table, leaving him cloaked in darkness just behind the sheet of illumination. He grabbed his Stoli and a glass and took a seat with his back facing the wall. Moments later, Missy had a new young man buying her drinks. Dmitri heard their flirty banter from across the bar and could tell each had pent up sexual frustration by the direction of their conversation. Missy's new target's hands were deeply tanned except for the bright stripe around his left ring finger. They would certainly use one another later. *Ahh, the joys of primal lust*, Dmitri thought.

The front door opened, and two young women entered—one beaming with excitement. The other appeared to be dragged there by the former. They both wore black work pants that accented their curves. Miss Bubbly wore a white tee shirt that hugged her chest, revealing remnants of a dark bra beneath. Her hair was curly and blond. Her face was painted with unnecessary layers of makeup and she all but skipped her way inside. Her friend, a brunette, wore a work shirt that had the words Ladybug Maids embroidered across the left breast with a white tee shirt peeking from beneath.

The couple took a seat at the bar. The bartender delicately placed a glass in front of Blondie and poured her a colorful mixed drink. He winked at her and made small talk. Dmitri listened to their conversation and began to admire the quiet conservative brunette who ordered bottled water. He licked his lips and touched the tip of his tongue on his incisors.

"You really should lighten up." Blondie's eyebrows bounced twice with anticipation as her head made an obvious jerk toward the handsome bartender. She bit her bottom lip and mouthed the words, He's cute.

"Sheila, you promised only one drink. I have to get home." The brunette's face was pouty.

"You're such a cock block," Sheila teased.

"Hey, you can stay, but I've got to change and get ready for work."

"Oh, my fucking gosh, Angela! You seriously need to get laid. You work two jobs and never enjoy yourself!"

"Sorry if I don't have men bending over backwards to pay my bills for me." Angela's words were fierce yet honest. She had no desire to sugarcoat anything.

Sheila must have known it. She shrugged and said, "A girl's gotta do what a girl's gotta do."

Angela peeked at her watch. Her feet bounced violently on the brass footstep that lined the base of the bar.

Sheila's elbows planted firmly on the bar and she leaned over to whisper something in the bartender's ear. Her feet dangled as she bent over the bar. His face stretched with a smile and he whispered back, "I get off at 2:30."

One of Sheila's legs bent at the knee. Her heel almost touching her butt. Giddy. Excited.

"You're on your own, girl." Angela snatched her water and darted for the door.

"Hey!" Sheila yelled. "Just think. Later, when you're wiping that old man's ass, mine will be getting spanked. YOLO!" Sheila's giggle squealed like a schoolgirl.

Angela's face twisted with disgust. "How are we even friends?"

Dmitri poured himself another glass of vodka and sat back in his dark corner. He no longer paid any attention to the conversation Sheila had with her lucky boy toy. He had heard enough. He pondered for a few moments on which young lady he would visit but couldn't decide. Dmitri plunged his pale hand deep inside of his pants pocket and retrieved a shiny gold coin. One side had a bearded Nicholas II. The other, an intricate crest. Dmitri flipped the gold five Roubles coin and caught it in his hand. He peered at his old, bearded friend and said, "Blondes have more fun, but brunettes remember it the next day."

Dmitri poured himself glass after glass, studying his prey from across the barroom. The time was just before one in the morning when Sheila began to yawn. The bar had become busy and her previously flirty Beau was consumed with the demands of his other patrons. Dmitri's eyes moved from Sheila, and spied the lone middle-aged woman still seated at the end of the bar. Her eyes connected with his, winked, and then dismissed him as she consumed her vodka.

Sheila stood up and adjusted her bra before paying her tab. She approached Dmitri with a confident stroll. The two locked eyes. Sheila's jaw fell slightly—her lips parted before she bit her bottom lip. Once at the door to the ladies' room, she turned to face Dmitri. He was watching her. She caught him and winked before disappearing inside the restroom.

Dmitri shook his head and thought, *This is too easy*. Minutes later, Sheila emerged with bright, glossy, red lipstick. Her hair slightly teased and her perfume stronger than when she entered. Their eyes met once again. Each with flames of desire fueling their drive. Sheila walked with calculated steps. Each was elegant and sexy as though she was prancing down a runway. As she passed Dmitri's table, she brushed it with her hand—her eyes never leaving his. She floated across the room until reaching the exit, but not before turning back to steal one last glance at the tall, dark-haired mystery man.

As she looked back, she deliberately flipped her hair over her shoulders. He smiled and gave a gentle nod before she disappeared into the dark night.

Dmitri approached the bar and paid the bartender. He waited a few moments before leaving the bar. Once outside he drew a deep breath in. His prey was not far. Her scent lingered like a blood trail, making his track too easy. He peered up at the crisp sky making way for a beautiful bright moon and smiled. Like a bloodhound, Dmitri took in Sheila's smell and walked ahead. The sidewalk was empty. The night was silent except for the occasional cab that raced by. Dmitri was an expert at tracking, paying attention to the change in winds, the odors left behind by surfaces touched by his mark, and the sounds offered by domesticated pets notifying him of recent nearby movement.

***

Every few steps Sheila took, she sneaked a peek behind her. Each turn, a disappointment. At one point, she even stopped along the sidewalk and waited. She knew how dangerous it was after dark in New Orleans, but she didn't care. The mission was her priority and physical satisfaction with the stranger was the mission.

Sheila entered her apartment building feeling frustrated. A quick glance back at the street revealed nothing. Discouraged, she was hoping to catch a glimpse of a tall, dark, and handsome man stalking her, but no such man was there. Her night was supposed to have ended with the company of a man. Much like a tigress ready to pounce, she had a deep yearning for satisfaction that felt unfulfilled. Sheila had a drive for sex that was unmatched by any man she had ever met before. Oftentimes, Sheila felt physically and mentally stressed when she went without releasing her sexual frustration. She knew exactly what she wanted and how to achieve it; seldom was she left with pent up sexual energy.

Clothes fell to the floor as she undressed and turned the shower on. Steam filled her bathroom as her mind drifted to the handsome man seated in the dark corner of the bar. She wondered if he was a regular there. She wondered if he would be there the next time she went. She was intrigued. Most of the time when she gave off signals like she did, men all but tripped over their feet just to capture her attention. But not him.

She soaped up, scrubbing the smoky bar aroma from her skin, careful not to wet her hair. The scent of cucumber melon soon invaded her senses and brought a smile to her face. Her mind drifted to a comforting place as the hot water massaged her breasts and rolled down her torso. She fantasized about the enigmatic knight in shining armor she had spied earlier. Her eyes closed as her hands lathered her soft skin with soap until all of her felt slick. The water soon grew cold—an indication that she'd lost track of time and had to cut her fantasy short.

The towels she used to dry her skin were soft and fluffy; a comforting shudder of pleasure made her smile as the feeling of clouds brushed against her body. Bed time meant she put on a pair of loose athletic shorts and a tank top. The stranger's square jaw remained etched in her mind as her thoughts raced. Every time she closed her eyes, he invaded her thoughts. She wanted badly to return to the bar in hope that he'd still be there. She stared at her front door, silently praying to hear a knock. She slipped into a role-playing fantasy as her mind was seized by lustful thoughts.

Something kept her focus staring at the door, like an invisible magnetic force on its other side. She took one step closer to the door and waited. She was calm. Comfortable. Relaxed. She reached for the doorknob cautiously, much like one would when expecting to face a blazing fire. Her hand gripped the knob and rotated it. The door cracked, revealing just a sliver of her face as she peeked through the thin opening. Her knees buckled.

Dmitri stood at her door. Something about his scent drove Sheila mad. His eyes told a story that she needed to hear. His smile was curious yet inviting. As Sheila stared into Dmitri's eyes, her walls all but disintegrated. She had no inhibitions. She was hypnotized by his authority—his every command. He charmed her without speaking. Sheila felt like a submissive slave, eager to please her dominant master. She stepped back and opened the door, "Please come inside."

Dmitri entered and caressed her shoulder. "Thank you for inviting me, my dear. My name is Dmitri."

She didn't remember speaking to Dmitri but was too overwhelmed by lust to try and figure anything out. She stepped closer to him, her eyes never breaking contact with his. She was inches from him, waiting for permission to touch him.

The carotid artery on her neck thumped. Dmitri smiled as the skin of her neck pulsated. He grabbed the back of her head, running his fingers through her hair and forcefully pulled her head back, extending her tender neck in a more desired position. A whimper escaped her parted lips as her eyes rolled back in her head. At that moment, she was prepared to do anything for his affection.

He knew it.

She knew it.

Dmitri ran his nose across her neck and took in her aroma. Goosebumps surfaced on her skin as his exhale tickled her like the softest feather. He gently grabbed her beneath her chin and arched her head upward toward his face. Her eyes remained closed. Dmitri pressed his lips against hers. His hand slid down her neck while they kissed.

"How badly do you want me, love?" Dmitri asked.

She whispered, "I want you. Now."

"Now? Mmm, my dear, that's no way to ask." Dmitri's fingers trailed down her neck and onto her chest just above her tank top. His finger slid inside the tank top and he tugged down, exposing her breasts. "You were saying?"

"Please. I want you now," Sheila begged, her breath soft and hot.

Dmitri nodded in approval. "First, you must tell me what you would do in order to obtain what you so strongly desire." He released the top of her shirt and ran his hand down the outside of her tank top until his hand touched the top of her shorts. "Will you do something for me first?"

Sheila nodded in anticipation. "Anything."

"Prove it to me. Write me a letter. I want to know what you would do to achieve ecstasy. Would you hurt for me?"

Sheila nodded without hesitation.

Dmitri smiled. "Good. Would you leave this Earth for me?"

"I would," she said.

"Write it for me while I disrobe, my love," Dmitri said as he unbuttoned his pants.

Sheila retrieved a pen and a sheet of paper.

"Something poetic," Dmitri insisted.

Soon, Dmitri was fully undressed. He watched as Sheila finished writing. Her hand trembled as she set the pen down. She pulled her tank top over her head and dropped it to the floor. She slid her shorts off and stepped out of them while staring at Dmitri the entire time.

With lightning speed, Dmitri embraced Sheila. One hand held the back of her head as he delicately pressed his lips against hers. The other hand pressed against her navel. What felt like magical fingers trailed down her torso then between her thighs.

First, she moaned, then screamed. Screams of pleasure. Screams of pain. Screams of ecstasy. Screams of euphoria. Every touch was applied with perfect pressure, delivering orgasmic tingles throughout her erogenous zones. Sheila had never felt pleasure like that before in her life. Every touch and every kiss sent joy through her entire body.

Chapter Four

Sensory Overload

C'mon universe, give me a good parking space. Something close to the entrance, in case I have to escape in a hurry. Katalina entered the parking lot of her favorite Italian restaurant, seeking for the perfect parking space; any parking space. The French Quarter in New Orleans is as unforgiving as any metropolitan city. She scanned the parking spaces from St. Charles Street and chewed her lip with anticipation. As if the universe granted her silent wish, she spied a newly vacated parking space at the front of the restaurant. The spot was directly beneath a burning bright light.

Thank you, universe, she thought. Katalina reverse-parked her Tahoe. She slid the transmission in park and grabbed her phone. She opened the app and navigated to the latest communication between her and Peter.

"Dating gods, don't fail me now," she whispered. "I promise I'll be on my best behavior. Just send me a winner for once. Please!"

This would be her third date attempt after signing up on a dating app in a two-month span. Each as miserable as the one before. Katalina was different in many ways than most women her age. Sure, she was cynical and pessimistic, but she couldn't help but shake the feeling of being a freak. Her entire life she'd been better, faster, smarter, more competitive and despite being physically superior, she was never accepted.

She managed to find everything possibly wrong with each man she had recently dated. Her last date's fingernails were black with grease and grime caked beneath. The skin on his hands was also stained black. He was a machinist—a hardworking man who smelled like a mixture of plastic, chemicals, and lubricants, covered up with cheap cologne. A man who worked with his hands for fifteen hours a day. She had cringed at the thought of him running his filthy hands against her skin.

Her heart began to race when she noticed the time. Seven o'clock on the dot. She pulled her visor down and opened the vanity mirror. The lights from the visor made her porcelain face glow. Her blue eyes sparkled in the reflection. Her lips, a lush and shiny red. She checked her teeth and ensured her eyeliner was perfectly applied.

She touched her nose to her wrist and drew in her essence. *Shit, I smell like gunpowder!* She dropped her phone in her purse and dug around. *I hate this tiny purse! Ugh, why does fashion have to be such a pain in my ass?*

Hidden beneath her Glock 43, she retrieved a tiny spray bottle of Jessica Simpson perfume. *Oh, thank God!* She sprayed her wrists, then her neck, then her chest and smelled her wrist again. *Mmm, much better.*

Katalina sprayed two quick bursts in her ponytail and thought, *Fuck it, why not?* She exited her SUV and took note of her surroundings like a paranoid criminal on the run. Nobody lurking behind vehicles—good. No cars randomly running—good. Katalina straightened her fitted dress, brushed her hands down her hips and glanced at her reflection in the window. She stroked her long fire-red hair and thought, *You got this girl. He's just a man. He puts his pants on, one leg at a time just like everyone else. Here goes nothing!*

Katalina tugged on the door and stepped inside. The restaurant offered a chilly air-conditioned welcome, a much-needed reprieve from the humid, hell-like temperatures New Orleans was known for. She took in the raw garlic smell and almost let out a whimper—she loved garlic. She smelled red meat being grilled, boiled pasta, sautéed meatballs in tomato sauce and the sweet aroma of Tiramisu stored in the cooler.

"Welcome to Irene's. Will you be dining alone, or are you meeting someone?"

Katalina smiled at the young hostess. "I'm meeting someone, but I'm not sure if he's here yet."

The doors opened and a tall man entered. His hair was dark-brown, and his complexion was deeply tanned, but it was a natural skin tone. The man's eyes were the color of an overcast ocean sky—gray, maybe hazel, but in the restaurant's lobby, they were gray. He wore a shiny silver suit and shiny leather shoes. She recognized his face from the dating app. The moment his eyes met hers, he smiled, exposing a set of brilliant white teeth. *Nope. Too perfect on the outside. Something must be wrong inside.*

"Miss Andrews?" he asked.

Katalina blushed and thought, *Impressed. Okay, he's got manners—check. He's got the looks—check.* She nodded and said, "Please call me Katalina. Mr. DeLuca?"

He returned a sheepish but heart-melting smile. "I'm Peter, but my friends call me Pete."

The hostess gave a polite smile and a subtle nod before she spoke. "Follow me, please."

Katalina looked at Pete who took a half-step back and offered his right hand as if to say, *After you, my lady. So far, so good*, she thought. Katalina's cynicism was screaming at her. On one shoulder, her angel was squinting with dagger-filled eyes saying, "If it seems too good to be true, it normally is." On her other shoulder, a red devil was saying, "C'mon, this could be the one. Your clock is ticking, you know? Plus, did you smell him? Oh, my goodness!"

"This place is beautiful," he said. "I've never heard about it."

"The Italian cuisine is authentic," Katalina answered.

She was trying to be classy, but it wasn't something she was good at. She could be well-mannered and respectful, but she hadn't ever been considered classy. Mostly, her occupation drew the worst out of her. She'd been accused of being too blunt and oftentimes too realistic. She caught herself staring at his face, his eyes, his forehead, his lips, and his chin. Anyone in Peter's shoes would be flattered if their date were reveling at such beauty. Her apparent adoration likely intoxicated Peter.

Katalina wasn't consumed with Pete's dapper looks. She was studying his body language—searching for micro gestures, cues that tell a non-verbal story. Subconscious movements, unbeknownst to Peter, that provide crucial insight into his true thoughts.

Katalina remembered how amazed she was when she first learned how to read people. Many of the micro-gestures were twitches of nerves; a sign of distress, often a result of uncomfortable stimuli. She just had to ask the right questions and wait for the show. Although the skill had served her well professionally, it equally sabotaged her personal life.

The server, Vincenzo, arrived and took the order. His accent was a thick blend of Italian and creole—a unique New Orleans drawl.

Katalina badly wanted to order a bourbon-neat to loosen up. Something strong to comfort her nerves, but instead she smiled, batted her eyes and said, "I'd love a glass of wine. Red please." Pete's right eyebrow gently crept up. One side of his mouth cracked a large smile much like the Grinch. As fast as it twitched, it was gone. He likely didn't even know his face moved.

Katalina squinted her eyes and questioned Peter's intentions. *Why did he smile like that? What is he thinking about? Is he judging me? Does he think I'm a light-weight?*

"I'll have the same, thank you," Pete replied.

"I'll be right back with a basket of garlic bread. Pardon me." Vincenzo disappeared into the kitchen with urgency.

Katalina heard something vibrate from across the table. The device startled Pete and he nearly jumped. His right hand darted to his inside jacket pocket and retrieved his phone. Pete's eyes blinked rapidly, and he said, "I'm sorry, it's my mother." Pete drummed away on his phone and tucked it back in his jacket pocket. Soon, Vincenzo returned with a steaming basket of bread and a bottle of wine. He poured the couple each a glass and asked if they were ready to order.

"Try the veal," Katalina said, still studying his face. Without looking up from his menu, Pete pursed his lips and nodded. "I'll have a ribeye, rare," Katalina said. The waiter was jotting in a notepad and paused. His eyes met Katalina's as he paid close attention to her. "Bloody," she said.

"I guess I'll have the veal," Pete said. "No garlic. I'm… Allergic."

The waiter scribbled on his notepad, said, "Excellent choice!" and disappeared.

"So, tell me, Katalina. What do you do for a living?"

Katalina wasn't ready for that question. She grabbed her glass of wine and held it up to her face—swirling the maroon liquid courage. *Okay, Kat. This can go a couple of ways. One, I tell him the truth and he runs like Forrest Gump or two, I skate around the truth and start our potential relationship on a bed of lies.* Her eyes met his. His face was impatient until he cracked another devilish smile.

Lies it is! The Kat-devil perched on her right shoulder laughed and high-fived her. "I'm in customer service." *That's it. That's all you get,* she thought.

Pete smiled; Katalina's eyes squinted.

Why is he smiling? she thought. W*hat's he thinking? Stop it, Kat! Give him a chance!* "What do you do, Mr. DeLuca?" Katalina tipped her wine glass up, then grabbed the bottle and filled her glass up again.

Pete smiled. That one was different—less genuine. "I own a used car dealership."

"Hmm," Katalina replied.

Peter's face changed from smug to defensive but before he could protest, his chest vibrated again. He grabbed his cell phone. The light illuminated his perfect face. Again, he smiled while he punched the glass screen on his phone. He looked like an excited little boy when he texted.

"Your mother again?" Katalina asked, her tone laden with suspicion.

"Yeah, I'm a momma's boy. She's just checking on me. She told me to be careful because of all the crazies out there."

"You can't be too careful, can you?" Katalina said.

Vincenzo returned with a worried look on his face. His thick Italian accent spewed concern. "Oh, signora, mi dispiace! Your wine bottle is empty."

Katalina knew what he'd said in Italian. She spoke five languages. Vincenzo snatched the empty wine bottle and darted to the kitchen. He returned before Katalina or Pete could form a new sentence. He topped Katalina's glass off and glanced at Pete's. He was nursing the wine, probably enjoying it like wine should be.

"So, tell me about your mother," Katalina asked.

Pete's eyes met hers. He had a deer-in-the-headlights look. She zeroed in on his face and watched closely. Pete drew in a sip of wine before answering.

"My mother?" Pete asked.

Answering a question with a question—classic stalling tactic, Katalina thought. She answered, "MmmHmm" with a crinkled and curious forehead. "Yes, I'd love to know about the woman who raised you."

"Well, my father died when I was thirteen. I don't know how she did it—raising all of us."

"You have siblings?"

"Six. All boys."

Katalina's face soured. Her brow furrowed and reflexes sent her hand brushing her inner thigh. "That poor woman!"

"Umm, it wasn't like she was raising the Mansons. We all turned out all right."

"Obviously," Katalina answered. "I didn't mean it like that. The thought of her vagina pushing out six boys. . ." Her face grimaced; a gesture she couldn't control.

Katalina had never been the type of girl to want kids. Even as a little girl, her ambitions and life goals were more career driven. She wasn't quite a Tomboy, but she definitely wasn't a girly-girl.

Vincenzo interrupted and delivered a beautiful steaming steak to Katalina. Pete's plate consisted of fried veal cutlet with a side of steamed vegetables.

"This looks delicious, Kat! Thanks for the recommendation."

"You're welcome. Tell me, Pete. How old are you?"

"Twenty-nine, just like my profile says."

"Have you ever been married? Do you have any kids? Are you a cheater? Have you ever been arrested? What's your credit score?"

Pete froze. His eyes scanned the table as if he had lost something. He appeared to be taken aback. "Who are you, Inspector Gadget?" he asked.

Shit! Chill out, Kat. At least enjoy your dinner. He hasn't done anything wrong. "I'm sorry, Pete. I'm really nervous and sometimes, as a defense mechanism, I start talking and can't stop. You don't have to answer any of those questions."

Pete's face relaxed. "That's okay. I've never been married. I don't have any kids that I know of." He let out an immature laugh. "And no, I've never been arrested. What about you?"

He conveniently left out the cheating answer.

"I'm twenty-nine, just like my profile says. I've never been married; I don't have any kids and I've never been arrested. We seem compatible." Katalina cut into her bleeding steak and closed her eyes with lustful anticipation. The aroma of iron mixed with sizzled fat sent pleasure signals up her spine. When she stabbed the steak and sliced her knife into the meat, blood oozed all over her plate.

"That's a bloody steak," Pete announced. "Aren't you worried about getting sick?"

Katalina gently placed a piece of raw meat on her tongue and slowly slid the fork tines from her lips. Pete's eyes were glued to her lips. When Katalina chewed, the blood from the steak absorbed in her mouth. She felt invigorated as if she'd been starving. She felt like a dehydrated desert dweller getting her first drink of water just before dying.

"I'm so turned on right now."

Katalina looked at Pete with piercing eyes. Suddenly, Katalina heard every sound with acute clarity. She smelled a host of fragrances from the perfume on the old lady seated at the table next to them, to the urine droplets on the waiter's shoes as he walked by. "Did you say something?" she asked.

"No. How's your steak?"

Katalina heard Pete's voice. Her eyes were closed when he said he was turned on, so she didn't see him say it, but it was his voice. He said it.

"Divine. I love steak."

"Gotta love a woman who wants meat in her mouth."

That time her eyes were open. His lips didn't move, but she heard it. Clear as day. *Dammit, Kat!* She knew it would happen. Every time she ate a rare steak that kind of stuff happened. Random, unexplainable things occurred. She wasn't positive, but Katalina felt stronger when she ate steak.

She felt primal.

Invincible.

A woman's voice shrieked from across the restaurant. The ambient noise level rose with gasps and raised voices shouted. "Somebody help him! He's choking!" Katalina thought about intervening. It was her duty to save lives. She pondered for a second and thought, *What if Pete asks how I know CPR? Shit, I've had too many to be certain that I'd even do it right. Hell, I might kill the poor man. I'd better sit this one out*, she thought.

Pete leapt to his feet and shouted, "I know CPR!" and ran toward the man who was clutching his throat with both hands. His eyes were large. His face turned a shade of maroon. Surely, he was watching his life escape before him. His wife, frantic and doing more harm than good was screaming. Katalina followed Pete to the table. She was careful to take calculated steps. She wasn't used to walking in heels sober, much-less with five glasses of wine in her.

Pete was the poster child for CPR. He approached the table and announced, "I know CPR. Can I help?" Katalina chuckled when she saw that. *He must have just watched a video*, she thought. Pete pointed to a woman on her phone and shouted, "You, call 911!" The lady on the phone looked around as if someone was playing a prank on her. She was already on the line with them. Pete stepped behind the choking man and placed his arms around his chest. It looked like a bear-hug. Soon, Pete was giving him abdominal thrusts. It took just six thrusts before the man spit out a piece of calamari that flew across the table. The second he hurled the food out, his breathing resumed. The entire restaurant erupted in clapping and chanted, *hero, hero, hero.*

The two returned to their table and Katalina said, "Wow. That was impressive. Where did you learn CPR from?"

"I'm a CPR instructor. I used to be a volunteer fireman and kept recertifying. Now I teach my staff every two years. It's my way of giving back." Pete's eyes drifted off.

He appeared to be zoned out for a second. Katalina heard every word he thought, so when he spoke, she knew he was being genuine. She rubbed her forehead, trying to shut out his inner thoughts, but it was futile.

"When I was a fireman, I made a difference. I was a better person." Pete poked at the food on his plate—teasing it, but never eating it.

"Why did you leave?" Katalina asked.

"Money. I wanted more out of life than what a fireman's salary offered."

Katalina sliced another piece of bloody steak. She smeared the bite in the pool of smoked blood that filled her plate and savored the taste. "More than personal satisfaction?"

His phone is about to go off, she thought to herself. Much like the parking space, as if she willed it to happen, Pete placed his utensils down and reached for his phone. This time, his grin was mischievous. "I'm with this gorgeous redhead. You know they say all redheads are nymphos, right? A few more drinks and I'll find out for myself!" Pete tucked his phone back in his jacket and grabbed his fork.

"Your mother must really be worried, Pete."

His eyes met hers. His body language suggested he was nervous. The tablecloth shook from his knee bouncing rapidly beneath the table. His eyes widened.

"Is she a nympho?" Katalina asked.

Pete's mouth was agape. Leg no longer bouncing. He squinted his eyes and gasped as if to say, *How could you?*

Katalina let out a laugh, "I'm just kidding! You should have seen your face!" Katalina cut another piece of raw meat from her plate and bit into it. She sucked the blood from the meat before chewing. "If you're going to last a second with me, you'll need to have a sense of humor and some thick skin."

Before long, the couple was flirting heavily with each other. Maybe it was the fifth glass of wine. Maybe it was the Kat devil egging her on. Or, maybe, Katalina was just tired of being alone. She had begun to retreat into reclusion and blame herself for failed dates. All she focused on in life was her job; being the best and serving justice to those oppressed. Her inhibitions were all but gone. "So, Pete? Does your name have a meaning?"

Pete smiled. Excited to answer, he said, "It means rock." His eyebrow arched in arrogance as if he had just stolen her heart.

"Oh? Well, Katalina means pure," she said, with defiance. *The two don't go together*, she thought.

"Hey, would you want to go back to my place for a nightcap?" Pete offered.

Katalina wanted to. She hadn't been with a man in several years. The bloody steak didn't help. It all but fueled the Kat devil on her shoulder who was shouting at her to let him get it in, saying things like, "Look at his hands; look at his broad chest; you know what they say about big hands…" But Katalina wanted to remain classy. She retrieved her cell phone and fired off a text message.

"Maybe next time, Pete," she said.

"But you're in no shape to drive. Why don't you let me drive you home?"

"I've got a ride. Thanks. This has been a lovely night. It's not that often that your date saves someone's life. *Hero*."

Pete smiled. Katalina knew his pride had been saved. "Can we do this again?" Pete asked. "I really like you."

Katalina smiled. She did enjoy the attention Pete gave her, despite his testosterone-driven motives. Besides, she knew most men thought the way he did. "I'd like that," she said.

"Can I have your number?"

Katalina shook her head slowly. Seductively. "Give me yours, Pete."

Vincenzo arrived and Pete settled the bill. Katalina turned her glass up and consumed the last sip of her wine before the couple walked out. The restaurant erupted in cheer once again for Pete the hero. The front doors opened, and the duo was slapped in the face with the day's high humidity. Pete instantly began to sweat. He stepped closer to Katalina, invading her personal space—something she was not used to. She fidgeted. Her gaze fell from his eyes to his lips. He grabbed her hand in his and tugged gently. She closed her eyes in anticipation. His cologne was still strong.

Katalina's heart skipped a beat—not from lust, but rather from the piercing horn that was blaring. She almost jumped out of her heels. The horn kept blowing.

"Oh, lover girl. Behold! Your ride has arrived!" the driver laughed hysterically.

Katalina closed her eyes in shame. *Seriously? I am going to kill him!*

"Should I be worried?" Pete asked.

"No, that's my coworker. He should be worried though!" Katalina turned toward her ride and shot him a pair of eyes that suggested he was about to be murdered. She returned to Pete and gave him a quick peck on his cheek. "I'll call you," she said.

Benoit Doucet sat laughing in his car. He was proud of his accomplishment. He had managed to make Katalina blush. She was normally the quick-witted one, but tonight he had the jump on her.

Katalina pulled the heels off her feet before approaching her ride. "Duce, what the fuck?"

"You're welcome. Hey, are you leaving your vehicle here overnight?"

"Nah, I'll take an Uber later and come get it."

Benoit shook his head. "Fearless."

***

Katalina entered her apartment after Benoit dropped her off and was met by her hairless cat, Casper. After a frustrating dinner, she leaned against the interior door and sighed. "What's wrong with me? I just want to be normal."

His meows sounded like something straight out of a horror movie. He was Katalina's true love—forever loyal and always affectionate. Immediately upon entering, she closed the door behind her and secured the deadbolt lock, the doorknob lock, a chain lock and an extra sliding bolt installed at the top. Hypervigilance is an unfortunate side-effect of cynical police officers.

"Alexa, play System of a Down." Heavy metal rock began blaring from her smart speaker. Surely her downstairs neighbor would soon be jabbing a broom handle against the ceiling to shut Katalina up. Her legs were muscular from years of running track both in high school and college. She was all-state champion every year she competed. She was "randomly" drug tested four times for performance enhancing drugs. She suspected it was because of how badly she'd outrun everyone. She broke records held by both sexes and had been recruited for the Olympics.

Katalina made her way to her bedroom and abruptly stopped halfway down the hall. Eyes were staring at her, burning her skin with judgment. The eyes came from a five-year old picture. She turned and faced the picture. "Don't you dare judge me," she said as if the picture was capable of speaking.

The picture was of herself. In it, she smiled proudly as she wore her class-a uniform. It had been taken on the day she graduated from the academy. The look in her eyes had been similar to all of the graduating rookies that day, eyes filled with excitement and wonder at becoming a cop, of each day saving the world in some small or huge way and unaware of the atrocities that waited for them out on the streets or how many innocent unsuspecting victims they would soon meet. That day seemed like a lifetime ago as she stared at the picture now.

Heavy metal music had become her form of therapy. The violent lyrics and ear-curdling screams relaxed her perhaps more than they should have. Her theory of policing also changed drastically from her academy days. She promised her instructors that she was going to change the face of the police department. *I'll get out of my car and actually talk to people. If someone has a flat tire, I'll be there to change it for them. I'll give respect in order to earn respect. I'll make the people love police as much as they love firemen.*

Katalina had been a property detective for the past year. She was given cases involving damaged or stolen property and had an excellent closure rate. Everyone inside her department called her The Janitor because she always cleaned up everyone else's mess.

Katalina was better at reading body language than anyone else in her department. During interrogations, she became a human lie detector and analyzed a suspect's words like an all-knowing wizard. Many of coworkers joked that she had psychic abilities. Her ability to see through bullshit kept many of her brothers and sisters in blue constantly on their toes when they were around her. Early on, her goal was to become a forensics investigator, but that changed and now she wanted more than anything to make the homicide team. Despite her perfect case closure rate, she'd never been taken seriously by her lieutenant. NOPD's bias was firmly cemented in her brain.

Chapter Five

Crescent City Myths

Katalina sat at a pub table just outside one of the many restaurants along the Outlet Connection on the Riverwalk. A greasy steaming slice of pizza and a diet Coke was all she could think about at that moment. The sun had long disappeared beyond the horizon and the mosquitoes were in full attack mode, thanks to Louisiana's tropical climate, winter was the thing of fairy tales along the southern coast. No sooner than she took her first bite of cheesy Italian ecstasy, a man sprinted down the Riverwalk before Katalina, his breathing rapid. As if in slow motion, she stole a glance of his face; it told a story of sheer terror. His eyes were bulging; his face stretched with horror.

"Son of a bitch!" she said to herself.

She looked to her side and saw people nervously watching her. Her shiny half-moon badge shone vibrantly in the full moon's reflection as it hung along her waist which meant she had to intervene.

She closed her eyes and sighed as she stood up. "Fine. Police! Stop!" Katalina screamed as she pushed ahead in full sprint along the Riverwalk.

Her fiery-orange hair was pulled tight into a ponytail that bounced back and forth with each step. The Riverwalk was dark except for tiny lights that lined the edge separating the brick deck from the Mighty Mississippi. The sprinter ahead of her didn't care that he crashed into bystanders as he fled. He was running for his life. Katalina closed the gap on the man ahead of her with ease. As she gained on him, his sheer size baffled her. Perhaps that's why he was so slow. His big cloddy feet were like concrete shoes.

"Police! Stop!" she yelled again.

Katalina grabbed his flailing arm in an attempt to stop his pursuit. He instinctively rotated and swung his fist toward her.

"Whoa, I'm here to help!" she shouted, but the man continued to resist her attempts to help and pushed forward. She stepped ahead of him and held her hand out in a stopping gesture. He stood over six feet tall and easily weighed over two hundred pounds. Judging from his clothing, he was homeless. Not to mention the foul odor emanating from his person.

He reached for Katalina. "We're going to die!"

Katalina grabbed his wrist as he reached for her throat. Vice-like pressure with a quick jolt rotated his arm upside down. The man fell to his knees and cried in pain.

"Nobody is going to die, sir. I'm here to help," she gestured down to her badge and the Glock on her hip. "I'm one of the good guys," she said.

He continued to fight and stood, despite his arm almost breaking and ignoring her commands. The giant towered over Katalina looking down upon her. He wildly swung his free arm and struck Katalina in her face. The impact was like a lightning bolt striking her head. A quick flash of light followed by searing pain across her cheekbone stunned her enough to release the grip on his wrist. Then he bolted ahead. Katalina shook her head, gathered her bearings and continued to give chase. Within seconds she was upon him and launched into the air like a flying squirrel. She cloaked his back and wrapped her tiny legs around his torso, digging her heels into his stomach. She hunched over his back and weaved her bony forearms between his neck and chin, then grabbed her own wrist and squeezed.

"Sir. Stop resisting!" she shouted.

The giant slowed to a stop. He tried to swat the tiny woman from his back, but he soon faded. First he fell to one knee, then he crumpled to the ground. Katalina wasted no time and hopped off of his back. She grabbed a pair of handcuffs and placed one on his left wrist. He was too broad to snap the other wrist in so she had to grab a second pair of handcuffs, connecting them before securing the runaway giant. She rolled him over just as he was waking up and sat him on his butt.

"I'm sorry if I hurt you. What are you running from?"

He looked up at Katalina, then peered behind her and said, "A vampire."

"A vampire?"

"I saw it with my own eyes. He sunk his teeth into this poor girl. The blood. It was awful."

"Where was this?"

"On Convention."

"Seriously? A vampire?" Katalina asked. "Sir, have you taken any drugs tonight?" Her eyes rolled.

"I don't do drugs!" he professed.

Katalina cocked her head sideways and arched an eyebrow. "Okay fine. Can you describe it?"

"He was a white guy. Black hair. His skin was pale… Just like yours." His eyes watered as they enlarged. "Oh no."

"Anything else? What was he wearing?"

The giant shrugged. "Please don't kill me!"

"Seriously, big man?" Her head shook in disbelief. "Only in the Big Easy," Katalina mumbled. "Okay, sir. Let's get you some help." Katalina released the man from hand restraints and helped him to his feet.

He rubbed his neck and said, "You're freakishly strong. You can't be but a hundred pounds soaking wet."

Katalina dismissed his comment. "Can you bring me to the girl?"

The giant's eyes almost burst from their sockets. His head shook violently before breaking into another full sprint.

"Sir, wait! Just show me where… Poor guy needs mental help." Katalina made a 180 turn. A small crowd of onlookers huddled nearby whispering. She heard every word:

"Police brutality. Oppressive cops. Poor man was just minding his business."

Katalina retraced her steps leading back to the string of restaurants, then back to Convention Street. She looked up at the buildings but no cameras were on display. "No bodies that I can see. No bloody massacres, and there sure as hell aren't any fucking vampires." She chuckled. "Good one, voodoo city. You got me."

Chapter Six

Dark Visitor

Katalina lay still in bed—paralyzed. Her eyes opened, but she was frozen. She struggled to breathe as if she was sucking air through a straw. Casper was screaming. Frequent, long meows. Not his normal hungry cries or his welcoming sounds. She couldn't see him because her back was glued to the bed. Her eyes worked fine, but her view was limited. She tried to scream but her mouth remained sealed. Her voice box didn't work.

Casper's meows were short and sharp now as if he were fussing at something. Soon, Katalina's heart rate drowned out all ambient sounds. Each beat was like a war cannon firing in rapid succession. She knew her body. She recognized what it was doing. Katalina had experienced this type of physiological response in her last on-duty shooting.

Her eyes darted toward the wall where her bedroom door sat. A shadow grew larger as it approached her room. Warm salty droplets ran down the sides of her face but she couldn't wipe them. She still couldn't move. The shadow appeared to be a silhouette. The head peered into her bedroom and stayed in the doorway. Katalina was helpless. She couldn't defend herself. She couldn't reach for a phone to call for help. She couldn't grab her gun that was tucked beneath the pillow next to her head.

Katalina let out a battle cry. A scream that broke through the paralysis. She sat up in bed. Her chest pounded through her saturated tee shirt. The normally bright red silk sheets were damp and dark with her sweat. Her bedroom was bright from the sunlight breaking through her blinds. The alarm clock displayed ten thirty. Casper pranced through her bedroom door with his tail flickering. His wicked-sounding meows were a message to his owner that he was hungry. He was always hungry.

Clarity slowly eased to the forefront of her brain. The fog that clouded her mind dissipated. Katalina scanned her room thinking alcohol must have caused such a realistic dream. The top of her dresser drawers only had a jewelry box on top. A worn paperback novel perched the edge of her bedside table. No bourbon. No wine glasses.

Katalina pondered while staring at the floor. She wanted to ignore all the signs, but she was too smart. Wicked dreams. Unexplainable power. Newfound love for the taste of blood.

She looked at her ceiling for inspiration and said, "Bring it."

Chapter Seven

Creatures

Katalina worked in a police department with horny disrespectful men, mostly who were married but always thought with the wrong head, so she was cautious in how she dressed. She couldn't help her athletic physique, so she tried to dress moderately. As a detective, she wore plain clothes as long as it was relatively respectful. She mainly wore blue jeans and cute shirts.

Within ten minutes she'd drawn a thin black line of mascara across her eyelids. A quick stroke across her tiny lips left them shiny and vibrant. Instinctively she caressed her right hip, touching the cold steel that was tucked snugly against her waist. She kept a tiny backup gun strapped to her ankle as she strolled into the precinct. Just like any other day, heads turned as she walked by. She heard the whispers—the wagers on who would get her in bed first. She also heard the disdain coming from jealous detectives. Angry whispers laden with foul thoughts.

Katalina had long suspected she was different-a freak if you will, and hearing others thoughts only solidified her fears. She knew she was different and it pained her to know she could do nothing about it.

Who did she sleep with to make it to homicide? Like she can really defend herself at one hundred pounds. One of us will always have to be there to save her ass.

Little did they know she could hear a pin drop from around the corner, but she kept her thoughts to herself and took a mental note of each coworker. Allies, enemies, and neutrals.

The bullpen sat as a shared space for the detectives in her department, a large open area inter-woven with cubicles and small glassed off rooms used for active detectives and supervisors. One side of the bullpen was for crimes against persons and the opposite side was for property crimes. There was a distinction. Only the best detectives made it to crimes against persons. The violent crimes; rapes, armed robberies, murder—anything involving the most heinous criminals out there. Two offices peered over the bullpen on Katalina's side. Sergeant Myron Daigle, a.k.a. 'The Salty Sarge', and Lieutenant Joe Esposito. The two were polar opposites. Daigle was an asshole who seemed to hate life. He was the ultimate cynic, whereas Esposito was a kinder, gentler person.

"Andrews! You don't look like death anymore." Benoit chuckled as Katalina sat next to him. He flipped through the case file from their last call-out. "Are we going to talk about what happened?"

Katalina shot Benoit a look of disgust. "Don't judge me, asshole! I have needs, too, you know."

Benoit's eyes widened as if he'd bitten off more than he could chew. "Um, I was talking about the suicide. We are still thinking this is a suicide, right?" Benoit slapped Sheila's case file on the desk between them.

Katalina closed her eyes and smacked her palm against her forehead then sighed. "I'm sorry, Duce."

Benoit laughed and said, "Kat, I don't care who you sleep with."

She punched him in his shoulder. "I haven't slept with anyone since college."

Benoit counted on his fingers and looked at Katalina with curiosity. Her eyes grew large. "Yeah. Six years. I'm basically a virgin again."

Benoit immediately regretted speaking. He grew uncomfortable with the direction of the conversation. "Kat, we've been partners for what? Three years now? You're like my little sister. I don't want to hear about that kind of shit, okay? Anyway. About our victim . . ."

"Yeah. About our victim. The medical examiner said almost all of her blood was drained out. Is that strange, or am I just being paranoid?"

Benoit shook his head and stared at his desk, "I don't know what to think anymore, Kat."

"Duce, the laceration on her arm was deep—like real deep. I've worked many suicides, and none cut to the bone. You've been in Homicide for seven years now, right? Have you ever seen anything like this?"

Benoit shot Katalina a look of uncertainty. "I've seen a lot. I mean, I've seen some shit. Voodoo, vampirism, cannibalism, witchcraft, serial killers, pedophiles, you name it."

Katalina's ears perked up. She fidgeted and couldn't help but wonder if he'd noticed her sneak a taste of Sheila's blood. "Vampirism? Like sleeping in coffins and hanging upside down stuff?"

Benoit laughed. "Not the theatrical stuff. Humans who 'think' they're vampires and drink other people's blood because they think it's cool."

"So, bullshit, basically?" Katalina asked.

"Not the voodoo or witchcraft. That shit's real."

"What's voodoo? Isn't it like witchcraft?"

"They're similar. Voodoo is more of a black magic teetering on the brink of demonic rituals. I could tell you some stories." Benoit studied Katalina's face when he said that. "But I've never seen any truth to vampirism. At least, not around here."

"How do you mean?" Katalina asked.

"New Orleans is rich with voodoo and witchcraft. I've seen it with my own eyes. Just a stroll down the French Quarter and you'll come across four or five voodoo shops. Some are BS sales gimmicks, but some are the real-deal."

An inquisitive Katalina was intrigued but cautious as she primed Benoit for answers. "But you don't *really* believe in that stuff, do you?"

Benoit closed his eyes and offered a genuine shake of his head.

"Ditto! Hey, Duce. Can I ask a personal question?"

"Of course. What's up?"

"What do you want more than anything in this world?"

Benoit thought for a moment. "I wish I could go back to before my dad died and spend more time with him. I'd give anything to tell him that I love him again."

Katalina's forehead crinkled. The corners of her mouth drooped. Moisture filled her eyelids. "Aww, Duce. He'd be so proud of you. I know he's watching over you, full of pride."

"What about you, Kat? What do you want?"

"I don't know. It's hard to follow that."

"Don't give me that shit, Kat. No judgment. I promise."

"My whole life, I've strived to be the best at everything I did. I won every competition and achieved every award that I set out to accomplish, yet nobody respects me. I just wish that for once, my peers recognized my hard work and accepted me as an equal. Hell, I'd settle for just not being looked down upon."

"You know I accept you, right Kat? You're the best partner I've ever had. Do you know why?"

"Cause I'm a bad bitch?" Katalina laughed.

"No, because you've earned it. You outwork everyone here. Run circles around all of us, and yes, you're a bad bitch." Benoit joined her laughter.

Shouting echoed from across the bullpen. "I fucking hate the judicial system!"

Katalina looked at Benoit who shrugged his shoulders. She hung her head to the side and looked beyond her partner at the homicide team on the other rotation. Castellano and his partner, Cabrera looked like two men on a mission.

"What's up with them?" Kat asked.

Benoit crinkled his forehead and offered a confused look.

The other squad of detectives stopped at Katalina's desk and threw a cell phone on her desk. "Do see that?" His accent had an Italian tune to it. "This fucking guy!" Castellano fussed. "This fucking guy. This piece of shit, Roseberry, rapes his own nephew and walks!"

Katalina grabbed the phone that read, Child Rapist Vindicated. "Who was the judge?" she asked.

Cabrera interjected, "Landry."

"Sierra Landry?"

"Mrs. Hug-a-Thug herself. The one and only," Cabrera answered.

"What happened?" Katalina asked.

"Fuck if I know! That kid even described Roseberry's dick to the jury! I'll tell you what happened. A lucky hot-shot defense attorney claimed that the chain of custody on the bloody sheets was compromised. Threw the whole thing out! You know, it's days like these that I wish we could go back to the time when the criminal justice system allowed an eye-for-an-eye. You know what? Fuck that. I bet Roseberry would enjoy getting raped."

Benoit spoke, "That's terrible, Cabrera." He looked at the angry team standing before him. "But he'll get his day. It may not be today, but you know what they say, 'you reap what you sow.'"

Cabrera looked at his partner, Castellano. "Yeah, I'd like to be the one to deliver the justice." His face was red with ire as Katalina swiped through the online news article.

Katalina was looking Cabrera in the eye and listening to his thoughts. "I'm gonna kill that mother fucker myself. Won't be the first time."

Castellano grabbed the cell phone from Katalina's hands and walked away. Cabrera followed, continuing with foul thoughts about Roseberry.

She watched as the pair strode down the hall, half joking about killing Roseberry. Castellano may have been joking, but Cabrera wasn't.

Chapter Eight

Demon Entry

"Hey, Duce. Forensics collected a couple of hair samples from Sheila's body," Katalina said.

Benoit's eyes widened. "And?"

"The hair was black. Both of them. They were different though. One was straight and one wavy. Sheila was a natural blonde," Kat said.

"How do you know she was a natural blonde?"

Kat stared at Benoit in disbelief. "You couldn't tell from her nudity? She's definitely a natural blonde."

Benoit's eyes clenched closed. "Kat! I don't want to hear that crap! Forget I asked!"

"Okay, okay, fine. Her eyebrows were blonde, Duce. That's how I know. That better? God you're such a pussy sometimes! Anyway, we'll run the DNA and hope to get a match."

"So, I'm guessing we're not chalking this up to suicide, are we?" Benoit asked.

Katalina shook her head. "Shhhh. I have a feeling, Duce. Sarge wants me to close the case—and I will, but I have to dig deeper. This will be our little secret."

Benoit massaged his temples and squeezed his eyes closed. "I'm going to be a meter maid if we get caught, Kat."

Kat shot Benoit a scowl. "Two can keep a secret if one's dead." A single eyebrow raised as the words left her mouth. She squinted and smiled at her teammate.

"You're the worst, Kat. Fine. I'll be your partner in crime."

A voice barked from across the bullpen. Duce looked in that direction, his eyes locking on Drake as he entered the pen. Drake dressed as Duce always saw him, in a black leather coat and a pair of jeans that fit a tad too tight and a bandanna that kept his hair out of his face. Tattoos covered every inch of his arms. Drake worked undercover in Narcotics and any officer with an ounce of sense could instantly see how deep he had gone. He'd been on the force for so long, many people couldn't remember when he had started. Drake only worked nights. Some say he was no better than the criminals he helped apprehend, but his drug, cash, and gun seizures were unmatched by any other narc in his department which became a justified reason for his superiors to overlook the obvious.

Drake wasn't the one doing the yelling. Another cop was responsible for the shouting as he followed Drake through the bullpen to reach another area of the precinct, accusing Drake of interfering on another case he had been working on. Not once did Drake look in the guy's location and only straight ahead.

Duce furtively pulled a small mirror out of the bottom drawer at his desk and aimed it to catch Drake as he walked past. Drake looked the same way he had the last time Duce had caught his reflection in the mirror, like a fiery red demon with his face ripped and torn and his teeth grotesquely rotten and his eyes a burning strange color of orange.

Nothing Duce saw prepared him for whatever he had seen in the mirror inside Sheila's apartment, but he kept watching Drake to be sure and until Drake exited the bullpen with his colleague still following closely behind him.

Damn!

Duce tossed the mirror back inside the drawer. What he'd seen at Sheila's apartment refused to leave his mind. Something had been inside that master bedroom—a man that moved extremely fast and had wings that could disappear. A demon, Duce thought, or what other people sometimes called ghosts.

For many, many years, New Orleans had some bad characters that lived inside it and he suspected that Drake may need to be added to the list. A website on the Dark Web had given some answers, but not all as to what he may have seen the night before. According to the site, ghosts in human form were seen in the same appearance as they looked on the day of their death, but this hadn't been what Benoit had seen. The thing he saw could have moved fast enough that it wouldn't be seen at all. Benoit suspected that the thing had allowed himself to be seen because it was shocking that he and Kat had been able to see it all.

Benoit knew why he could see things other people couldn't. What he couldn't understand is how Kat had been able to not only see it, but feel its presence. The way she drew her pistol and aimed at it had frightened the thing off, although Benoit suspected that the escape had nothing to do with the fear of death and only that it had been seen. And the way it had landed on her Tahoe then came back twice to get closer to her.

It's that part that frightened him because for years he suspected that Kat was different, not because she could run fast or exert a lot of energy and not get tired or because she loved bloody, close to raw steak. As her partner and only friend, he knew that Kat was keeping secrets about herself and he wondered if that secret was tied to what he'd seen last night.

He stared at Kat a moment. Playtime had ended and she had absorbed herself into the file. Reaching again for the mirror, he sat in a way so she didn't see it then held it in a position to catch her reflection. He saw the desk and the many objects on top of it including the file, but not Kat. He looked up and saw her still sitting there. His heart raced. Kat looked directly at him. He waited until she looked down again then stared into the mirror. A page in the file flipped over, but Kat's fingers or reflection couldn't be seen. Benoit almost flipped out of his chair.

Several people looked in his direction. Benoit righted his chair while still sitting in it and stared at Kat. Her eyes were on him. Concern could be seen inside them.

"You all right?" she asked.

Benoit tossed her the mirror.

Kat looked puzzled as she held it then stared into the mirror and studied her teeth to make sure makeup hadn't got on them. She fingered her hair then licked her lips.

"I got something on me?" she asked with furrowed brows.

Damn, Benoit thought. Either Kat was good at pretending or didn't see her reflection the same way he saw it.

"Nope," he said, then forced a smile as his heart tried its best to race out of his chest. His leg bounced nervously on the tip of his foot as he thought about the things he'd come across on the Dark Web the night before. Creatures of the night were known to have wings and handsome human appearances—creatures that didn't have reflections when they looked into mirrors. Creatures the Dark Web said were real living vampires.

But Kat didn't have wings. He knew this because he's seen her in a bikini before. The creatures of the night weren't able to come out in daytime, but Kat sat in the direct rays that were coming into the bullpen from a nearby window. Kat loved garlic and ordered more of it every time she visited her favorite Italian restaurant.

But Kat loves bloody meat, Benoit reminded himself then stood rapidly onto his feet. She ate bloody steak all the time and possibly every day. At twenty-nine years old, she looked no older than twenty-one or twenty-two and since he'd known her she hadn't aged. There had to be a reason she didn't have a reflection today when she had had one on the many other occasions he had taken a peek at her. A winged creature. Kat sensing its presence and reacting. It had to be connected and the reason she had no reflection today. Kat also had an unusual hue of hair. All this time, he and everyone else thought she dyed it. Lots of comments had been made about it—comments that Kat had never corrected. Now he wondered if her hair color was natural—a deep red hue similar to the Phoenix character from the X-Men comic books.

"What the hell's wrong with you?" Kat asked annoyed as she sat tall and stared at him.

Benoit asked himself a question he had never asked before. Did other people see Kat the way he did or did he see more because of his gift?

"I need to go to the restroom," he announced then hurried to the door that led to a long hall that had many doors on both sides of it.

Halfway down he reached the restroom and splashed his face with water. When he stared at himself in the mirror, he wondered if it could be true. Could Kat be a creature of the night? Could such a thing even be possible? Had they evolved and sunlight no longer threatened them? These questions had to be answered because it was the only way to explain why she had no reflection or did her not having a reflection mean she wasn't a vampire but something else?

Later that evening, his search turned up nothing. For hours he perused the Internet and Dark Web only to conclude that nothing about Kat fell under the category of a vampire or any other supernatural creature.

He studied his reflection in the mirror for quite a few minutes before convincing himself that he hadn't been wrong about Kat and there was definitely something different about her.

Chapter Nine

The Jungle

The precinct sat twenty minutes from her apartment depending on traffic. A call came through the SUV's Bluetooth. Duce's name appeared across the face of the radio. Katalina quickly accepted the call. "Sup, Duce? Why in the hell are you calling so early?"

"Good morning to you, too," he countered. "Skip the office and head to the 300 block of Lombard. We have a body."

"I'll be there in a few," she answered.

The 300 block of Lombard was known for its gang activity and violence. Many of the houses were run-down and were a far cry from livable, yet families kept them rented as a means to survive. Dusty cars that had stopped working years ago sat parked in yards like lawn ornaments. Toddlers wearing nothing more than diapers ran along the sidewalks while family members sat on their porch and watched the road. Every person she passed took a moment to stare at her and her vehicle because residents in this area were more than leery of the police. Back in the 90s, cop cars were pelted with glass bottles and even bricks. During that time, the precinct instituted a new protocol that didn't allow cops to leave their units without having backup. More than twenty years later and the contention between the police and civilians had not improved.

An angry mob waited at the address she'd been given. Neighbors had gathered to loudly voice their opinions about what they saw as yet another injustice. Quite a few officers from her department had already arrived, allowing Katalina to reach the scene without incident. She ducked under the yellow crime scene tape and stood in front of Benoit. "What's up?" she asked.

"This isn't our scene," he answered. "It's Cabrera and Castellano's. We're just here to help in any way they need us."

Katalina nodded knowing the nature of their request. The jungle, as the area was commonly called, was a place that required reinforcements no matter what type of call. She got closer and approached Cabrera as he squatted and took pictures of the victim.

"Joseph Paddio," Cabrera said, "one of the heads of the organization."

"Which family?" Katalina questioned.

Cabrera looked at her then stood up. "YBK. Rumor is they're on the extreme side of violent.

"Worse than the Marcello Family?" she asked, intrigued by what the answer would be.

Cabrera smiled. "A lot more violent and with less respect. This was ballsy. I suspect someone close to him is our suspect. No rival gang would dare penetrate the jungle."

"Those pictures—they're for your private collection?" Kat asked. "Why do you look so happy that someone punched Paddio's number?"

He looked over shoulder then whispered, "This mother fucker live-streamed a gang rape of a teenager. Yeah, he was arrested. In fact, it was my case, but wouldn't you know he fucking walked?"

"What? How? You said it was live-streamed!"

Cabrera shot Katalina a less-than-amused look. "One of the jury members went missing and, as of yet, still hasn't been found. Needless to say, his terrorist antics worked because the vote wasn't unanimous, and he walked out of the courtroom a free man."

"What idiot thought a unanimous jury is the best thing for the people? All it takes is one juror to crack and boom! Case closed and the bad guy walks."

Paddio lay sprawled across his back porch with a deep laceration across his throat. His neck looked like an open mouth in the midst of a scream. The white sticking out of it was his spinal cord, the wound had gone that deep and had been made that wide. As she stared down at the gruesomeness of it, her stomach twisted in hunger. Beads of sweat dotted her upper lip. Seeing the blood had given her a craving for it and this time not in the form a steak.

Benoit had come closer.

"You okay, Kat?" he asked.

Katalina drew in a deep breath and let it out. "I need to eat, is all."

"Eat? That's what's on your mind right now? Food?" Benoit studied her carefully.

Katalina heard him, but her attention had focused on a bullet-style surveillance camera. "Surely that's not working," she said.

Benoit smirked. "I bet there are plenty more on the property and all of them are being viewed remotely right now by the YBK family."

Katalina entered the residence, surprised to see how nicely furnished it sat. Large flat-screen TVs were inside every room along with gaming consoles and surround sound stereo systems. In the master bedroom, she located a monitor displaying several different cameras. A few keystrokes later, and she had accessed the hard drive and was manipulating the recorder. She rewound the footage and found a frame where Paddio stood on his back porch and pressed play. The video showed him smoking a cigar while he was on his cell phone. He appeared to be yelling.

Milliseconds later, the feed showed a blurry swipe across the front of it followed by Paddio on the ground bleeding out. She rewound and replayed the frame twenty times and each time the moments leading up to Paddio's death only displayed a blur. She dug in and prepared to watch hours of video. Every camera was to be viewed for an hour prior to the murder, but the footage was useless. No arguments. No fights. Nothing out of the ordinary seemed to jump out so she packed the DVR up and exited the residence.

"Duce, I'm going to deliver this to forensics and see if they can enhance the video."

She was escorted to her vehicle by three officers. Her drive out of the jungle was safe. Too many angry onlookers remained at the residence versus paying any attention to her.

Chapter Ten

Dark Killer

As a man entered the Carousel Bar, a couple that had been leaving noticed the cold look in the man's eyes. Dressed in a tailored suit that draped him perfectly along with the kind of jewelry he wore, they saw him as someone successful and possibly enigmatic and looked away just as he looked at them.

Dmitri couldn't care less about the couple. Tonight his desire was specific. Walking to the bar, he didn't wait in line like the others. As soon as his eyes made contact with the bartender's, the bartender stopped what he was doing and urged Dmitri closer.

"Vodka," Dmitri said.

"Straight?" the bartender asked.

Dmitri's eyes filled with loathing. The bartender saw this and reached for a bottle of Grey Goose on the shelf behind him. Dmitri admonished the bartender in a gravelly voice. "Stoli. The entire bottle."

The bartender tried to look fearless as he grabbed a clean glass and the bottle and set both on the counter, then waited for Dmitri to hand over the right amount of money before the bottle exchanged hands. As Dmitri walked away, the bartender stared down a moment wondering what just happened: Why he had stopped to help Dmitri first and why he had acted frightened when normally he never turned down a good fight?

As Dmitri walked to the darkest corner of the room, he noticed that all of the tables had been taken. That didn't matter. The closer he got to the table he normally sat at, its occupants got up, grabbed their drinks, and vacated the table then stared at each other while wearing smiles of shock as to why they had gotten up in the first place.

On nights like these, Dmitri chose The Carousel for its classier clientele although on some occasions women like the one he'd picked up the night before somehow managed to get inside and not be shown out by the bouncer. Usually, he didn't hunt so soon, but it had been hard to get the red headed detective out of his mind. Even now he wondered if landing on her Tahoe had been a coincidence or if she had somehow lured him.

Twice he had gotten close and twice she seemed to have sensed his presence. That's what struck him as odd, that and her partner seeming to have special gifts. But how could two witches live in New Orleans and he not know anything about them when it proved wise to keep tabs on such things?

He opened the bottle of Stoli and poured a generous amount. A brunette sat alone at the end of the bar. Jewelry that caught the muted light draped her neck. Their eyes met. She gave a wink. He gave a nod, his smile infectious. He flagged down a waiter and had another of whatever she was drinking be brought to her and for the bill to be brought to him.

Minutes passed. The woman received her drink. The waiter leaned close to her ear to tell the woman who had paid for the drink. With a flirtatious smile, the woman looked at Dmitri.

Come to me, love, he thought.

The woman stood with poise. Her posture perfectly erect. Her steps eloquently made as if she'd taken ballet her entire life. She sat next to him. "Thank you for the drink."

"My pleasure. I'm Dmitri." He extended his hand. She embraced it with a light touch. Her face flashed a smile without her realizing it.

"Chloe. I haven't seen you in here before. Are you new to the area?"

"You could say that." Dmitri turned to face Chloe. His burning eyes intently on hers. Her eyes fixated on his and then she sat amorously frozen.

"Tell me your real name and what you're doing here," Dmitri whispered.

"Erica Fontenot. I'm working." The trance broke after the words left her mouth. Looking around, she sat momentarily confused.

Dmitri thought to himself, *A lady of the night. How fun that might be.*

"You're beautiful, Chloe. What's a beautiful woman like you doing in a place like this all alone?"

Chloe had regained her composure and once again fell into character. When she looked at Dmitri, she was overwhelmed by his appearance. She reveled in how handsome he was and sensed she might be putty in his hands.

"Just looking for some good company," she said coyly.

"For Mr. Right or Mr. Right Now?" he asked.

Chloe shrugged. "Depends. What are you looking for?"

Dmitri thought for a moment. Prostitutes were street-smart. Playing a game of cat-and-mouse might tell how slick she could be. "Let's cut to the chase, Chloe. How much for an hour?"

"Two thousand," she answered.

An attractive brunette took a seat next to Chloe. She ordered vodka-neat then stared at Dmitri. "What about me?"

Chloe looked at her, then back to Dmitri and then back at her and smiled, "Just you? Or both of you?"

The brunette whispered something in Chloe's ear, then paid her tab. Chloe stood up with thirsty eyes, licked her lips, and disappeared from the bar while Dmitri and the brunette finished their drinks.

The moment she entered her apartment, she kicked off her stilettos then pulled her dress over her head. Underneath she wore matching red lace panties and bra and seemed proud to show them off. After taking off her diamond necklace, she motioned for Dmitri to follow her to the bedroom. Inside of it, she opened a drawer, exposing multiple erotic toys. A leather flogger and nipple clamps were pulled out.

"You like pain, my love?" Dmitri asked.

Chloe gave a slow nod. "I want you." She couldn't resist another second. Dmitri grabbed her hand and pressed it against his erection. Her brows arched when her hand caressed the huge bulge in his crotch.

"Not yet," Dmitri insisted.

He ran his hand through her hair and peered into eyes that had become needy. The look was never the same. Each woman had their own look of arousal and he remembered every last one of them like photographs ingrained in his brain. Complete obedience fueled his intentions. Grabbing her head and tilting it to one side, exposed her neck in the most carnal way. The blood that rushed through her veins reminded him that he no longer had a beating heart. This caused his breathing to grow rapid and his incisors to emerge. Every ounce of his being wanted to bite and suck, but Dmitri practiced discipline. The method he'd mastered while feeding had served him well for many years.

"Please, Dmitri," Chloe begged, her lips parted, her breaths coming out in quick short pants.

"Please, what, my love?"

"Take me," she whimpered, unable to control her thoughts or how she felt.

"In time," Dmitri cautioned. "Get ready to experience pleasure beyond your wildest imagination, but first you must do something for me."

Chloe got on her knees and reached for his zipper.

"No, no, my love," he chastised gently then took her hand and lifted her on her feet again. "Not that. Be patient and you'll have your pleasure." Staring intently into her eyes, he took further control. "You'll write a letter. Tell me what you want in that letter. Tell me you're willing to die to get it. Understood?"

Chloe walked in a robotic gait to reach her bedside dresser. Moments later, she stood in front of him again. "It's done."

Dmitri removed all of his clothing. Chloe slowly licked her lips as she peeled off her underwear. Dmitri lay back on the bed. Chloe straddled him with urgent fervor.

The two lay in bed, Chloe sore and exhausted from intense physical exertion.

Dmitri turned to her and said, "Before you fall asleep, my love. Grab a knife out of your kitchen then come back to me and slice open your wrists."

Chloe exited the bed, still fully nude and barely able to walk steady. She returned with a large kitchen knife and laid beside Dmitri as he nodded in approval. Chloe stabbed the knife in her wrist and sliced the length of her forearm, digging almost to the bone. Blood spewed and showered her bare body.

Dmitri grabbed her wrist and took it into his mouth. He drank until his stomach distended, then dropped Chloe's lifeless arm beside her. Soon, he passed Chloe's arm to his beautiful dark-haired vixen who emerged and drank the beautiful nectar.

Chapter Eleven

Second Visit

A scream woke Katalina out of a deep sleep. Pressure mounted on her chest, making it hard for her to breathe. The paralysis had reared its ugly head again, pinning her down with invisible restraints. She couldn't see anything, but she felt a dark presence. It stood over her watching—a sadistic puppet master toying with its prey. She badly wanted to see it—to know what had such an uncontrollable stronghold over her. Katalina was stronger than any man she'd ever engaged. Some people secretly called her sir because of her dominance, but tonight she was stripped down to a scared little girl that was unable to gather her composure.

A shadow appeared on the ceiling near the doorway. It moved closer like fog creeping into a cemetery and with each inch it took Katalina's fear grew worse. Katalina knew that ninety-five percent of fear was baseless, yet tears streamed down her face. She needed help, but was kept silenced. This time, not even Casper's annoying screaming was there to comfort her.

A partial silhouette of a giant figure appeared in Katalina's field of view. It was solid black with no identifiable features. It was as if a large being had draped a black sheet over its head and lurked in the shadows. The figure raised a limb—an arm perhaps because it rose laterally. Katalina heard a scream followed by the raised limb thrusting down violently.

Katalina's screams broke through. The invisible force field lifted and she sat up as quickly as she could. Once again, her sheets were fully saturated. Her chest rose and fell like an accordion. She stepped over the side of her bed and inhaled—no scent out of the ordinary. She listened intently—no sounds to be heard.

Grabbing the gun from under her pillow, she stood on her feet. Her knees were wobbly and her hands trembled as she crept closer to her open bedroom door. She squeezed the trigger on her gun. Three pounds of pressure—four needed for the gun to fire. A simple jolt of nerves could destroy whatever the gun pointed at. Whoever was in her apartment would soon meet their demise. Had someone gotten inside her apartment? Were they now hiding? The shadow had been all-telling. She couldn't have been alone and if someone was there they would soon feel a bullet from her gun. She took a moment to gather her bearings. She drew a deep breath in to try and slow her heart rate.

Her cell phone buzzed from her nightstand. Katalina stared at it nervously, its sound having taken her by surprise. A breathy gasp came out of her when Casper waltzed inside of the room. So convinced she hadn't been alone, she would have shot at anything that moved. Thank God that phone had rung or she could have hurt her beloved cat. She got closer to the bedside table and saw that Benoit was calling.

"What's up, Duce? It's two a.m."

"Suit up, sunshine, time to clock in. The Riverdale Apartments, number 413."
Katalina sat at the edge of her bed and rubbed her forehead. The dreams seemed to be getting more detailed; and more frequent. Something didn't set right with her. Never in her life had she had nightmares like these. Why now?

Chapter Twelve

Staged

Benoit studied the leather-bound grimoire with curious awe. Someone had it wrapped years before to protect it. The writing inside appeared ancient, filled with intricate designs and sketches that looked similar to hieroglyphics. The writing was in English. He'd practiced basic spells for three years and had made great headway—small things like good luck spells, confidence builders, and healing spells, but his most prized secret was the little glimpses—little flashes of pictures that told an instant story of what was to come.

The grimoire was a gift, handed down throughout the generations. Benoit was able to see glimpses of the future. He knew when his phone was going to ring. He knew when people were going to speak to him. He sensed bad intentions among peers. He also sensed purity and positivity. But lately, his partner had consumed his mind. The tiny seemingly delicate detective who defied physical odds intrigued him.

Benoit was visited by an ancestor in his dreams—a witch doctor from Malawi. He came in peace and prophesied that Benoit was a lone warrior in a world filled with despicable creatures—creatures that only he had the power to combat. His visitor told Benoit to harness the power of animals to improve his strengths. He also learned to avoid cash as it was believed to break any spells being cast. The visitor didn't allow Benoit to speak and only to listen.

Benoit stood in his bathroom staring at his reflection in the mirror. An indigo aura surrounded him. He hadn't ever seen an aura before. Indigo auras cloak people who are sensitive to others' energy. They tend to know things before they happen, hear things before they're said and to have lucid dreams.

Benoit turned his head and waited for his cell phone to illuminate. *Someone died*, he thought. Seconds later, the phone rang. The patrol sergeant had called to let him know they had another body and where he and Katalina could find it. Benoit caressed the open page on the grimoire before leaving his apartment. *Clarity please.*

Twenty minutes after receiving the call, Benoit arrived at the crime scene. Less than two minutes later, Katalina parked her car next to his. "Kat, why do you always look like shit? Do you ever get any sleep?"

"Eh. I'm a night owl. I prefer the dark. I get a lot done at night."

Benoit couldn't help but get suspicious. *A night dweller.*

"Thanks, Duce. Nice to see you, too, dick. As a matter of fact, lately I've been sleeping horribly."

"Why? Nightmares? Stress? Body aches?"

"The first one," Katalina answered then averted her gaze along the street. "Lately, they've been getting more intense."

"They have drugs for that, you know? Over the counter stuff and not the strong shit. It looks to me like you could use at least one good night of sleep. Shall we get to it and see what we're going to find this time?"

A city cop guarded apartment 413 and handed the crime scene log for them to sign-in and add the time of their arrival.

"What do we have?" Benoit asked.

"Looks like a suicide, but you're the expert."

Benoit felt Katalina staring at him because the side of his face was burning. He looked at Katalina who had a look of suspicion—her eyebrows arched high across her forehead.

Benoit heard a growl. "You hungry, Kat?"

"Famished," she answered.

"You don't sleep. You don't eat. What is it that you do when you're home alone?"

"You'll never know," she joked.

The crime had taken place inside of a bedroom.

Benoit spoke first. "Okay, everyone out. We've got this. Good job securing the scene."

A forensics agent handed him a pair of nitrile gloves and then quickly put them on. After he heard Katalina snapping on a pair, he decided that now was the time for an inappropriate joke. "No, Kat. I won't bend over. What is your fetish with anal exams?"

Katalina tilted her head slightly to one side and stared at him with narrowed eyes. "You know that's exactly what you want."

"Nope!" Benoit said and offered a smile. "You've got issues."

The victim was a middle-age woman that lay naked on the bed covered in blood, her hair fanned neatly over the pillows as if the position of her head had been staged. Benoit looked at her arm, split open from the wrist to the bend. Her tendons and bones exposed. The knife still pierced in her flesh.

"You see that, Kat?"

"Somebody fixed her hair," Katalina answered.

"The wound," he clarified. "This is the second victim with their arm gorged this way."

Benoit walked into the master bathroom while Katalina studied the body. It was tidy. Several bras hung from a rack behind the door. A loofa hung from the shower head. Several bottles of perfume covered the sink. Benoit entered the living room and discovered a hand-written note:

I can no longer bear the overwhelming desire. I need you and will go to the ends of the Earth to quench my thirst. I hope to meet you on the other side.

"I found the note," Benoit alerted.

"A suicide note?" Katalina yelled from the bedroom.

Benoit brought it to Katalina who was radiating. He instantly recognized her aura—red. "You are radiating a red color, Kat."

"Huh?"

"Your aura. It's red. A red aura indicates a passionate, unapologetic, and adventurous person. They are generally unafraid of death and need adrenaline-inducing activities. I don't remember seeing your aura before."

"That sounds like some Sigmund Freud shit." She took the note and read it aloud. "No way this is coincidence, Duce! The same wound. A poetic note. Both women fully nude. No way. Do you know why most women don't commit suicide by shooting themselves?"

Benoit shook his head, "No, but I bet you're going to tell me, aren't you?"

"It's believed they want to be remembered as attractive when they're found," she answered. "Being found naked?" She gave a quick shake of her head. "I don't think that's how our last victims wanted to be found. Having their nudity stared at by a bunch of cops? Ninety percent of women who commit suicide do it by hanging themselves while they're still clothed. Make sure forensics sweeps this body. Something tells me they're going to discover jet-black hair again."

Benoit searched the residence and discovered a checkbook. "Kat, let me look at that suicide note again." He compared the handwritings. "It's definitely her handwriting. According to her checks, her name is Erica Fontenot."

Benoit found a cell phone and scrolled through its pictures. "I think our victim is a call girl judging from the selfies inside her phone and a good one at that, judging from the balance of her checking account."

Benoit returned to the body and opened her closed eyelids. Erica's dead eyes stared into a blank distance. He gazed in her eyes—waiting for something. He touched her forehead and closed his eyes. In his mind he recited a chant to a shaman. A breeze flowed through the room, giving him a chill. His eyes opened. He felt refreshed—informed.

His Zen state was interrupted by two voices entering the apartment, "Kat, forensics is here. Let's wrap this up."

Chapter Thirteen

The Hispanic

"Suit up sunshine, time to clock in. The Riverdale Apartments, number 413."

The dream she had before Benoit's call shook her to the core—a more intense dream that made her feel physically drained. But exhausted or not, work never ended and getting out of bed that very minute was something she had to do. To revitalize herself, she padded carefully to the kitchen with her pistol still in hand although she no longer suspected someone else inside her home. The spell had broken. Her thoughts were now clear. All of it had only been a dream; an eerily real dream.

After grabbing a diet Coke out of the fridge, she guzzled some of it then went back into her bedroom and got dressed, wearing comfortable attire for the night: a pair of jeans and a police tee shirt. Her badge was worn in plain sight. It hung from a necklace down the front of her shirt. As she exited her apartment, each step she took, it felt like the grip of the puppet master lessened until it finally disappeared. She raced to Riverdale apartments, secretly hoping to beat Benoit. Everything was a competition to Katalina, although she never admitted it out loud.

"Shit! He beat me," she mumbled as she pulled up next to Benoit's car. She sneaked a peek at herself in her rearview mirror and groaned.

"Hello, Death," she said to herself then hopped out of her SUV knowing Benoit would have something smart ass to say then gave him like for like after he did.

She'd been walking in front of him to reach the crime scene when the smell of blood made her mouth water. The smell felt like a drug, like pure ecstasy. She closed her eyes and licked her lips. A thunderous roar escaped her stomach just as she was approaching the entrance.

"You hungry, Kat?" Benoit asked.

"Famished!" she answered then said a few more things under her breath. The moment they entered the building she felt that familiar feeling of being watched. She studied every inch of every wall hoping to find where those prying eyes were coming from. When she finally reached the crime scene and donned a pair of nitrile gloves, she stared at the bedroom window, certain it had been left open, but after she got closer she noticed that it not only sat closed, but locked.

The victim is what she focused on next. She got close enough to examine the wound while Benoit searched the apartment for evidence and clues. Tasting the blood became too much of an urge. Using two fingers, she wiped along the wound then placed her fingers in her mouth.

Her eyes closed in satisfaction. She no longer felt bone exhausted, but fully refreshed and invigorated. No. More than that. She felt powerful, invincible then stared at the bedroom when Benoit yelled out he found a note.

***

Katalina and Benoit were interrupted by the radio traffic that blared, "Headquarters to 1115 Alpha, we're receiving a report of a signal 30 at 125 Ridgeview Drive, Apartment 24."

She gave Benoit a look, her face sour. "Are you fucking kidding me? A homicide? Looks like I won't be getting any sleep any time soon."

Benoit smiled. "C'mon, sunshine, let's go do what we do best."

The team arrived on Ridgeview Drive and replayed the same scenario that they always did. Yellow crime scene tape surrounded the apartment. Curious mobs of neighbors gathered outside the cordon while uniformed patrol jotted names and phone numbers down. Angry bystanders shouted police injustice while eyewitnesses kept the street code and kept their mouths shut.

Katalina approached the officer who maintained the crime scene log and got a whiff of iron. She looked at Benoit who was beside her and said, "It's a bloody one." She scribbled her time of arrival on the officer's log and dipped under the tape.

"Kat, we need to talk. In private," Benoit whispered.

"Nobody seen nothin'," the perimeter officer interrupted as he sucked his teeth.

"What's going on with you?" Benoit asked.

"Nothing. I'm just tired and hungry. Chill." Katalina fidgeted. Half curious and half concerned about whatever her partner was inferring.

Benoit stood face-to-face with Katalina and peered into her eyes. Much like an admonishing grandfather looking down the brim of his nose. "You know you can tell me anything, right?"

"It's fine, Duce. I'm just going through some shit. Thanks for the concern, but I'm a big girl," Katalina said as she pushed forward past Benoit.

The apartments were on the lower end of the economic spectrum. The mortar between the bricks, once white, now blackened. Cream-colored wood panels met the bricks that used to be bright white. "Yeah but they're sure quick to call when they're the victims," Katalina said. Benoit and Kat entered the apartment and found a white male laying in a pool of dark red blood; his neck gouged from ear-to-ear with his eyes still open. "I recognize him, Duce," Katalina said.

"How? Worked a case with him?"

"No, he's the pedophile who got off on a technicality. Cabrera and Castellano's case."

"No freaking way?" Benoit's face lit up with surprise.

A uniformed supervisor approached with a driver's license. "Kyle Roseberry," he said as he handed Benoit the ID card.

"Thanks, Sarge. Any witnesses?"

"A neighbor said they saw a Hispanic-looking man with dark features walk behind the building sometime earlier, but we don't have anything concrete yet."

Cabrera looks Hispanic. He said he wanted to kill him—well, he thought it.

"Thanks," she said. Katalina turned to Benoit. "I'm going to take a look around the apartment."

Her stomach growled. She suddenly felt like she was starving but had to ignore her stomach pains. The smell of fresh iron made her want to devour the blood inside, but too many eyes were lurking around.

Be disciplined, Kat, she thought.

Katalina entered his bedroom and was drawn to an open laptop beside his bed. The images displayed made her blood boil. Sweat surfaced on the base of her neck, but she took a controlled breath in and thought, *Kat, he's already dead. No need to get yourself all worked up*.

Katalina exited the bedroom and told Benoit, "That computer needs to be analyzed by the ICAC team." She mumbled under her breath, "Sick fucker."

"Internet Crimes Against Children?" Benoit asked.

"Yep. Seems he was back to his old habits." She looked down at the corpse and shook her head, "I guess someone else knew it too and took justice into their own hands."

Benoit asked, "Any surveillance?"

"I'll start the canvass," Katalina said as she exited the apartment.

It was dark outside, and no cameras obviously stood out to her. The crowd had dwindled since her arrival. Most were in the parking lot in front of the building, but something caught her eye. Movement along the rear corner of the building, near a tree line. She focused and saw a dark-complected male disappear behind the building. He had thick black hair and a deep bronzed skin tone. Instant nausea set in as Katalina clutched her stomach.

Hatred filled her entire being. He didn't belong.

She advanced toward the corner of the building; her hand resting on her Glock. The smell of a gym locker room consumed her nostrils. Putrid. Foul. Katalina crept to the corner, easing to the edge of the bricks. Her heart raced. Something was just around the corner. She knew it. She felt it like a headache gripping her skull. Katalina held her breath and peeked around the corner.

Nothing.

The wind rustled the leaves on the many trees that boxed her in, but no suspicious sounds were made. No twigs or sticks crackling as if someone were running through the woods. No animals being spooked. *I must be getting tired*, she thought.

The mystery man was gone. Katalina continued her walk around the building and emerged on the other side. She returned to the crowded parking lot and searched for the man she'd just seen, to no avail. Her right hand rubbed the back of her neck; a prickling feeling pinched her skin as the hair stood up. A hand touched her shoulder and she let out a scream. She almost jumped out of her shoes.

"Whoa, Kat. I'm sorry," Benoit said. "Let's wrap this up. We'll come back during daylight hours and get a better look. Crime scene is taking over anyway."

"Was there a murder weapon?" Katalina asked.

"Nope."

Chapter Fourteen

Redemption

On the following day, Dmitri's hunger drove him back to The Carousel. He was cocky and thought, *I didn't even get to hunt last night. That was too easy.* So, he dressed in his usual semi-formal attire. Blazer, slacks, and shiny Italian shoes. His long black hair dangled along the sides of his pale face.

Dmitri took a seat in one of the dark corners with his bottle of vodka already in hand. He eyeballed every woman that entered. With his senses heightened, he listened to conversations from across the room—the witty sexual banter and cheesy pickup lines. His seat was near the hallway leading to the restrooms, so every person who went to the bathroom had to pass within feet of him. But he secretly wanted to see the detective. He wanted to taste her, satisfy her, then kill her. Something about her made him determined.

A heavy-set girl with layers of makeup approached. They made eye contact and she smiled. Dmitri smelled her blood as she passed him. He became aroused and adjusted his pants as they tightened around his crotch. A smile stretched across his face.

It must be her time of the month, he thought. Every ounce of his being wanted to burst into the restroom and take her—violate her, then drain her. But it was early, and many people were walking past to reach the restrooms. *Be smart Dmitri*, he thought. *She'll return and fall in love. They all do.*

Dmitri had two loves in his life: a burning desire for sexual escapades and blood. He enjoyed pleasuring women. His supernatural gifts extended to his sexual performances. He always pleasured his victims before killing them. It was his offering before taking their lives.

The girl emerged from the restroom. Dmitri heard someone call her Chastity. *How fitting*, he thought. She walked past him and didn't make eye contact. He stared at her plump rear and licked his growing incisors. He focused and forced his way into her thoughts. Her stroll slowed. She stopped as if she'd had an epiphany. *That's right, Chastity. You should turn around and speak to me. You have something I desire.*

Chastity turned on command and stepped toward Dmitri. Her eyes fixated on his. She was drawn to him like a magnet. Chastity leaned over Dmitri's table—both arms locked as her hands gripped the tabletop. Her head hung, her eyes twinkled. She opened her mouth to speak but was interrupted by a man's voice.

"Babe. What's going on here? Who is this?"

Chastity ignored him and continued her trance-like gaze. Dmitri squinted his eyes and invaded her mind. "This is my new friend, Blaze. I'd like to bring him home with us." Chastity turned her lustful eyes to her boyfriend. She gently nibbled her bottom lip and whispered, "I want this." Chastity reached for Blaze's belt and tugged. She pulled his stomach against hers and rose on her toes. She kissed his neck and took his ear lobe into her mouth.

Dmitri reveled in his conquest. Without trying, he'd wrangled two unsuspecting lovebirds into his web. He extended his right hand to Blaze. "I'm Dmitri, nice to meet you. Have a seat and enjoy a drink, on me."

Chapter Fifteen

Hello Handsome

Katalina and Benoit entered The Carousel and jumped right into action, beginning with the bartender. She produced a photograph of Erica. "Hi, I'm Detective Andrews. This is my partner, Detective Benoit. Have you seen this woman before?"

The bartender studied the picture and immediately recognized her. His eyes nervously darted across the room. Katalina noticed and zeroed in on his eyes. "Yes. Her name is Chloe. She's a regular."

Katalina looked at Benoit and sniffed him again. He shot her a pair of eyes that suggested he wanted to kill her. He gritted his teeth and spoke, lips barely parted, "I'm wearing deodorant, Kat!"

Katalina laughed and said, "When was the last time she was here?"

"Last night," he answered.

"Who was she here with?"

The bartender thought for a moment. He shook his head and said, "I don't remember. She was alone, I think."

"C'mon, think harder. She was a prostitute and she came here to meet her Johns."

The bartender shrugged his shoulders, offering no facial expression.

"Okay, are there any other regulars here tonight?"

The bartender studied the room and pointed to a man seated in the corner. The man was with two other people: a younger lady and a younger man. The trio appeared to be having a good time. The girl was hanging all over both men.

Katalina approached the table and felt a familiar invisible grip squeeze her. She was fixated on the older man with dark hair. "Excuse me, sorry to interrupt, but can I have a word?" Katalina asked. Her frigid eyes locked on Dmitri's fiery eyes.

Chastity and Blaze's chokehold was released when Dmitri focused on Katalina. The couple rose from their chairs looking dazed and confused. They disappeared across the barroom while Katalina questioned Dmitri.

"I'm Detective Andrews." Katalina extended her hand toward Dmitri. She grew scared. Her head suddenly felt pressure as if she had a cold. She noticed Dmitri focusing on her eyes as if he was trying to stare through her. *Creeper. Does he know me?* she thought.

"Dmitri. Pleased to meet you, detective. To what do I owe the pleasure?"

Katalina produced a photo of Erica and asked, "Do you know this woman?"

Dmitri took the picture and analyzed it, studying the woman he fed on just hours before while Katalina studied his expressionless face. He shook his head and said, "I don't know her."

Katalina paid close attention to his hands. The picture remained perfectly still in his fingers. No nervous shaking. No wavering. She was drawn to Dmitri. His chiseled face and burning eyes were attractive to her, but she fidgeted as she sat. Her eyes darted throughout the bar as if trying to catch a glimpse of an elusive fly. She anxiously studied every person, every sound, and every smell. Her heightened synapses were on fire with warning signs and anxious stabs in her head caused confusion. She stood up and searched for Benoit. He was across the bar talking to other patrons. "Will you excuse me, Dmitri?"

"Wait. Do you have a card or something? Her picture looks familiar and perhaps if something comes to mind, I could reach out to you?"

Katalina wanted to ask Dmitri a thousand questions, like what kind of music he liked or what his favorite movie was or what his sign was. She wanted to get to know him on a personal level. Something about him was enigmatic yet charming. Katalina produced a business card and did something she'd never done before. She scribbled her cell phone number on the back without even realizing it. When she handed the card to Dmitri, his fingers brushed against hers and she felt a foreign warmth. Not physical warmth. In fact his fingers were icy, but a welcoming warmth. Her heart fluttered. As she stepped away, she rose on the balls of her feet—almost skipping.

Benoit came into her field of view and stepped toward her. He spoke cautiously, "What is up, Kat? Your smile pains me. Did you get a lead or something?"

"Hmm?" Katalina dismissed his questions and wandered right past him as if he wasn't standing in front of her.

"Earth to Katalina. Hello?" Benoit snapped his fingers in her direction. "Well, a few people saw her last night. She was indeed a regular, but everyone here knows her as Chloe. She left alone last night. No surveillance cameras.

Katalina reached for her phone in her back pocket. She checked it several times while Benoit spoke to her. She moved around the room questioning different patrons and stole a peek at Dmitri every chance she could. Sometimes he returned the glance and made eye contact. If her heart had a mouth it was smiling.

Chapter Sixteen

Dirty Thoughts

Katalina sprawled across her couch and opened a paperback novel. She snuggled beneath a warm fleece blanket and enjoyed a sip of Sangria. Casper leapt onto her lap, his tail flickered, and he begged to be covered. Katalina lifted her leg, exposing a small entry beneath the covers. Casper crept in and plopped in between her legs. He had to touch her. Her skin against his provided wonderful warmth. Seconds later the sound of a fine-tuned motor emanated from beneath the blanket as Casper purred—his sign of complete surrender and comfort.

The novel was graphic and sexual with an emphasis on romance and Katalina couldn't help but think about the dark-haired mystery man from The Carousel. Each scene in the book, the main character felt seduced and had no control around her beau, ultimately surrendering and allowing him to have his way with her. She didn't feel used though, in fact, she was using him as much as he used her. Katalina fantasized about being the main character and Dmitri being her beau. She took another sip of Sangria and stared at her phone, hoping a foreign number would appear. Dmitri's number.

She thought about tapping into her investigative database and doing some digging. Someone that handsome and dapper must have a checkered past.

Hopefully he's a bad boy, she thought. *Shit, I don't even know his last name or if Dmitri is even his real name*. Katalina opened her dating app on her phone and did a search on Dmitri. *That's an uncommon name*, she thought. Katalina had a message notification inside the app. Her heart rate increased. *No fucking way*. She nibbled on her bottom lip, anxious to see who messaged her. She hoped Dmitri somehow found her. Fate somehow aligned the stars for her.

When Katalina pressed the notification on her phone, Pete's picture showed up. His message read, "Missing you!"

Katalina's face stretched with a warm smile. She enjoyed his company, albeit his deep desire to molest her. *Who am I kidding? I need it as much as he does*, she thought. *Besides, what guy doesn't think that way?* Truth be told, Katalina had a high sex drive and needed a man who could keep up. She closed the application and sent Pete a text message:

"Hey. I'd love to catch a movie. If you're available and still interested, let me know."

Pete responded, "I'd love that!!! Just say when!"

Katalina loved reading his text message. The exclamation points made her feel special. She was a stickler for punctuation and knew he was genuine the second she read it.

"Well, Casper. What do you think?"

Casper let out a piercing scream.

"Okay, all you really want is food." Katalina sent a text message back to Pete, "Meet me at the Grand Theater at 8:45 sharp. My pick."

Pete responded, "I can't wait!"

Katalina didn't take long to get ready. She only wore eyeliner and mascara. Her lips were painted a vibrant red. She curled pieces of her neon orange hair and it fell beautifully against her shoulders, but she knew the curls would straighten within the hour.

Do I dress comfortably? Or Sexy? Let's meet in the middle. Katalina had gone all out on their first date at Irene's. She hadn't worn a dress in years. *Tonight, he gets a more realistic version of Katalina*, she thought.

She chose a pair of Buckle jeans that stretched like yoga pants. The jeans hugged her every curve but gave her the comfort of lounging around her apartment. She wore a dressy black bralette beneath a gray sweater that wrapped around her shoulders, exposing the black straps against her milky white skin, and was long enough to grace her thighs.

Katalina arrived at The Grand Theater just before 8:45 pm. She reverse parked beneath a parking lot street light and checked her surroundings before exiting. An uncomfortable feeling surrounded her. That strange feeling of being watched. The hair on the back of her neck stood. Something was close. She closed her eyes and tried to push the feelings away—chalking it up to second-date nerves, but she couldn't. From the driver's seat, Katalina peered into every vehicle in her field of view. She hoped to catch a creep watching her. That would put her mind at ease. The mere fact that something had control over her drove her insane.

She sent a text to Pete, "Black Tahoe backed into a space on row three."

He responded, "Just pulled in!"

A silver truck pulled into a parking space near Katalina and Pete emerged. He was dressed handsomely, with jeans and a short sleeve Polo shirt with a leather jacket. Katalina exited her vehicle and walked toward Pete. His cologne, Aqua di Gio, drove Katalina mad. She inhaled and closed her eyes with pleasure. Her nervous eyes met his and the two embraced.

He held her tight and said, "I've missed you!"

Katalina melted. She felt safe in his arms. She belonged in his arms. The couple strode into the theater, hand-in-hand.

"What are we watching?" Pete asked.

Katalina looked up at Pete and said, "Since it's the holiday season, I thought we'd watch a classic. *It's a Wonderful Life.*"

Pete smiled. "I see we share the holiday spirit! This movie is a classic. Great choice!" They entered the auditorium and all but had it to themselves. Only three or four other people shared their nostalgia.

Chapter Seventeen

Thirsty

Dmitri obsessed over Katalina. Never in his life had he ever experienced someone whose mind he couldn't infiltrate who wasn't a vampire. "Victoria, my dear."

His beautiful brunette vixen who shared Eric's blood appeared. "Yes?"

"That detective. Miss Andrews, from The Carousel…"

Victoria grinned as if she knew what was coming. "Mmm Hmm?"

"Did you notice anything peculiar about her?"

Victoria answered, "Oh, like the fact that we can't read her?"

Dmitri's eyes squinted. The muscles in his jaw flared out like little wings as he exhaled, "I don't know what to make of it. Witch maybe?"

Victoria shrugged and said, "I don't know, but I do want to taste a sample. Please arrange a meeting."

"I do have her number," Dmitri responded, "but I think I'd rather play first."

Victoria's eyes widened. She pressed her thin lips together in anticipation. "Oh, I love a chase! But you'll have to really charm her. You can't force it on this one."

Dmitri's head tilted. His mind drifted into deep thought as he pondered his next move. "Let's take a stroll."

"I thought you'd never ask. I'm famished!"

"Would you like a snack first, dear?" Dmitri asked.

Victoria answered, "I'd rather wait for the mysterious redhead."

"Well, then. I know where she is. Shall we?"

Dmitri and Victoria lurked behind trees in the dark that surrounded the movie theater. Their stomachs growled with each young vibrant teenager who entered. Some just under the age of consent, being dropped off by their parents. "I do love the vitality that comes from these younger ones," Dmitri whispered.

"There she is, Dmitri. Aww, would you look at that. She's backing into her parking space like a good little driver."

Dmitri nodded. "Try to get in again," he said. "So will I." His head shook with frustration, "Nothing! What is it with her?"

"Looks like you've finally met your match, Dmitri."

"Challenge accepted."

"Who is that? A boyfriend?" Victoria asked. She listened to Pete's thoughts.

I'm the luckiest guy on Earth right now. I wonder if she likes my cologne. God, she looks gorgeous!

"Yes, definitely her boyfriend, Dmitri."

Dmitri released a low primal growl. "We'll see how he fares when tested."

Dmitri and Victoria took seats at the opposite end of the theater. Each hidden beneath darkness. Each listening intently on Pete's inner thoughts as he watched the movie.

Victoria communicated with Dmitri telepathically, "He has good intentions."

"It's a facade. He's a man. That goodie two-shoes shit will wear off. Just you watch. And I'll be there to pick up the pieces. I'll be the hero's hero."

Katalina leaned over into Pete's arms. His hand gripped her shoulder. Dmitri seethed behind them. He focused on the couple and heard Katalina whisper in Pete's ear, "I needed this. Thank you."

Jealousy coursed through Dmitri. Anger moved through him like a glacier that burned everything it touched with the deadliest coldest heat. He drummed on his cell phone.

He sent Katalina a text message as a test. "Hey, there. Hoping we can meet up. Maybe get a drink. Truly yours, Dmitri."

He watched Katalina closely as she reached for her purse. She took a quick look at her phone and dismissed it instantly, dropping it back into her purse without a second thought.

The movie ended and the parking lot sat empty. Katalina and Pete walked toward their vehicles hand-in-hand. With each breath they took, white condensation poured into the cold air. Victoria emerged from the darkness and stood ready behind Pete's truck.

Chapter Eighteen

Step Aside

Katalina hooked her arm with Pete's as they walked out of the theater. "I really enjoyed tonight," she said. "I've been dealing with a lot of stress lately, so a night like this one was very much needed."

"The pleasure was all mine," Pete answered and gave a smile. "I hope we can do this again sometime soon."

Katalina slowed almost to a stop. The invisible force had returned. Something heavy pressed against her on all sides making it nearly impossible to take another step while her heart beat uncontrollably fast inside her chest. They had reached their cars. She could sense something wrong. Just as her eyes started to scan the parking lot, a brunette stepped forward with a hammer in her hand, her eyes murderous and fixed on Pete.

"Who is she?" Victoria asked in the voice of a jealous jilted lover.

Instinctively, Pete stepped in front of Katalina, not wanting her to get hurt by someone that looked crazy and dangerous. When he spoke, a plea could be heard in his voice. "Ma'am, we don't want any trouble. I think you have me mistaken for someone else." After he spoke, he saw that the windows of his truck had been busted out and that the passenger door had been smashed with something heavy and riddled with pock marks.

Katalina recognized Pete's fear and that he was experiencing—catatonic shock. She'd seen this many times in victims throughout her career. The shock left him almost completely immobile. His thoughts warned he didn't know the armed woman. Katalina grew defensive. The need to protect him became an insuperable urge.

There was only a small distance between them and the crazy woman. Katalina wanted to grip her pistol from the small of her back, but her arms and legs refused to budge; something she'd never experienced before, despite her numerous fight-or-flight encounters. Without warning, the crazy woman lunged, striking Pete in the head with the hammer. The sound of a disturbing crack filled the air. As if everything happened in slow motion, a deep gash opened on Pete's hair, spraying warm blood on Katalina's face with the speed of a watermelon exploding.

The aroma of blood shook Katalina to her core. As if her eyes were forced to watch everything as it happened, she saw Victoria parted her lips as her incisors grew long into two sharp fangs. The growl Victoria made as she stared down at Pete collapsed on the ground broke the spell Katalina had been under. Her hand reached instinctively toward the small of her back. Muscle memory controlled her subconscious movements. Her proficiency was laser-sharp; evidence of hours of training. With her arms extended in a perfect isosceles triangle, both of her hands gripped the firearm. Her knuckles turned white. The barrel was pointed at Victoria as Katalina kept both eyes open.

No hesitation.

No second guessing.

Katalina squeezed the trigger, waiting for an explosion. With each squeeze after the sound of a gun firing disturbed the night for several streets away. The muzzle flash filled the darkness. Katalina didn't stop shooting until the slide on her Glock locked back indicating she'd shot her last round.

Victoria didn't fall. Katalina's eyes grew large, her jaw clenched tight. Fear, excitement, hunger, protection, and ire filled her senses. After she licked a splatter of blood from her lips, she grew enraged. Her skin itched as her blood flowed through her veins, pumping much needed oxygen to all of her organs. A sense of numbness and invincibility fueled her courage.

Stepping over Pete's body, she punched Victoria in the face then spun swiftly on the balls of her heels before leaping into the air while turning in a three-hundred-and-sixty degree circle and sending a strong kick into Victoria's stomach.

The kick sent Victoria flying backward then flipping and tumbling on the pavement. When she stood, her eyes glowed in an unusual color. With surprise showing on her face, she parted her lips to expose her fangs. In an incalculable speed she lunged toward Katalina only to be met with a powerful punch that connected to her temple.

When Victoria found herself being knocked several feet across the air again and landing on her back, she grabbed a broken bottle out of the gutter and tossed it like a boomerang at Katalina's thigh in the hopes that the pain would bring Katalina down.

The jagged, sharp edges of the glass pierced Katalina's thigh, but she didn't flinch. She felt no pain. Victoria didn't back down either. In a flash, she was on her feet lunging at Katalina while at the same time throwing a punch. The punch landed on Katalina's jaw and knocked her back a few steps.

Before she could recover, a kick forced the broken bottle deeper into her thigh until it struck the bone. Victoria ran to her hammer, the toss she made similar to a boomerang. With each twirl, the weight of the hammer cut through the air making the sound of a fast spinning blade.

Katalina lifted her left arm to block her face. The head of the hammer shattered her forearm, the impact causing the steel mallet to break off after the wooden handle splintered. Without thinking, Katalina gripped the broken off handle, piercing its sharp end into Victoria's chest.

The sound that filled the air was similar to two freight trains colliding. Victoria dropped onto her knees with disbelief showing in her eyes, and then she collapsed onto the ground as her body shriveled in size. When it got smaller than humanly possible, a red essence lifted out of it and flew inside of Katalina's body. The laceration on her thigh disappeared. The broken bottle shattered into tiny pieces after it dropped to the ground.

Katalina turned to Pete then hurried to him. Although he lay motionless, he was still breathing. She checked his pulse and found it very faint, then she crawled closer to her fallen purse, grabbed her cell phone and dialed 911. She then called Benoit and breathed a sigh of relief after he told her he was nearby. It took only minutes for him to arrive and, thankfully, before the police and paramedics.

Benoit hurried out of his car to reach the male body he saw on the ground, but Katalina pulled him away.

"That's not what I need you for," she stressed, then pulled him closer to the body of the deranged, hammer-toting woman.

At first, Benoit couldn't tell what he was looking at and only that whatever it was, it was dead. And then despite the size or how shriveled the corpse appeared, he realized he was staring down at what used to be a woman.

"What the hell?" he shrieked, falling back on his heels to put distance between him and what lay on the ground.

"It's a vampire, Duce. A fucking vampire! How can I explain this to anyone at the precinct?"

Benoit stared at the piece of wood sticking out of the corpse's now tiny chest. After seeing it, he took only seconds to regain his composure. Closing his eyes and lowering his chin, he waited until calm filled him and then he started to meditate.

Katalina cradled Pete's head in her lap. "Everything is going to be okay," she whispered.

Sirens blared louder as they grew closer. The first responders and paramedics pulled up at the same time. The medic in charge asked Katalina questions about what happened.

"He was mugged. He was struck with something large."

"Okay, ma'am, step back. We've got this." The medics exchanged medical lingo and worked tirelessly, stabilizing Pete before loading him into the ambulance.

"Wait! Where are you taking him?" she asked.

"Tulane Medical. They have the best trauma team in the state." The medics blazed away in a fury, leaving Katalina and Benoit to themselves.

Katalina stared at the ground then jumped onto her feet and faced Benoit. "Where is she?" she whispered.

"Where is who?" Benoit whispered back, the look in his eyes more than conspiratorial.

***

Katalina and Benoit were walking to her Tahoe when a sudden gust of wind slammed into them and rocked the Tahoe vigorously from side to side. It just had come out of nowhere causing both of them to look up at the sky. Benoit got Katalina's attention then gave a gesture for her to keep going. As she drove away, she noticed how her body felt strong, healthy, and capable of anything.

Before tonight, if someone had told her that vampires were real, she would have laughed in their face. Now, as she drove she stared at the pedestrians she drove past and wondered if they were human or something else. What she couldn't stop thinking about was how she had been able to kill a vampire. Each time she stared down at her jeans and saw a tear but no wound underneath, anxiety and fear coursed through her, forcing her to focus on the road or risk causing a collision.

Chapter Nineteen

Markus the Elder

Vozrozhdeniya (Voz) Island, Uzbekistan

Markus held up his fist to stop the two other elders from advancing. He tilted his head and gazed into the dark distance. No life had inhabited the island since the mid-1980s. Voz Island, dubbed Anthrax Island, was an abandoned top secret biowarfare testing site controlled by the Russians through the mid-to-late twentieth century. Only people wearing heavy-duty biological protective gear could step foot on the island otherwise death was imminent.

The two elders, Amelia and Viktor, focused on Markus—their eyes a deep and lush red, burned with curiosity. They knew what was happening, but they patiently waited.

Markus turned to his comrades. "We've lost one. Victoria. She belonged to Dmitri."

"Was it Dmitri?" Viktor asked.

Markus shook his head.

"Another vampire?" Viktor inquired in a skeptic tone.

Markus pursed his lips then let out a breath. "Not one I recognize. A female with red hair."

"Human?" Amelia asked in disbelief.

"Get Dmitri here," Markus insisted. "It's urgent." He turned to face Viktor. "This female has an uncanny resemblance to Erik." Markus glared at Viktor. "You remember Erik, yes? How about Ivanka, his pregnant human? I recall you telling me that you dispatched them both." He trembled with anger as he glared at Viktor.

Viktor's eyes darted between Markus and Amelia. "I did. I tore their heads off and burned them both. Coincidence. There is no way possible—"

Markus interrupted Viktor's plea with a simple wave of his hand, his eyes bitter with disdain. "Do you doubt me, Viktor?"

Viktor hung his head. "No, but I know what I did and—"

"You ensure Dmitri is here with a full report on Victoria."

Markus vanished, leaving Viktor and Amelia to themselves. They dared not speak an ill word of Markus, for he was the grand elder of Europe.

Chapter Twenty

Disposal

Dmitri emerged from the shadows beyond Benoit and Katalina. He observed Katalina pleading with her friend; frantically pacing back and forth. He needed to snatch Victoria's body without being detected but the witch posed a problem. Not to mention the redheaded enigma who somehow killed a vampire before him. Whatever she was.

Dmitri wisped in like the wind, just behind Benoit. He held his breath, assuming the witch would sense his presence or worse, get a glance of him. Dmitri wasn't prepared for that kind of encounter. He'd never battled a witch before and had only heard stories of their exquisite destruction tactics; something that frightened him greatly. At the right moment he had rushed closer and stole Victoria's body before anyone noticed.

Dmitri approached Sylvain's on Chartres Street. Tourists formed a line outside the front door, waiting for a chance to experience the notorious haunted restaurant so Dmitri crept to the rear of the building. He reached a cellar door that was separated from the antebellum-style structure and delivered Victoria's body to a sentry standing guard. The entryway was much like a separate basement entrance which was odd considering New Orleans was beneath sea level.

Once inside, he descended multiple levels until he reached a long winding hallway with little entryways cut out; each with a room, much like a medieval whorehouse. Moans of pleasure could be heard from behind each door. Humans whispering and begging to be satisfied. Vampires intoxicated beyond control. The rooms were a safe haven where vampires brought willing human prey to feed on without the threat of discovery. American vampires didn't kill humans without cause. It was an American vampire rule Dmitri despised and ignored. Little pipettes containing traces of blood lay scattered throughout the rooms, most crushed after their contents were consumed.

The end of the hallway opened up to a barroom. No humans were allowed into the barroom—only the feeding rooms leading up to the bar. Dmitri entered the room and took note of his company. He was easily the youngest vampire in the room.

He knew it. He also knew that they were aware.

Dmitri approached the bartender, Maks. A vampire who had tended the bar since its inception in 1886. "Where's Victoria?" Maks asked.

Dmitri's head hung. He inhaled cautiously. "Stoli please." Maks poured Dmitri a glass and handed it to him.

"What did you do this time, Dmitri?" Maks asked.

Dmitri's eyes tried to remain calm, but they stole glances in each direction as he spoke. "Whatever do you mean?"

Maks delivered a look of disgust. "No idea, Dmitri?" He shook his head in disapproval. "You are not in Europe, Dmitri!" Maks' head shook in disbelief. "There are consequences here in America." Maks clenched his jaw and wiped the bar. His top lip quivered; his tongue could be seen wiping his fangs beneath his top lip despite trying to hide them. Each stroke of the rag shook the ancient cypress frame. "Did anyone follow you here?"

Dmitri's face twisted with ire. He gripped the glass, his knuckles white, and hurled the glass in Maks' direction. Maks didn't flinch. The glass flew by his head and shattered against the wall behind him.

"Dmitri, you've been called for by the elders in Europe."

Dmitri froze the moment those words left Maks' mouth. He stared at the dirty bar top and drew an imaginary picture with his right index finger. He knew not to whisper, for every vampire in the bar could hear each word. Dmitri's hands shook for the first time since being turned. His eyes shifted left then right.

"Dmitri, don't return here until after you've spoken to the elders. You're not welcome until your business there is done."

"You're siding with the European faction? You're weak, Maks."

Maks' eyes grew cold as he bore down on Viktor. "You may not value your existence, but I do. I know better than to defy the elders."

Dmitri nodded his head, tipped his glass up and vanished from the barroom. When he emerged from the cellar doors, the sentry was still standing guard, minus Victoria's corpse. The two exchanged glances—the sentry offered a friendly nod, reassuring Dmitri it was done.

Chapter Twenty-One

The Elders

The three elders conversed deep in an underground bunker beneath the abandoned radio station that blared Russian propaganda. A scene from the 1950s as snippets of Joseph Stalin played over and over through the loudspeakers.

"He's here," Markus whispered.

Viktor and Amelia sat, impatient for Dmitri's arrival. A vampire's magic was rendered useless on the island. Only the elders maintained such a privilege because they absorbed all of the power like a magnet. When vampires departed the island, their power returned.

Dmitri entered the ruins and walked what seemed a lifetime until reaching the rusted pipe fence that surrounded the radio station. A ship graveyard surrounded the island, rich with decrepit ancient fishing boats that once proudly produced 44,000 tons of fish per year, now relegated to a vast desert that was once the massive lake's floor.

Upon arrival, he knelt before the troika. Markus spoke, "Dmitri, lad. It disturbs me that I had to call for you. Were you not going to come on your own?"

"It happened so quickly, your highness. I barely disposed of the body without detection."

Viktor spoke, "How so?"

Amelia's eyes widened. Her face turned to Viktor. She stared in awe, mouth agape.

Markus cocked his head sideways when Viktor spoke. Only the grand elder reserved the right to ask questions, but Dmitri spilled anyway. "We were just messing with some humans…"

"We?" Markus asked.

"Yes. Victoria and I. You know, just torturing them before feeding," Dmitri said.

"Who is *them*?"

"A woman named Katalina and some man she'd spent the evening with."

A smile stretched across Markus' face. His burning eyes twinkled. "You know only one name, Dmitri?" Dmitri's head remained hung low as it slowly swayed back and forth. "Describe this Katalina."

Dmitri shrugged his shoulders as if dismissing the question. "Young woman. Red hair. Pale skin. She's a police officer in New Orleans."

Markus, Amelia, and Viktor went silent. The tension could be cut with a knife.

"In America?" Amelia asked.

Dmitri lowered his head and nodded.

"Dmitri, you're not stupid. You know the consequences for going outside your territory, don't you?"

Dmitri remained silent.

Markus spoke, "And her surname?"

"Andrews." Dmitri's palms rose facing up in confusion, wondering why that was even a question.

"Tell me about Victoria's demise," Markus said.

"Victoria destroyed the man. Killed him, I think. That upset Katalina. She… she…"

"Yes, Dmitri. Tell me how this human killed a vampire," Markus said with passive-aggressive sarcasm.

Dmitri hadn't had a chance to process what he witnessed. It was evident by the pauses before his answer. "Victoria did what she was supposed to do, but Katalina was somehow stronger and faster."

"Stronger than a vampire? A human?" Markus shook his head, sucking his teeth in disappointment. Dmitri's head rose, seeking answers to the nonsense that spewed from his lips.

"Is there anything else, Dmitri?"

"There was a witch. A brown-skinned human who cast a weak invisibility spell to cloak Victoria's body from other humans in the area."

"Did she see you? The witch?" Markus asked.

"He. The witch is a man, and no." Dmitri answered.

"Did you kill him?"

"No."

"A witch strong enough to cast a spell, witnessed one of our kind dead, and you did nothing? A human killed one of our kind—a high crime by all accounts, and you did nothing?"

Dmitri remained silent, knowing the questions had been rhetorical.

"You shall return to America and clean up this mess. Need I remind you what happens if you can't right your wrongs, Dmitri?"

Dmitri shook his head. "No your highness."

Markus waved his hand as if to sweep floating crumbs away from his face; his head slightly cocked away from Dmitri and his face sour with disgust. "Run along, Dmitri. I expect all loose ends to be tied up immediately, otherwise Viktor will tie them up for you."

Dmitri nodded, his eyes never leaving the floor beneath him.

"You're dismissed," Markus ordered as he watched Dmitri disappear through the primary tunnel of the dungeon. He turned to Viktor and said, "He has two days."

"Shall we notify Rainey?" Viktor asked.

Markus glared at Viktor yet remained silent. Viktor sighed and shook his head without speaking another word.

Chapter Twenty-Two

Katalina's Homecoming

Katalina grabbed two perfectly wrapped gifts from under her Christmas tree. She stepped out of her apartment barely bundled up. Christmas Eve in New Orleans was mild to say the least. In fact, just after noon the sun finally burned through the overcast sky, and folks could be seen wiping sweat from their foreheads.

Katalina looked up at the marvelous blue sky and asked, "Would it be so hard to surprise us with a little powder for once?"

Her phone rang through the speakers in her SUV. "Hey, Mom! I'm on my way."

"Oh, hon, it's just past lunchtime and I was beginning to worry," her mother said.

Katalina hadn't visited home since Father's Day. Getting out of the city was a tough task. "I know, I'm so sorry. I'll be there in twenty minutes. Mom, did you bake a pumpkin pie?"

"Max! Get away from those! Yes, hon, but if you don't hurry, there may not be any left."

"You tell Dad that we will fight if he eats all of those pies," Katalina yelled, half laughing.

"Well, there's a pumpkin and a pecan. He may think he can eat them all, but he ain't the young man he used to be. I'll see you soon honey."

"Okay, Mom. See you soon."

Street activity in New Orleans stayed busy throughout the year because of heavy tourism and Christmas brought the same number of tourists as the summer. Streetlamps throughout the French Quarter had been decorated with either boasted sleighs, candy canes, mistletoe, or crosses. Each pole had vibrant red or green lights twisting from top to bottom. Businesses downtown had white lights strewn around the doors and windows and along the Mighty Mississippi River, the docks were decorated with red and white striped ribbons. Even the iconic riverboat that slowly churned up the river was decorated with the holiday spirit.

Katalina arrived at her parent's house and smiled. She drew in a deep breath of fresh country air and immediately grew nostalgic. Her eyes squinted like half-moons when she saw the front door and windows sprayed with fake snow. Her parents loved the holiday season as much as she did. When she walked in, her mother all but screamed and ran toward her—still wearing her apron. Her dad was seated in his favorite recliner watching football. The sweet aroma of cinnamon, sugar, and pumpkin spice enveloped her when she entered.

"What's for lunch?" Katalina asked.

"Oh, the usual. Deboned turkey roll, rice dressing, cornbread dressing, candied yams, cranberry sauce, pumpkin pie, and pecan pie," her mother boasted.

Katalina smiled and waited. She also smelled the raw steak sitting out on the counter that her mother forgot to mention. "Anything else?" she asked.

"I almost forgot! Your steak, my dear. I was waiting for you to get here because I know you like it rare."

Her father took a drink from a dark brown bottle with a blue and silver wrapper, "Only my girl would want a steak for Christmas!"

Katalina peered at her dad, still reclined on his chair. Her mouth slightly agape and her hands propped on her hips. "Daddy! I would have eaten anything Mom cooked." She smiled at her mother. "But I was really looking forward to the ribeye!"

All three laughed. Katalina tucked the two gifts she brought beneath the magnificent tree staged in the corner. It was a live tree, also sprayed with fake snow. The tree had homemade ornaments that Katalina had made throughout grade school along with a little police car, but the majority of the ornaments were Disney characters collected over the years.

"Everyone take a seat. Lunch is ready," her mother announced as she arranged plates and glasses around.

"You know, Mom. I love how you haven't changed the dining room table in all these years," Katalina said.

The table was a modest homemade farm-style that seated four. Once seated, they all held hands and blessed the food, followed by a sign of the cross and an "amen" after. Her mother and father's plate were similar, each with perfectly measured portions of food. Katalina had a plate that mirrored theirs. She also had a plate with a luscious steak soaked in blood beside the traditional plate.

"I don't know how you can eat so much and remain so tiny," her dad noted.

"High metabolism, Daddy," she answered.

"You'd better enjoy that shit because once you hit thirty-five, your metabolism sets sail."

Katalina shrugged as she eye-balled her plates, almost dismissing his comment. She carefully cut into the delight that caused a trickle of saliva to escape one corner of her mouth. With each slice of her knife, blood dripped from the steak. She took the piece of flesh into her mouth and moaned as if she'd been starving.

"You look just like her," her mother said.

"Who?" Katalina asked.

"Your mother, Ivanka," she answered.

Her dad chimed in, "She looks like Erik, too. Spitting image." Each eye had tears as they admired the beautiful woman before them.

Katalina chewed and enjoyed her chunk of heaven before speaking. "What were they like?"

"Ivanka was a strong woman. She was a waitress in Belarus and emigrated there from Croatia. She was beautiful—looked just like you. She spoke several languages and was the smartest person I knew. When you were growing in her belly, she used to read books to you in different languages. She played music from all over the world, hoping you would be cultured," her mother said.

"And your father, Erik. He was an honest man. People respected him. Nobody ever messed with Erik, not even the Russian mafia. He pursued your mother for months before she even acknowledged him. You got the best traits from each of them. They would be proud of you if they were still alive, my dear," her father said.

Katalina smiled. "Was he smart, too?"

Her father grinned. "He read every book in his bookstore. Nobody knew more than Erik, but he wasn't cocky! He was a humble man, always helping a friend or neighbor. They don't make 'em like that anymore."

As Katalina devoured her steak, she couldn't help but hear her adopted parents' thoughts.

"I hope we've made them proud," her mother thought.

"You did," Katalina said out loud.

"I did what, hon?" her mother answered.

Katalina's eyes darted back and forth from her mother to her father. "You did an amazing job on this meal!" Her father nodded in approval. Her mother blushed. "One day, I'd like to visit where they lived," Katalina said.

"Just be careful. A pretty girl like you all alone across the world…" Her dad shook his head. Thoughts of women being kidnapped filled his head.

"I'm pretty tough, ya know?" Katalina offered. "I'd be just fine, dad."

Before long, her father announced, "Let's open gifts!" as he plopped back down in his recliner, fresh beer in hand.

"Okay, me first." Katalina handed her mother a present, her eyes twinkled with anticipation.

"What's this?" her mother asked.

"It's a plane ticket! To Europe!" Katalina shouted.

Her mother bit her lip and glanced at her father who cracked a sheepish smile. Katalina fidgeted in her seat, barely able to contain her excitement. "I know none of us have ever been, but I think it'll be so much fun! We can visit the town my mother was born in, where she and dad met, and maybe even where his bookstore was!"

Both of her parents had tears again. Her mother pursed her lips as the corners of her mouth drooped. "This is beautiful, Katalina. You shouldn't have."

"Don't worry about the cost. It's not like I have a man or kids or anything!"

All three chuckled.

Her father squinted in suspicion. "About that. When are you going to find yourself a nice man?"

"Um, let's not have this conversation. Soon enough, okay?"

Her father shook a finger at her. "I have a special gift for you, my dear." He stood from his recliner and produced a rectangular box.

"I can see you wrapped this, daddy. Hey, E for effort, right?" Katalina shook the box and heard a light rattle. "It's kinda heavy." She tore the loosely wrapped box open and smiled. "Ammunition?" She inspected the box closely and pulled the plastic tray that held fifty bullets out. "Ooh, hollow points. Nice, dad!"

"Honey, those bullets are special. A friend of mine gave them to me. They were specifically made just for you."

"What does that mean?" Katalina asked as she pulled a single round from the tray and analyzed it.

"I have a friend who works in one of those voodoo shops in the bayou. He gave them to me and said that these were for all of the monsters out there. I know you deal with some unsavory characters, honey."

"Thank you, daddy! And tell your friend I said thanks."

The bullets appeared to be ordinary. The name brand was a popular manufacturer. She smiled and retrieved the Glock from her purse. She ejected each round from the magazine and replaced them with her new bullets. Her dad smiled.

The trio settled in and put a Christmas movie on the television. Within minutes a low purr slipped through her dad's lips.

"It doesn't take much." Katalina's mother looked over at her husband. "The minute his head hits the pillow, he is usually out."

She and her mother talked for the rest of the afternoon. Before long daylight no longer intruded the frosted windows.

"I have to get home," Katalina pouted.

Her father stirred from his chair and groaned.

She kissed his forehead and whispered, "Merry Christmas, Daddy." She hugged her mother and said, "I'll call you when I get back to my apartment, Mom. I love you."

Katalina opened the door and scanned from left to right, a tactical readiness she'd committed to muscle-memory. She stepped forward from the comfort of her parent's home and was immediately restrained as if a powerful gust of wind pushed against her. She took note of the bushes in her mother's yard not moving. Her eyes darted to the tree line just beyond the driveway—no movement.

No wind.

She stood on her mother's doorstep for a few moments. The air smelled like a campfire with a hint of musk. The road was dry. It was a mild, comfortable evening. Satisfied nothing was an immediate threat, Katalina pressed the button on her key fob. Her park lights flashed, and she entered her Tahoe. Her mother waved from the doorstep. Her hand touched her mouth, followed by a wave.

"I love you too, Mom," Katalina said to herself as her fingers spasmed in the windshield waving back.

Chapter Twenty-Three

Make Him Wait

A foreign phone number displayed across Katalina's phone. "Nope. Not today telemarketers, I'm not answering," Katalina fussed as she drove. "If it's important, you can leave a voicemail."

Katalina's phone dinged as she backed into her parking space. The tone indicated a voicemail had been left. She peered up to the window overlooking the parking lot hoping to see her hairless companion, Casper, but he was long gone. Once the sun went down, Casper needn't stay perched on the windowsill. No sun equals no Casper. She grabbed her phone and listened to the voicemail:

"Detective Andrews, this is Dmitri. We met a while back at The Carousel. You told me to call if I remembered anything. I'd like to meet somewhere and talk to you."

Katalina's face stretched; the corners of her mouth almost touched each ear. *Why the different number?* she wondered. *Maybe it's a new phone*, she rationalized.

Just as soon as suspicion entered her brain, it rushed away. *Merry Christmas to me,* she thought. His voice sounded wise. His accent, maybe European. She pictured his handsome face and intriguing eyes and wondered what he looked like without a shirt on. Then she remembered the main character in her latest erotica novel as being a well-dressed hitman from the east coast and thought, H*e could assassinate me anytime—*

Her cell phone chimed. A text message interrupted her fantasy. The notification banner read: TEXT MESSAGE RECEIVED FROM DUCE. Katalina opened her phone to read Benoit's message: Merry Christmas, partner.

She responded in kind and made her way upstairs. The moment she opened the door, Casper was there screaming at her. "Merry Christmas to you, Casper," she said. She stared at her cell phone and struggled. *Do I call back tonight or wait a day or so?*

 Casper circled his empty food bowl and shrieked. Katalina looked at her watch and thought, S*hit it's late. I'll wait.* "C'mon, Casper. Tonight, you get wet food. That's a nice little Christmas gift isn't it? What's that you say? Okay, sure, I'll pour myself some bourbon. Looks like we're both winning tonight!"

Katalina laughed; she spoke to Casper as if he were human. She ran a hot bath and grabbed a paperback. Before stepping in the tub, she glanced at her phone once more. *Make him wait, Kat*, she thought.

Chapter Twenty-Four

Come to Me

An hour passed and Dmitri's cell phone remained silent. His jaw muscles flared as a low growl escaped his exhale. *You don't want to come willingly? Don't fret my dear, I'll arrange a forced meeting*, Dmitri thought.

Dmitri watched her closely as she exited the house. She wore a backpack and locked the door behind her. Her brown hair looked black in the dark. She turned and scanned to her left and right before stepping off the front porch. Her walk was determined and brisk. She crossed the street while digging in her front pants pocket. Soon, she produced a set of keys and pressed the button. Brake lights illuminated from a car parked along the side of the street followed by a horn chirping. She stopped and stared at the ground near the front driver's side.

Action, he thought as he appeared beside her. "Oh my, you've got a flat tire. Do you need help changing it?"

She looked up at Dmitri and paused before speaking. She appeared awestruck as she stared at the tall dark-haired man before her.

Dmitri's desire to be wanted by women was almost as intense as his need for blood. He stood there with a cocky smile that most women found irresistible.

Angela's eyes looked down at the flat tire. She scanned everywhere around her. Several porches had lights on that helped to illuminate the street after dark. Each exhale sent trails of condensation disappearing into the cool air.

"I have roadside assistance. I'll be fine," she said as she pecked away on her cell phone.

Before Dmitri could protest, someone answered her phone call. She gave them her name and rattled off a number with both letters and numerals.

"Yes, Angela Stratton. Three hours? You've got to be shitting me?"

Dmitri admired her bold personality. Angela had a take-charge attitude; something he had enjoyed from the first time he'd seen her.

"Ma'am, why don't you let me change the tire. I'll be done in ten minutes," Dmitri offered.

Angela looked at him from head to toe and bit her lip. She pressed her lips together as if weighing a difficult decision and said, "You know what? Never mind. I'll just change my own tire and you can bet your ass I'll be cancelling this bullshit racket as soon as I get home!" She pressed a button on her phone and slid it in her back pocket. "Sure. You're not a serial killer, are you?" she asked the handsome mysterious savior.

"I don't eat cereal, ma'am," he answered in the most certain voice. The two laughed together. "How about this: you sit in your car and lock the doors while I change the tire. Hell, call a friend and have a conversation while I get dirty," Dmitri said.

Angela's stone-cold face softened a bit. Her shoulders slouched slightly, and she cracked a smile. "That sounds like a pretty good deal." She sat down in the driver's seat, locked the doors, and popped the trunk. "I don't have any money. I can't pay you," she yelled from inside.

Dmitri walked to the rear of her vehicle and watched her watch him in her mirror. He smiled and dug around her trunk searching for a floor jack. He listened closely to her thoughts and smiled when he heard them.

God, he's handsome. Pretend to be tough. Play hard to get. He's sexy!

Dmitri smiled, impressed yet again. A quick search revealed the donut, floor jack, and the lug wrench neatly tucked in her trunk. Dmitri's senses were superhuman. Her breathing, her heartbeat, and every fidget she made, he heard including a spraying noise followed by a sweet fragrance. Dmitri knelt beside her front driver's side tire and went to work. Once the tire was off, he heard the front driver window rolling down. The smell of spearmint rushed into his nostrils and gentle smacking sounds could be heard as she chewed a fresh stick of gum. Every few seconds a little snap could be heard as she popped her gum.

Dmitri stood after the tire was changed. He noticed her lipstick was touched up. "How's that for timing?" he asked. "Surely better than three hours."

"You said ten minutes. It's been thirteen." She sounded tough.

Dmitri tossed the flat tire and tools in her trunk. He approached her window and asked, "You wouldn't happen to have a napkin or some hand sanitizer?" He showed his greasy hands like a blackjack dealer.

Angela sucked her teeth and said, "Sorry, I don't. I could give you a ride to your place, if you'd like. It's the least I can do."

"My place is far. I'd hate to—"

"I don't live far!" she interrupted. "Maybe you could get cleaned up there?" Her eyes were wide. Her jaw bounced rapidly as she chewed.

Dmitri offered a warm smile and said, "That's so kind of you. You're not going to abduct me, are you? Keep me locked in your place and do bad things to me?"

Angela smiled. Her tongue brushed her lips. *Now that's a thought.* She may not have realized it, but the moment he asked the questions, her shoulders slightly shrugged as if considering it. Dmitri surely noticed.

"I promise I won't abduct you. Hop in."

Dmitri entered Angela's car and extended the seat back to accommodate his long legs. He turned to Angela and peered into her eyes.

"You're too kind. Thank you," Dmitri said as they drove away.

Angela opened her front door and walked inside. Dmitri waited like a gentleman and watched her from behind. She turned and offered a cute smile. "Well, don't just stand there. Come in!"

Dmitri entered and walked past her as he took note of her living room. Several pictures decorated a shelf but none of Angela and an adult male. Just pictures of her and handicap children. The residence definitely had zero masculinity. *She lives alone*, Dmitri thought.

She shut the door behind them and locked the deadbolt. Dmitri washed his hands in her kitchen sink. After drying them, he raised them eye-level and admired how clean they were and mumbled, "I wouldn't dare tarnish such a beautiful body with filthy hands." He turned to face Angela who remained still near the door; a thousand thoughts rushing through her brain:

Do I offer him wine? Is it too soon to slip away for a shower? Do I have clean matching underwear? It's been so long, I'll probably fuck it up anyway. God he's hot!

He stepped closer, his face inches from hers and smiled. Angela's heartbeat rose. Her breathing grew heavier. She gulped trying to wet her throat. "Why don't you get cleaned up yourself?" Dmitri asked.

She breathed a sigh of relief. Her forehead crinkled slightly as she looked up at him. "Are you sure you don't mind? I'll be quick!"

Dmitri shook his head. "Please. Take your time."

He heard the water from the shower spraying and heard Angela singing from inside. He wandered around her home and located a box of refrigerated wine that seemed perfect for the occasion. Her refrigerator was bare. Her pantry also bare. Dmitri noticed a notepad and an ink pen on her countertop and grabbed it.

He heard the water stop and returned to the bedroom. Angela emerged and stood in the doorway wrapped in a white towel; her hair shiny and wavy with steam shrouding her silhouette. He drilled into her eyes and asked, "When was the last time you've been with a man?"

In a monotone voice, she answered, "Over a year."

"That's too bad," he said. "Come here and sit beside me." He handed Angela the notepad and ink pen from the kitchen counter and said, "Write this for me: I can't bear to live like this anymore."

Angela wrote the sentence then looked at Dmitri.

"Now, place it on the table beside the bed and tell me, what is it you want more than anything at this very moment?"

Her head turned to meet his gaze. She didn't speak verbally, but her thoughts betrayed her silence. *For you to take me. Make me scream in pleasure.*

Dmitri stood before Angela who remained seated on her bed. He reached for the corner of the towel that was tucked between her breasts and lightly tugged. The towel fell and wrapped around her waist. "I most certainly will," he answered.

Angela sat erect; her posture pulled her shoulders back, her breasts perched upward. Dmitri took a step backward and kicked his shoes off. He slowly unbuckled his belt while maintaining eye-contact with her. He unbuttoned his shirt and when he opened it up, Angela let a whimper escape her lips. His taut skin hugged the wavy muscles all the way beneath his navel. Dmitri unzipped his pants and let them fall to the floor. He wore no underwear and stood proud before his latest prize. "How, my dear, shall we proceed?"

Angela didn't speak. She simply stared at Dmitri.

"Love, that's a question," Dmitri said, "and questions beg to be answered."

She laid her back on the bed. Her feet followed. She laid there fully exposed as Dmitri watched in anticipation. He knelt onto the bed and gently separated her legs. He began kissing her feet and slowly worked his way upward providing soft butterfly kisses. Once he reached her inner thigh she reached down and gripped a handful of his hair. She spread her legs wider apart and thrust her hips upward while simultaneously pulling his hair.

Dmitri stopped when he reached the middle of her thigh. Each beat of Angela's heart sent a surge of blood rushing through her femoral artery. Dmitri extended his hand up the rest of her leg, gently massaging with each inch. His incisors extended and at the moment Angela let out a loud whimper.

Chapter Twenty-Five

Break in the Case

Her eyes opened. Complete darkness surrounded her. No sounds heard. No scents. She couldn't move. The familiar torture chamber trapped Katalina yet again. Her chest squeezed with pressure. Her breathing required every ounce of energy she had. The silhouette appeared in her doorway. This time it was crisper. Her eyes moved, but her head remained frozen. Soon, she heard sounds—a voice, but she couldn't comprehend what it was saying. It was a male voice.

"Mne zhal."

An arm appeared to extend from the silhouette. It fell with force. Katalina gasped while sitting up in bed. She thought for a moment, trying to clear the fog from her head.

"Mne zhal," she repeated.

She recognized the Russian language. "I'm sorry? What the hell?" She stood and cautiously walked around her apartment, peering into each room as if a surprise lurked behind each door.

DING!

Katalina turned her attention to her nightstand and saw her cell phone glowing. *Please be Mr. Tall, Dark, and Handsome*, she thought. She grabbed her phone and growled, "Ugh. It's too fucking early for this shit!" She pressed a button on her phone and listened to it ring. Ring. Ring.

"Hey, Kat. We've got another body. Call me when you're leaving. I'll give you the address. Oh, and Merry Christmas again!"

"Really, Duce? Merry Christmas? Can you do some of that voodoo shit you talked about and turn time back so I can enjoy another relaxing day without work?"

"I don't know anything about voodoo, Kat," Benoit said.

"Whatever, Duce. Give me a few minutes to throw something on and I'll call you back."

Thirty minutes later Katalina met Benoit outside and said, "What do we have?"

Benoit gave her a suspicious look and said, "You're not gonna believe this shit, Kat. Another suicide."

Katalina stopped and turned to Benoit. "White female victim? Nude? Suicide note?"

Benoit nodded. "Check, check, and check."

Katalina shook her head, her brow furrowing. "Do you believe me now? I told you there's more to it! I knew it!" She pulled a pair of nitrile gloves out of her back pocket and stretched them onto her hands creating a slapping sound.

"Don't even ask," Benoit barked.

Katalina laughed, palms facing up. "What?"

She entered the home and scribbled on the required entry-form. A supervisor on scene led the team to the back bedroom.

Katalina's head cocked slightly. "This one's different." The victim was indeed nude laying on a bed. The comforter was disheveled. Her left thigh had a laceration about five inches long. The cut was deep, and the wound was gaping. "Duce, notice anything peculiar?"

Benoit nodded. "No blood."

"None! Not a drop on the bed. None on her leg. None!" Katalina shouted. "If she sliced her femoral artery, there would be blood splattered all the way across the room, painted everywhere!" She stepped closer to Benoit and whispered, "We've got ourselves a vampi—"

"Shh!" Benoit shushed her. His right index finger almost touched her lips. Katalina swatted his hand as if he was delivering a punch. Her eyes grew large. "For now, let's just do our jobs," Benoit said.

Katalina's eyes darted across the room. She looked at a pile of clothes in the bathroom and moved them around with her shoe. The black collared shirt piqued her attention. LADYBUGS MAID SERVICE was embroidered across the breast. She looked at Benoit who was analyzing the body.

"No signs of a struggle," Benoit mumbled.

"Check her fingernails."

Benoit's focus went to her hands. "No skin under her fingernails, but…"

"But what?" Katalina yelled.

"Black hair wrapped around her fingers."

"She has black hair though."

Benoit shook his head. "No, she has brown hair. Long. This is solid black and isn't as long as hers. This is someone else's hair, Kat."

"Okay, Duce, let's recap. White female. Nude. Apparent suicide. Black hair left at the scene, obviously not hers. She just so happened to work for the same company as Sheila from a few weeks back. Blood drained."

Benoit shook his head in disbelief and mouthed the words, *What the fuck?*

Both Benoit and Katalina's phones chimed with a notification. She retrieved her phone and opened the email. A grainy picture of a Hispanic or Indian was displayed. The heading read, PERSON OF INTEREST IN HOMICIDE. The synopsis made Katalina smile, "Duce! This was taken from the DVR we retrieved from the Paddio murder. This person was lurking around the back porch just hours before!"

Benoit looked at his phone and smiled. "Yep. He definitely looks out of place. Good job, Kat!"

Chapter Twenty-Six

Date Night

A foreign phone number displayed across her cell phone again. She looked up and balled one fist with a smile on her face. "Hello?"

"Detective Andrews? Hi, this is Dmitri. We met a few weeks back at The Carousel. I was wondering if we could meet sometime to talk?"

"Hi, Dmitri. I remember you. Sure, when is a good time to meet up?"

"I work days and can't get away. Are you available after dark? I could come to the station, or perhaps we could talk over coffee? Café DuMonde?"

"I love coffee. How's seven?"

"I'll see you there. Thanks, Detective."

Katalina looked at her watch. 3 p.m.

"Whoa, Kat. You're glowing! Are you pregnant?" Benoit laughed.

"Don't wish that shit on me, asshole. You know, certain 'things' have to happen in order to get pregnant."

Benoit shook his head and covered his ears. "Speaking of… you know. How's Peter?"

"Still in a coma. I'm actually going to visit him tomorrow. Whatever happened with that whole situation?"

Benoit had a puzzled look. "So, about that. I don't really know. One second she was there and the next… gone."

"What do you mean, gone?"

Benoit's shoulders rose. "I mean, it disappeared."

"Yeah, but you put that spell on it to make it disappear, right?"

"Not quite. I tried to place an invisibility cloaking spell over the body. I didn't destroy it or make it disappear." Benoit's face was stretched wide. His eyebrows arched high on his forehead. "Your guess is as good as mine."

"Well, I'm meeting with a potential witness from a few weeks back. Remember that black haired fellow at The Carousel? He reached out to talk to me."

Benoit interrupted, "At the station, correct?"

Katalina inhaled and pressed her lips together. "Well, about that…"

"Kat!"

"Duce, I'm a big girl, ya know. I can handle myself just fine. You saw what I did to that vam—"

"Okay, got it. Just, be careful. That's all I'm asking. Where are you meeting him?"

Katalina sucked her teeth. "Ugh, really, Duce?"

"Just work with me here, Kat. Please."

"Okay, whatever. The French Quarter. Café DuMonde."

***

Katalina stopped off at her apartment before heading to the café. She threw on a fresh shirt and passed a quick roll of deodorant under her arms. She spritzed some perfume on her neck and touched her lipstick up.

"Casper, wish me luck. This one's tall, dark, and mysterious. Mmmm. Something about bad boys." She opened her refrigerator and grabbed a slice of cold pizza before hitting the road.

Katalina parked along the side of the street a block up from the café and walked. The streetlights were still decorated with Christmas décor. The businesses were decorated with dull burning colorful lights. Most closed at five, but Café DuMonde was lit up with lights surrounding its signature green and white striped canopy.

As she approached along the sidewalk, she grew paranoid. Kat stole a peek behind her out of habit to check her surroundings. Nothing appeared out of the ordinary. Her heart rate picked up. The familiar strain of being smothered enveloped her. Katalina stopped before reaching the café and looked around. Something wasn't right.

Like always, parking in the French Quarter was more than a chore. All of the streets sat narrower than streets of other cities and all of them had been revised to have one-way traffic. There were no nearby parking garages or lots. More parking spaces could be found after you reach Canal or Rampart Streets of which both sat on the Quarter's perimeter. But inside the Quarter, finding a parking spot had a lot to do with luck. This evening, Katalina had no such luck and ended up parking a few streets over from her destination.

A disappointed driver stared at her as she climbed out of her Tahoe. *I got here first, buddy,* Katalina thought. *You think I'm just going to give it to you because you're a tourist and I live here? Good luck with that.*

Crowded sidewalks were something she'd long gotten used to. To reach Café DuMonde, she had to thread her way through soldiers on furlough drinking beer and looking patriotic while wearing their military uniform, of families taking in all the sights and taking lots of pictures, of hucksters that danced or sang or drew caricatures to earn a few bucks. A lot of tourists that had visited the city solely for Christmas had already moved on, but plenty more had arrived to take their place causing Jackson Square to sit full with people that had traveled to the city from all over the world.

It was as Katalina was walking past one of the Pontabla buildings that she stopped suddenly and stared around. It was back—the strange feeling she got that sometimes made her feel paralyzed. Nothing seemed out of the ordinary, but she knew not to trust that instinct this time. The last time she did a deranged woman appeared toting a hammer and now Pete lay in a coma.

What triggered her defenses was the fast beating of her heart. It didn't beat this way because she was afraid, but because it always beat this way when a dark presence had come too close, she realized that now.

At that moment, her body not only felt under strain but as if something was trying to smother her while enveloping every inch of her. Something wasn't right—something was off kilter. Everything inside her brain warned her of danger. After pulling out her pistol, she ejected its magazine and stared at the shiny new rounds her father had given her. Special bullets. That's what she might need now that she knew without a doubt that vampires lived inside New Orleans.

She listened to random voices from around the corner—all were jovial. She inhaled—just the smell of fresh ground coffee. *You got this, Kat. Head on a swivel. This could be a big break, or a hot night cap. Either way, seize the moment!*

Katalina spotted Dmitri from two hundred feet away. He sat taller than everyone else. His hair, shiny and black, was pulled back into a ponytail.

She holstered her weapon before she approached. "Hi, Dmitri, thanks for meeting with me."

"The pleasure is all mine. I took the liberty of ordering for you. I hope you don't mind. If you don't like it, I'll drink it."

"I'm sure I'll drink whatever's in front of me."

"It's a cold-brew iced coffee with a splash of French vanilla flavoring," Dmitri said.

"I would have taken it black," Katalina answered.

"You seem like a direct woman, so I assumed your coffee was basic."

"You assumed right. Thanks." Katalina found herself staring at Dmitri, mesmerized by his beauty. His teeth were perfect; straight and a brilliant white. His jaw was chiseled. His eyes were just as mysterious the rest of him. She stole a glance at his hands and smiled. She thought, *Large, not too smooth and not too rough. No ring. No tan line from a ring. Nice.*

"Forgive me for being so direct, but you don't look like the cop type," Dmitri said.

"Oh? What's that look like?"

"You know. Mean, hard, angry, ugly."

Katalina blushed. A smile escaped. "Um, thank you? But I am mean. And hard. And angry. The ugly, well…"

"No chance. You're beautiful. I'm guessing your ancestry comes from Europe. Norway perhaps. Maybe even Ireland."

Impressive, she thought. "I'm not sure," she answered. "So, tell me, what did you want to talk to me about?"

Dmitri offered a half-smile. "Right. Direct. I like that. After we met that night, I started replaying the night in my head and I remember a woman at the bar. A lady I didn't recognize. I don't know, it may be nothing, but she kept staring at me. It kind of made me uncomfortable."

Katalina tilted her head as she listened. She nodded, offering her full attention.

"Aren't you going to write this down?" Dmitri asked.

She shook her head. "Nope." She tapped her temple and said, "It's all stored up here. Go ahead though. Describe her please."

"She was maybe in her forties. Very pretty. She had brown hair and dark brown eyes."

"Do you know her name by chance?"

Dmitri shook his head. "No."

"Well, perhaps she paid her tab with a credit card. I'll check with the bartender. I have to ask, why didn't you just tell me that over the phone?"

Dmitri smirked. "And miss a chance to see you in person again?"

Katalina's heart skipped a beat. His smile appeared genuine. "That's nice of you to say."

"I'll keep a lookout for her and if I see her again, maybe I can strike up a conversation and get her name and number."

"No! I mean, I'll take care of that. It's my job." *Shit Kat! That was desperate*, she thought. She noticed Dmitri was staring at her; his eyes squinting as if trying to look through her. Her head hurt—an immediate headache smacked her in the face.

"Detective Andrews, do you—"

"Katalina. My name is Katalina."

He smiled. "That's a beautiful name. I've not heard it before. Well, Katalina, are you seeing anyone?"

"I was…"

"Were? His loss."

"It's a long story. I was seeing this guy. Well, kinda. We went on two dates. He was in an accident." Katalina averted her gaze.

"I'm sorry to hear that," Dmitri said.

"It's okay. He's still hanging on." She looked at Dmitri. "Coma."

"I'm sorry for being so forward. There's something about you that intrigues me. I mean, aside from the beauty. I think there's something here. Something I can't explain."

Her face turned pink. Her hand touched her chest. "Don't apologize. I'm enjoying talking to you, too."

"Well, forgive my manners. If you ever want to hang out again and here's my number." He slid her a folded-up piece of paper. "You should probably get home. You know what they say about New Orleans after dark; all the ghouls and goblins come out to play. Especially in the French Quarter."

"I'm aware. And thank you for the concern, but remember the mean, hard, and angry part earlier. I got this."

Dmitri laughed. "I'm sure you do. Good night, Katalina. I hope to hear from you soon."

"Goodnight, Dmitri. Thanks again for the coffee. Maybe next time we'll shoot for something a bit stronger?"

"I'd love that," Dmitri said.

Katalina walked away from Dmitri with butterflies fluttering in her stomach. As she walked away, she turned to sneak a peek at Dmitri. He was staring at her as she walked away. She smiled and bit her bottom lip. She strode down the sidewalk toward her vehicle.

Chapter Twenty-Seven

Jealousy

Katalina arrived at Tulane Hospital and pressed the eighth floor on the elevator. She walked to room 843 and peeked in. The room sat vacant. No patient. No Pete. She turned and walked to the nurse's station, "Hey, my friend was in that room. I guess they moved him. Can you tell me where he is?"

The nurse punched the keys on her computer. Her eyes scanned the screen and she asked, "What's his name?"

"Peter DeLuca."

The nurse looked up from her monitor at Katalina and shook her head, "I'm sorry ma'am, but he passed away last night."

"What? But his vitals were strong and—"

"Are you family?" the nurse asked gently.

Katalina shook her head. "No, just a friend."

"I can't give out any more information. I'm sorry for your loss."

Katalina walked away from the nurse's station in a daze. Normally she heard sounds from a mile away, but at that moment, everything was quiet. Her vision, normally acute, was blurred. When she reached her vehicle, she called Benoit.

"Duce, he died." She didn't cry, but her voice was softer than usual.

"Who died, Kat? The dark-haired witness?"

"No. Pete. He passed away last night."

"What? But I thought…"

"Me, too."

"I'm sorry, Kat."

"Hey, are you busy right now?" she asked. "I could really use some company."

The phone went silent for a few seconds before Benoit answered, "I've always got time for you, Kat. Grab a six-pack. I've got some leftover Chinese food you can help me get rid of. I know how you're always hungry."

Katalina smiled. "I'll be there in twenty!"

She exited the hospital's main entrance and was struck with a powerful gust of wind. It was cold outside, and the wind cut through her clothes like a laser. Her pace slowed as she approached her vehicle. The hairs on the back of her neck rose.

She turned in a flash to catch a glimpse of whoever was following her but all she saw was the sliding double glass doors. Nobody was outside between her and the entrance. Her stomach lurched, threatening to upheave the diet Coke sloshing around inside it. She scanned the parking lot looking for threats. It was dark out and the parking lot sat scattered with cars. As she walked toward her car, her hand eased toward her waist where her gun was neatly tucked. Once at the driver's door, she caught a glimpse of a glare that wisped by on the other side of her vehicle, followed by another gust of wind. She entered quickly and locked the doors. The instant she sat back in her seat; the pressure dissipated.

Katalina arrived at Benoit's place and rapped on the door. When he opened the door, she smelled peanut oil and chicken fried rice. She also smelled a unique burnt smell that reminded her of cinnamon.

"Excuse the mess. You know, bachelor pad," Benoit said.

The home was immaculate. Benoit had a bookshelf that stretched from floor to ceiling and was jammed packed with books of all shapes and sizes. Katalina spied a couple of wooden figures that were sitting on the same bookshelves. The one that caught her eye resembled a tribal warrior holding what appeared to be a severed head.

"Did you bring the beer?" Benoit asked.

Katalina held up a six-pack of Coors Lite bottles. "Sure did!"

"Coors Lite?" Benoit asked. "I pegged you for a Bud Lite kinda girl, but I'm not complaining. Thanks, Kat!" Benoit brought Katalina a steaming oyster pail filled with golden fried rice. "Chop sticks?" Benoit asked.

Katalina laughed. "How about a fork, Duce?"

They ate and each downed a beer before Benoit addressed the elephant in the room. "I'm sorry about Pete. I know you liked him."

Katalina stopped chewing and stared at Benoit—her head slowly rocking back and forth. "I just don't get it, Duce. Lately, I'm so confused. I mean, a fucking vampire?"

"Tell me what happened, Kat. Tell me about that night," Benoit asked.

Katalina inhaled and stared Benoit in his eyes as she spoke. "She appeared out of nowhere. She was angry. It felt like her presence tried to crush me. Her eyes were dark with evil, almost black. She moved with lightning speed and precision. Each strike was as powerful as a bear. I shot her, Duce. I fucking emptied my magazine in her and it didn't faze her."

"With department issued hollow points?" Benoit asked.

"Yes. Golden Sabre bonded hollow points. You know, the bear-killing rounds that the chief thinks are as good as kryptonite."

Benoit nodded, careful not to upset Katalina. "How did you kill her?"

"First, she crushed Pete's skull with a steel mallet. He tried to be honorable. He stepped between us and shielded me. I should have shielded him though. Anyway, after crushing Pete's head in, she threw the mallet at me. It was like a bullet coming toward me and I just covered my face. The mallet struck my arm and broke in half—the steel portion flew to the ground. I grabbed the broken handle and before I knew it, she was charging at me like a freight train. Instinctively, I extended my arms to protect myself and she slammed into the wooden handle. The instant it pierced her she died."

Benoit said, "You went toe-to-toe with a vampire and won. How is that possible?"

Katalina shrugged her shoulders and said, "I don't know. I guess I'm a bad bitch." She laughed trying to lighten the mood, but Benoit remained focused.

"No doubt. I've always known that. But vampires? It's the twenty-first century, Kat! I've never heard of a real vampire. Everything I've ever known about them comes from movies and books."

"This changes everything, Duce. Everything we thought we knew is questionable," Katalina said.

"We can't say a word about this to anyone, Kat."

"Uh, no way!"

"Let's take this to the backyard," Benoit offered. "I've got a chiminea and some firewood that needs burning. Grab a few beers and meet me out back."

The backyard was illuminated by several strings of party lights. Katalina watched as he gathered an armful of wood and knelt beside the fire pit. She took a seat in a handmade Adirondack chair and enjoyed an ice-cold beer. She watched in awe as Benoit shaved slivers of wood and piled them into a miniature teepee inside the bowl of the chiminea. He then broke apart smaller pieces of wood followed by larger pieces and before long a beautiful fire blazed before her eyes.

"Tada!" Benoit took a theatrical bow with an infectious grin across his face.

"You deserve a beer for that!" Katalina extended an ice-cold bottle to Benoit. "That was some impressive shit, Duce! I mean, you're like a regular caveman with your fire-making skills! What other outdoorsy shit can you do?"

Benoit took a seat next to Katalina and tipped his bottle up followed by an "Ahhh. Well, I can fish, and I think I can build a pretty decent shelter. I don't hunt. I don't believe in harming animals."

"No shit?"

"No shit. Animals are magical creatures. They have healing powers and—"

A rustling noise interrupted Benoit's sentence. Katalina's attention quickly focused on the wood line beyond the fire pit.

"Did you hear that?" Benoit asked.

Katalina rose to her feet and squinted, trying to see in the dark. The sound of shattering glass behind them startled her. Instinctively, she grabbed her gun and tucked it against her chest. She heard Benoit mumbling next to her. "Duce, are you okay?"

No answer.

The fire pit exploded in an epic blaze and illuminated Benoit whose eyes were closed with his hands extended ahead of his body as he continued his chant. The backyard was fully lit, almost mimicking daylight from the monster inferno. The trees flipped and flopped from hurricane-force winds, displaying a beautiful performance of shadows dancing on the grass, yet it was the middle of the winter.

Katalina advanced toward the tree line where the winds seemed to taunt her, leaving Benoit behind to say whatever prayer he was rattling off. Soon she was outside the protective glow of the fiery light. She listened intently and heard insects chirping, wind blowing, and of course, she still heard Benoit fifty yards behind as he mumbled. Each step was carefully placed across the unlevel forest floor. She heard a snap and felt her footing slightly give way. A fallen branch had snapped in half when she took her last step. She bent down and retrieved a piece of the branch and stuffed it in her waistband at the small of her back as a secondary weapon.

The sound of wind sweeping by, snapped Katalina into focus. Her attention intensified behind her toward the house as the whizzing sound blew by her. She looked in Benoit's direction and saw a speedy blur swipe across her peripheral. Benoit let out a roar and his arms flailed over his head. The second his arms extended, Katalina felt like an invisible train ran her over.

Her hair blew wildly as if she was standing behind a turbine jet engine; the force was so strong that she closed her eyes to protect them from flying debris. The gust lasted seconds and the instant she was physically able to, she ran to Benoit as he swayed unsteadily. His legs trembled. His hands fell to his sides appearing to search for some stability.

Katalina grabbed Benoit and said, "Here, Duce. Have a seat." as she tried to guide him into a lawn chair.

"No, Kat. We need to get inside."

Katalina escorted Benoit back inside his house and closed the door behind them. Benoit appeared to regain his composure as he took a seat in the living room. She ran to the door and locked it.

"Don't worry about that, Kat," Benoit said.

"What? Why? Someone just tried to attack you! Where's your gun?"

"Kat. Calm down."

"Calm down? Duce, we need to do something. Somebody just—"

"Kat, we're inside now and we're safe."

"How can you say th—"

"It was a vampire, Kat. They can't come inside without being invited."

"A vampire? How do you know?"

Benoit said, "Turn on the light please." and removed his shirt. He had two perfectly symmetrical scrape marks on his right shoulder muscle that led to two puncture wounds. "I suspected it the moment the lights burst so I was somewhat prepared."

"Prepared? How the fuck can you be prepared, Duce?"

"Whatever it was attacked me. I have no doubt it wanted to bite my neck, but I was able to ward it off in just enough time." He rotated his bleeding shoulder to emphasize his perfect timing.

"And this business of it not being invited inside? Seriously, Duce?"

Benoit looked at Katalina without expression. "You're gonna have to trust me on this one. And what about you?"

Katalina's palms rose as she shrugged her shoulders. "What?"

"I'm pretty sure you have a wooden stake stuffed in your waistband."

"Fuck off, Duce. This shit works, okay?"

Benoit smiled and said, "As does not inviting them inside."

Chapter Twenty-Eight

Mission

"All right, troops, shut up and gather around," Sergeant Daigle barked at the team. He passed out stapled operations plans to everyone seated in the briefing room. "Tonight, we're assisting vice on an operation along the docks. This is their show. We're just support. Kat and Benoit, you two are on surveillance. You'll each be an observer to the sniper team in the control unit of a crane overlooking the docks. Gonzalez and Carlin, you're the cover team. Narcotics will be the contact team. The targets are in your packets. Intel says a shipment of machine guns is set to arrive by boat just past midnight."

"Machine guns," Kat whispered to Benoit. "Shouldn't that be for ATF? Why the hell is narcotics involved?"

"Where there's guns, there's dope, Kat. You know how they are. Cowboys," Benoit said. "Besides, I'd rather be paired up with S.W.A.T. than narcotics anyway."

Katalina nodded and looked around the room at the S.W.A.T. operators who lined the back of the room. The sheer size of those men was enough to make even the most hardened criminal soil his pants.

She whispered to Benoit, "Duce, their muscles have muscles! I mean seriously, their veins are almost as big as my arm! And that one keeps eyeballing me. What the fuck's his problem?"

"Kat, chill. They're on our team."

"Thank God," Kat said.

"Okay, team, we're on channel six. Keep off the radio except for the surveillance team. Saddle up, lock and load, and remember that every bullet has a dollar attached to it, so don't fuck anything up. Dismissed," Sgt. Daigle waved his hand and the entire room of cops prepared to deploy.

"Duce, I have to hit the restroom," Kat said.

Benoit shook his head and smiled. "Every time."

"What? I can't help it. I'm… Regular," Kat said.

"Nah, I think it's the nerves. Happens to the best of us. No judgment, do your thing."

Katalina ascended to the control center of the crane she was assigned to. Her teammate, Lasalle, was a quiet operator wearing black balaclava, a black lite tactical vest, black pants and black boots. He looked like a ninja with a bunch of tactical gear.

Lasalle unzipped his rifle bag and produced a Remington 700 LTR bolt action rifle. He extended the bipod legs and adjusted the scope as he peered down toward the lane that separated the massive containers lined along the dock.

He handed Katalina a pair of digital binoculars and said, "What's the range from here to the water?"

She pressed the power button and heard a beep. She admired the high-tech gadget before peering through them. The sight picture was crystal clear. In the right lens a number was displayed. "The water is 120 yards away."

Lasalle said, "Okay, now what's the range at the Carnival cruise liner to your east?"

Katalina turned to her left and said, "312."

"Roger." Lasalle turned the dial on his scope and it made little clicking sounds as he rotated the knob. "Okay, Andrews, the boat should be coming from the east just beyond the cruise liner. If I were driving, I'd dock right there." He pointed due north.

"Got it," Kat said.

About 50 yards to Katalina's west, Benoit was in another crane with a second sniper covering the west. The night was eerily silent—only the waves crashing against the bank of the Mississippi river made sounds. The docks were like a ghost town. All workers were likely sound asleep before their early morning alarm clocks would steal them from their beds. Off in the distance a humming noise entered the silence steadily growing louder.

The radio silence was broken when Katalina spoke on her portable. "All teams standby. I've got a boat approaching from the east."

Lasalle whispered, "Right on time."

The boat pulled alongside the docks almost directly in front of Katalina's team. She updated the team. "I've got two white males exiting the boat. One white male is staying on board. The two are carrying duffel bags. They match the suspects in the briefing."

Her radio crackled before a voice came over the radio waves. "Roger. That's our targets. Nobody engages. I want to wait until they meet up with someone and take them all down."

Katalina didn't recognize the voice. *Probably someone from vice*, she thought. She peered through the rangefinder binoculars and watched as the two targets approached the shipping containers beneath them. "Team, I've lost visual on the two. They've disappeared."

Benoit's voice added in, "Sniper team two, we've also lost a visual."

The strange voice returned, "Make your way to the ground and prepare to cover our assets from below."

"Roger that," Katalina responded, followed by Benoit's acknowledgement. She looked at Lasalle who was zipping his rifle bag up and preparing to descend.

"Move it, Andrews!"

The vice supervisor barked, "Contact team, move in!"

Katalina was climbing down a 200 foot ladder and couldn't talk on her radio. She was just above Lasalle who was moving like water. She heard thumping in rapid succession as his boots touched each rung. Finally, after what seemed an eternity, she reached the bottom. Lasalle was nowhere to be found. The entire team was out of sight. No sounds heard. She pressed the mic on her radio. "Alpha spotter to control, update?"

Silence.

"Alpha spotter to any member of the TNT?"

Silence.

"Does anyone read this radio?" she asked.

Her chest instantly hurt. Pressurized from the inside out. The familiar feeling of being watched enveloped her. She heard footsteps and reached for her gun, spinning in the one swift motion. In a flash her Glock was trained at Benoit who was feet behind her.

"Whoa! What the fuck, Kat?" His hands elevated above his head.

"Dammit, Duce. I almost shot you!" She lowered her gun but kept it tucked against her chest, "Did you hear my radio traffic?"

"I heard nothing. I also keyed up. Did you not hear me?" Benoit asked.

Katalina shook her head. "Nope. Where's the team?"

"I don't know. My sniper slid down the crane like a freaking fireman and before I knew it, he was out of sight."

Katalina looked at Benoit, her eyes searching for a hint of normalcy, but Benoit offered no such thing. "I only saw the two disappear that way." Katalina motioned a single thumb behind her back.

"What about the third target who stayed aboard?"

Katalina's eyes grew large and she jogged toward the boat. Benoit trotted behind her. The two slowed as they approached the edge of the dock where the boat pulled in. She trained her gun forward—arms fully extended as she peered over the edge toward the water.

Benoit instinctively turned to cover her six—his back facing hers. Katalina's left hand released the grip of the gun and clutched her stomach. Her skin developed goosebumps. The hair on the back of her neck stood. "Boat's clear, Duce, let's hop down and conduct a security sweep."

"You go ahead. I'll stay up here and cover the docks. Hurry up!"

Katalina once again climbed down a rickety ladder that led from the dock to the boat below. She shouted, "Duce, you good?"

"I'm good!" He shouted back.

She stepped onto the boat and grabbed a flashlight from her hip. The light burned bright and illuminated the red speedboat. She approached the cabin and noticed a backpack on the floor stuffed beneath the console. Katalina did a quick scan around her before kneeling down to analyze the bag. It was jam-packed full to the brim. She unzipped the bag and noticed hundreds of tiny glass vials of what appeared to be blood with the word VOZ printed on them.

The boat rocked with each rolling wave then leaned hard on one side as a gale of torrid wind slammed against it. Salty water crashed on top of the deck like a hard spraying fountain. Katalina blinked to keep water out of her eyes as she repositioned her feet to stay upright. Leaving the bag behind wasn't an option. Lowering her weapon, she grabbed the bag and slid it onto her back. Grabbing her pistol and standing upright again, she found herself face to face with a man.

Aiming her pistol at him didn't frighten him. A look of superiority came into his eyes—a look that warned how confident he was that he would survive this ordeal but she wouldn't.

"Don't move!" Katalina threatened to assert her authority between the two of them.

The man threatened her in return with a new look that came into his eyes. "You think that gun can hurt me?" he asked as he took a step closer.

"Don't move," Katalina cautioned. "One more step and I will shoot you."

The stranger didn't raise his hands. Instead, he smiled a sadistic grin. Katalina felt something was off. "Don't move!" she shouted.

The stranger laughed and said, "That won't hurt me, little girl." and he took a step closer to her.

"One more step and I'll light you up! Do not move!"

"Give me the bag," he said. "We can do this the hard way…or the *hard* way." There's going to be a lot of pissed off vampires if they don't get their… *fix*." Sharp fangs extended as he parted his lips. When he lunged, he did so too swiftly for her to see it as it happened. Instincts took over. *Pop! Pop!* As she squeezed off two rounds, she took two rapid steps back.

The man dropped at her feet, his fangs slowly retracting to normal size back into his gums. A red essence lifted out of his body and disappeared inside her stomach. She heard footsteps, breathing, a rapid heartbeat, and smelled the personal scent of the man approaching.

Benoit stood atop the dock peering down. "Kat! You okay? Are you hit?" He didn't wait for an answer and disappeared as he found a way to reach her.

The vampire at her feet burned like paper on a bed of hot coals. That made three times now that she had come in contact with vampires—three times when only months ago she believed they were a myth.

Benoit hurried onto the boat then hurried faster to reach her across the deck. After he got close and saw something burning, he stopped and studied the corpse before holding Katalina's gaze intently, "Another one?" he asked in disbelief.

"Another one," she confirmed with suspicion showing in her eyes.

Benoit's mouth parted, his eyes grew intense. "How did you kill it?" he asked, taking several steps closer to her.

"I shot him," Katalina answered matter-of-fact then holstered her weapon. "Help me toss him over. I don't want to have to explain this in my report."

Benoit gingerly touched his foot on the boat and extended his arms to secure his balance. "You know I can't swim, right?" He looked down at the desiccated corpse then back at Katalina.

Benoit's forehead creased. His eyes went from Katalina's face to the pile of wrinkled skin then back again. "I heard gunshots."

"Yeah, I shot him," Kat said.

"What? How? I thought you couldn't—"

"Me either, but here we are," Katalina said. She holstered her gun and said, "C'mon, Duce. Help me toss him over."

Benoit's lips parted in disgust. His mouth slightly agape. His chin quivered, "You want me to…"

"Yes. Don't be a pussy. C'mon, hurry up!"

"Are you sure he's dead? What if he's playing possum? Should you stake him?"

"Duce, look at him. He's fucking shriveled up." She bent down and grabbed his shirt just above his shoulders. Benoit grabbed his feet. Katalina said, "On three." as the duo swung the bag of bones back and forth. "One, two, three!"

They stomped the small fire out then lifted what was left of the vampire and tossed him into the Mississippi. To make sure their deed was done, they stared over the deck to make certain the currents of the river had sucked the body under. After that, they stared at one another, giving each other a knowing look.

"Let's go find the team," Benoit said.

"Or at least what happened to them," Katalina countered.

Chapter Twenty-Nine

Vigilante

Days had gone past—days that had played out like any other typical day. Sleep constantly evaded her, but that night she didn't have any trouble and miraculously fell asleep as soon as her head rested against the pillows. She couldn't be certain how many hours had passed.

One minute she'd been in a deep sleep, the next she woke up with her body feeling as if it had been imprisoned. Her vision was crisp. She smelled the faint scent of human body odor and old musty clothing. She was used to her recurring nightmares; she knew exactly what was to occur. Despite knowing she was paralyzed, she still tried to move—only her eyes moved freely.

The backdrop was black and soon the silhouette of a person appeared in her field of view. The figure took on human form with a head and shoulders. It stood tall and the air that surrounded him beamed with confidence as if a puppet master knowingly introduced fear into an unsuspecting victim. She could hear words being formed as if it was holding a conversation, but she couldn't comprehend the words being spoken.

The being moved and turned slightly, exposing a glimpse of a human face. His profile displayed pale skin and a pointed nose. The single eye that she was able to look at was cold and dark. It didn't look at her, instead only momentarily it turned to its right then back forward again, peering away from her. It raised a hand and struck down with a swiping motion.

When the paralysis wore off, the visual was gone. She didn't launch out of her bed like before; she knew better. Whatever it was had left, but this time it left a visual in her head. Katalina's mind was as sharp as an idiot savant's and her memory was unparalleled. "What are you trying to tell me?" She prepared for work with a new motive. New direction. Once she arrived at work, she dove straight into the intelligence database scouring mugshots dating back to when she was a child. Then, she flipped through hundreds of pages of old Polaroid pictures from a time before digital technology.

Nothing.

Katalina's stomach twisted in knots. So much that her knees buckled. Her left hand clutched her waist while her right anchored atop the desk keeping her upright. She smelled body odor and cigarette smoke. She spun around, prepared to catch a glimpse of something supernatural, but nobody was behind her.

Soon, she heard a familiar voice from down the hall laughing and her face grimaced. Drake's presence made her angry. She despised him and everything he stood for, so she turned back to her search and ignored his existence.

Drake's voice was clear as he walked past Katalina. "I would punish that strawberry ass in a heartbeat."

Her eyes rose from the photo album with disgust as she turned her head in just enough time to catch a glimpse of Drake walking past her; his eyes glued to her butt that was perfectly on display as she bent over the desk. She wanted to bite her tongue, but she was beyond being friendly.

"Hey, Drake," she called as she turned to face him. He stopped; eyebrows arched, and the corners of his mouth fully stretched across his face. "What is it that they call you on the streets?"

"The Punisher," he boasted.

"Oh? Is that in reference to you punishing the criminals out there?" Katalina asked.

Drake grabbed his crotch and adjusted himself. "That's not all I punish, if you know what I mean. Call me sometime and you can come on a ride-along and find out for yourself."

Katalina stared into his green eyes and listened. Her top lip quivered at the sound of his violent and sexual thoughts. "You do a lot of work on Bourbon Street, don't you?" she asked.

"That's right," he said.

"Well, the talk in the ladies room here at the precinct and on Bourbon is that you couldn't punish a virgin with your tiny dick. I sure hope your tongue works because your other nickname on the streets is 'The Disappointment'. Oh, and Drake. You stink. Lay off the cocaine and cigarettes. You're making me sick."

Drake's face grimaced. "Fuck you, bitch!"

"No, thanks. I have enough disappointment in my life. I don't need a strung out, baby-penis, dirty cop with little-man syndrome leaving me unsatisfied."

Drake's eyes blazed with fire. His carotid artery rattled. "You don't know who you're fucking with!"

"On the contrary. I know who I'm *not* fucking with," Katalina said as she pointed below his waist. "Don't you have some rights to violate or some drugs to 'confiscate'?" Her fingers gestured in air quotations as she walked away. She went to Sergeant Daigle's desk, but he wasn't there, so she continued to the lieutenant's office and knocked.

"Come in."

"Excuse me, sir. Who on the force is a forensic artist?"

The lieutenant thought for a second before his eyes widened. "I think that Rankin still does that. I think he still works for Captain Hatley at the academy."

Katalina smiled. "Thank you, sir." She returned to her desk and phoned the training academy, "Is Rankin working today?"

"This is Rankin. Who's this?"

"This is Detective Andrews." Before she finished pronouncing her last name, she heard Rankin exhale. "I'm sorry, is this a bad time?" she asked.

"Whatcha got, Andrews?"

"Are you still a forensic artist?"

"I am," he said.

"Good. When are you free? I'd like to describe someone I saw and see if maybe you could sketch him out for me?"

"If you saw him, why do you need me to sketch him?" Rankin asked.

"Well, I only saw his profile and—"

"Profile? As in the side of his face? I can't do shit with a profile. Get me something more and we'll see what I can do, but until then, you're shit out of luck." Rankin hung the phone up.

Katalina returned to the Polaroid pictures and computer database. She narrowed her search down to white males. Unfortunately, that returned hundreds of thousands of results. She was a patient woman, but after two hours of looking through pictures, her eyes began to hurt. She checked her watch, and it was just after 10 p.m. She had clocked off two hours ago and was frustrated.

Cabrera and Castellano were discussing several cases from across the bull pen when Castellano happened to look up and made eye contact with her.

"Late night?" he asked.

"Just wrapping up some loose ends," Katalina answered. "What about you guys? Why are you still here so late?"

"A new case," Cabrera explained. "We think we have a vigilante on our hands. We've had a string of murders lately, all of them some very bad guys in the neighborhood. It seems like someone is taking them out one by one."

Katalina narrowed her eyes. "Bad guys with the same MO?"

"Nope," Cabrera answered, liking that her first thought had been the same as his. "A rapist, a child molester, a drug dealer, and a murderer. Four different MOs. Four different cases with evidence that suggests they all could have been done by the same killer."

Katalina shrugged her shoulders, palms facing up, as her head shook in confusion.

"Our first victim was a child rapist who was identified in court by the victim. He even pointed out a birthmark on his dick and he got off on a technicality. The second was on bail for an armed robbery where the store clerk died of a heart attack. The third victim was a drug dealer who gang-raped an abducted girl, and the last victim was drunk and crashed his vehicle into a car, killing everyone inside."

"Hmm." Katalina's eyes squinted. "Method of death?" she asked.

"Someone sliced their throats," Cabrera said.

"We're talking gruesome scenes," Castellano added.

Her stomach was growling, and she had to get home to feed Casper. "Well, just shout if you guys need anything from us." She grabbed her phone and saw a text message from an unknown number:

"Thinking of you, D."

Chapter Thirty

Giving In

She smiled and her mind went to a dirty place as she pictured Dmitri wearing only a towel wrapped around his waist with water glistening his chest. She responded:

"Wanna get a drink?"

"I'm at the 21st Amendment, wishing you were with me."

"I'll be there in twenty."

"Can't wait."

Katalina stopped by her apartment on the way to the bar. She was greeted by her loving Sphynx who seemed less-than-amused at her late return. She fed him and rolled on some fresh deodorant. She touched up her red lipstick and sprayed a fresh spritz of perfume on her neck.

"Don't wait up, Casper. Momma might be late."

Katalina arrived at the 21st Amendment and was carded at the door. She smiled at the bouncer who checked her ID. *He thinks I'm under 21. How cute,* she thought. As she entered, she observed guns hanging on the wall behind the bartender. Pictures of mobsters along with prohibition-era photos scattered across the walls.

Inside it was dimly lit and a live jazz band played soothing music. She located Dmitri tucked away in a corner. Her chest pressurized, but she discounted it; chalking it up to nerves. She suddenly felt as if she wasn't alone—as if perhaps a supernatural predator was within the crowd. She tried to listen to every conversation being had but it was too much—too many different tones and interruptions. Her eyes drifted to Dmitri again and before she knew it, she was standing next to him.

"Hi, there," she said.

"Welcome. You look radiant," Dmitri said. "I ordered you an Old Fashioned."

"You didn't slip anything into it, did you?" Katalina joked.

"No ma'am, I'm not desperate. I want to win your affection fair and square."

Katalina took a seat next to Dmitri and said, "You take the first sip."

Dmitri didn't hesitate and consumed the entire drink. He waved at the waitress and summoned her over.

"Ma'am, whatever the beautiful lady is having please."

Katalina smiled and said, "I'll have a bourbon, neat."

The bartender asked, "House or top shelf?"

"Do you carry Buffalo Trace?"

The waitress winked at Katalina and said, "Coming right up."

Katalina stared intensely into Dmitri's eyes and said, "I have a question. Let's say you're on top of a bridge that crosses over a railroad track and just below you see a family of five tied to the tracks. You don't have enough time to get to the bottom of the bridge to save them, but next to you is a largely obese man who you suspect if thrown over onto the tracks, could derail the train and save the family, but ultimately kill the innocent overweight man. What do you do?"

Dmitri pondered for a second and looked at Katalina who was reveling in her superiority. "So, sacrifice an innocent obese man to save a family of five? Nah, the father of the family is an alcoholic. The mother an adulterer. Of the three children, statistically, one of them would end up as a violent criminal. The second would be a heartless bully who crushes innocent lives and the third… Who cares about the third? The rest of the family outweighs the third. So, my philosophy, professor, I would not murder the obese innocent man. Do you have something against fat people, Miss Andrews?" Dmitri laughed.

Katalina smiled—impressed at the thought put into Dmitri's answer. The waitress delivered her drink along with a bottle of Stoli. Dmitri smiled and said, "I can't drink brown."

"So, tell me, Dmitri, do you like jazz?"

"I do. I prefer the likes of John Coltrane, Miles Davis, and Billie Holliday. Now them," Dmitri closed his eyes and bobbed his head as if the music was playing in his ears, "they were true masters of their craft."

"I would have loved to listen to them play live," Katalina said.

"It's even better than you could imagine," Dmitri mumbled. Katalina squinted her eyes and stared at Dmitri. The detective in her had questions but the girl on a date wanted to just admire the sexy confident man before her. She caught herself gazing in his eyes and realized he caught her before aggressively turning her head away. She was embarrassed at how she felt. A hardened woman like herself wasn't used to feeling vulnerable.

Katalina stood up and said, "Excuse me." and walked over to the bar, leaving Dmitri to himself. *Walk away. Let him watch you. Show him what could be his*, she thought.

When she reached the crowded bar, she squeezed in between two men. One turned to her and smiled. He made small talk—"Hi. I'm Mike."—before extending his hand to her.

Politely, she shook his hand and answered, "I'm Katalina."

"What's a pretty girl like you doing alone in a bar?"

"I'm not alone. I'm with a friend," she said.

"Really? Can I buy you a drink?"

Katalina gave Mike a disgusted look. Her face soured as if she licked a lime. "No. I'm fine. I don't think my friend would appreciate that."

Mike smirked. "I don't think you have a friend here. In fact, I think you're just playing hard to get, but hey, I'll play. I can chase with the best of them."

Katalina jerked her head back and arched one eyebrow. "You think I'm lying?"

"Perhaps. I know that if I were your date, I wouldn't let you go to the bar alone," Mike said.

"Possessive much? I bet that's why you're single, Mike."

"Who said I'm single?"

"Does this shit ever work? I mean seriously, Mike, this has to be the most pathetic attempt I've ever heard. I would rather accept a proposition from a married man before entertaining a single second with you, and I don't believe in wrecking homes!"

"Excuse me," Dmitri interrupted.

But before he could finish his sentence, Mike cut him off, "Fuck off asshole." and gently shoved Dmitri back.

Katalina, sensing what was about to happen, stood between the two and kissed Dmitri on his mouth. Her kiss was aggressive as if she were trying to remove his lips. When their faces separated a string of saliva stretched, attached to their mouths. Katalina grabbed Dmitri's hand and escorted him back to their table. She turned to check her six and saw Mike giving them the middle finger.

"The nerve of most men. To think that they can just objectify women and treat them like possessions. It pisses me off! I had half a mind to kick his ass. Good thing I didn't have a buzz yet, otherwise he'd have ruined it!"

"Katalina. That kiss…"

"Was it too aggressive? Did I hurt you? Did I bite you? I'm sorry."

"No! Don't be sorry. I loved it, I just wonder was it part of a show, or did you really want to kiss me?"

Katalina shrugged her shoulders and said, "Eh, kind of both. I wanted to kiss you and I wanted to piss him off."

"I'm not complaining. Trust me. I'm just wondering where we stand after that."

"Well, thank you for coming to my rescue, Dmitri. That was very gentlemanly of you. I could have handled myself, but I do appreciate the effort. And they say chivalry is dead."

***

Dmitri was normally a stoic man who allowed little expression to escape his face, but he was indeed smiling. Without taking his eyes off of Katalina, he heard Mike from across the bar talking about him.

"Fucking cock block is lucky I'm on probation. Bartender! I need another one!"

"So, Miss Andrews, tell me some things about you. What's your favorite thing to eat? Wait, let me guess. Salad?"

Katalina laughed. "Um, no chance. Guess again."

"Forgive my assumption, and I mean this as a compliment, but you're a tiny little thing. That's why I said salad."

"Thanks—I guess, but not even close," she said.

"Okay, okay. If not salad, then soup?"

"You suck. I eat like a bear preparing for hibernation. Anything and everything. I may have a tapeworm because no matter what I eat, or how much, I remain this size."

"You know, most women would kill to be in your shoes."

Katalina nodded and grinned. "Yes, I know. My absolute favorite thing to eat is steak."

"I think I'm in love," Dmitri professed.

"Yep, the bloodier the better. Just drag it across the grill once on each side and let me devour it. How's that for girly?"

Dmitri heard Mike tell someone he was headed to the latrine and told Katalina, "You'll have to excuse me. My eyeballs are floating. I have to hit the men's room."

Katalina smirked and said, "If you shake more than twice, you're playing with it."

Dmitri pursed his lips and pondered for a second before saying, "Guilty!"

They both laughed as he disappeared into the darkened crowd. He entered the restroom and noticed one person using a urinal. It wasn't Mike.

There were two stalls; one open and one closed. Dmitri stepped at a vacant urinal and pretended to pee while he waited for the other bystander to disappear. Once he was satisfied they were alone, Dmitri locked the door. He leaned against the sink and waited for Mike to exit the stall. Mike emerged and his face immediately scowled.

"Well, isn't this my lucky day?" he asked.

"Or mine," Dmitri answered.

Mike rotated his head sideways until it cracked then repeated the other way. He swung his arms across his chest as if to stretch them out and said, "You're about to get the beating of a lifetime. You should've just let me take care of that little redhead for you." Mike lunged toward Dmitri and swung his fist wildly.

Dmitri side-stepped with no effort.

Mike went stumbling forward, then turned and squared back up to Dmitri.

"You are an idiot," Dmitri mumbled.

Mike let out a growl and charged at Dmitri. Once again, Dmitri simply side-stepped him, which sent him tripping head over heels forward until he crashed into the wall. Mike stood tall, face still facing the wall and began to speak.

Dmitri advanced toward Mike and grabbed a fist full of his hair. He violently shoved Mike's face into the tile wall three times. Each time, Mike left artwork splattered across the wall. His knees buckled, but Dmitri held him up.

"No, sir. You don't get to give up that easily," Dmitri said.

He grabbed Mike by the shoulders and threw him into an open stall. His back crumpled against the toilet; the back of his head smashed against the wall, leaving a perfectly round hole. Dmitri followed in a flash and tore into Mike's neck. His bite was so strong that his top and bottom teeth touched after biting through Mike's skin. Dmitri ripped a mouthful of flesh out and spit it onto the floor. He went back to his neck and fed. Mike's body was limp.

After, Dmitri closed the stall from the inside and locked it. He peered at himself in the mirror and retrieved a handkerchief from his inside coat pocket and ran water over it. He dabbed a few obvious specks of blood from his clothing and then wiped his face clean from any of

Mike's blood. He patted his hair and ran his hand across it, ensuring it remained perfectly in place. Dmitri smiled in the mirror, adjusted his coat and exited the bathroom.

"I'm terribly sorry. The line in the men's room was long."

"Good thing you came back when you did. I was about to go find Mike and take him up on his offer!" Katalina giggled.

Dmitri laughed and grabbed his bottle. "This feels a little light. You didn't…"

"Yeah right. That's what I want you to see. Me throwing up after mixing clear and brown liquors," Katalina said.

"Well, if you do throw up, I'll hold your hair back."

Katalina glanced at her watch and made a pouty face before saying, "It's getting late. I have to be at the office in just a few hours and—"

Dmitri grabbed her hand and pulled it closer to him. He offered a seductive smile and gently kissed the top of her hand before saying, "You know, we could just stay up all night. I surely could use the company and you—"

"And I what?" Katalina chirped.

"And you wouldn't be as tired. You know how it is, just getting a few hours of sleep. I know I wake up groggy and would rather just push through."

"Oh? And where do you propose we enjoy each other's company for the next few hours?" Katalina asked.

"Well, I hadn't put much thought into it. How about your place?"

Katalina stood up, her hand still inside of Dmitri's, and walked closer to him. She bent over, grabbed both sides of his face, and kissed his soft lips. "Although you did earn some major points trying to rescue me from Mike, I'm not ready for a night cap. Let's let this play out organically. Are you a patient man, Dmitri?" Katalina stood straight, her lips wet from the kiss and smiled.

Dmitri tugged her hand again and pulled her into another kiss, this time a bit more forceful. "You have no idea how patient I am. I can wait a millennium, my love."

Katalina winked at him and said, "We'll see." as she walked away.

Dmitri stared as she disappeared in the crowd, but not before she glanced back and shot him a cute smile.

It was cold outside and the streets were well-lit from street lights. She walked a block to the parking garage where she parked. With each step, she heard footsteps walking in cadence with hers. She turned quickly and was struck with a wisping wind. Nothing in sight. Katalina continued to the parking garage and entered the stairwell. She parked on the second floor and only had to round one flight of stairs before reaching her car. When she reached the stairwell door, she felt it. Something was just beyond the steel door opposite her. She hoped it was Dmitri, but something about her feeling was ominous.

Katalina opened the door holding her breath. Her nerves took control of her hands and rattled them. She stepped forward and scanned both directions.

Nothing.

She shook her head and said to herself, *Dammit, Kat, chill out*. She spied her car and speed-walked to it. She heard more footsteps and felt another breeze. A woman appeared between her and her Tahoe. Katalina didn't need to see fangs to know it was a vampire. She felt hatred building up inside and just knew it. Red enveloped her eyes as instant aggression took control of her body.

"I believe you have something that I want," the woman said.

"What's that? Beauty? Intelligence? A life?" Katalina laughed.

The vampire opened her mouth and hissed. Her fangs protruded in a proud display of superiority, much like a lion before roaring.

Katalina balled her fists and prepared to battle the undead woman before her. "You won't be the first vampire I've destroyed this week," Katalina said.

The vampire closed her mouth, shutting off her hissing sound. Katalina detected the concern in her face—the hesitation. Then, she nodded and blew the vampire a kiss before mouthing the words, "Come getcha some."

The vampire flashed toward Katalina with supernatural speed. She side-stepped and delivered an elbow strike to her assailant. The impact knocked the vampire to her back. The crash echoed throughout the parking garage. She jumped up and again rushed Katalina, this time screaming like a wild banshee.

"Give me the backpack!"

Katalina squatted, then spun around with her leg extended. The vampire approached fast and had her legs swept from beneath her causing her to tumble forward like a gymnast. She landed face-first and slid across the pavement. She stood and faced Katalina; her dirty face, ripped and torn, instantly healed before her. Again, the vampire hissed and lowered her center of gravity, preparing to launch again.

Katalina felt a slight pinch on her neck and spun to her right. As she turned, she felt her flesh tearing. Behind her stood another vampire—a male who had just bitten her. His mouth had a trickle of blood from Katalina's neck, but he stood dazed and appeared confused. His pupils were fully dilated and stared downward. His shoulders slumped, his knees buckled, and he swayed much like an intoxicated person about to pass out.

Katalina jumped behind him and grabbed his head. She wrenched with all her might without even realizing what she was doing. The sheer force of her blow tore his head off like a perforated sheet of paper. His body crumpled to the ground; his essence escaped his corpse and absorbed into Katalina's body. She reveled in power as she inhaled his red essence, but only for a second until she regained her composure.

Twenty feet in front of her she heard a mumble, "You're a…"

The female vampire stood trembling. Her eyes wide and full of terror. She seemed to have shrunk with fear before attempting to flee. In what seemed like slow motion to Katalina, the vampire turned and ran, but time hadn't slowed down any; in fact, time was on Katalina's side. She sprinted to the tiny demon's disappearing silhouette and ran her down. Katalina stood before the vampire and extended her arm. The deserter ran directly into her arm and was lifted by her throat into the air; her arms hanging limp, her feet dangling.

Katalina's eyes were black with ire. Something powerful consumed her. Unaware of the strange force that took control of her, she squeezed the vampire's neck until her fingers touched. Her fingers pierced the vampire's flesh until she gripped a spinal cord, and a quick jerk of her hand snapped the vertebrae causing the vampire to fall to the ground—headless. Katalina stood over the shrinking body and breathed in her essence.

Katalina's senses were acutely enhanced. Before, she was faster than anyone she faced off against. Her hearing was crisp and amplified. Her olfactory sense was like that of a bloodhound, but now they were taken to another level. She had a sense of power and knowing, much like drinking information from a powerful hose, she drank from a magical elixir that enhanced everything about her.

She sat in her car feeling refreshed and satisfied. A sense of accomplishment showered her, accompanied with a rush of euphoria. Almost immediately, her mind went to Dmitri. She wondered what he would think of her barbaric acts.

He'd probably think I'm crazy for saying the word vampire, she thought. *It's best he's kept in the dark.* She immediately fantasized about him lying naked in the dark, begging for her to ravage his body. Suddenly, her emotions were heightened—especially her sexual hormones. She couldn't wait to get home to soak in a hot bath and continue her fantasy about Dmitri.

Chapter Thirty-One

Goodbye

Katalina walked into the precinct a little slower than usual. She'd only had a few hours of sleep and although tired she managed a smile. She could hear everyone's discussions, their whispers and even some of their thoughts, but she was checked out. She had one thing on her mind—Dmitri. She wondered what he was thinking about after she left him.

How much longer did he stay? Did he try to follow her home? Did any bar flies try to close in on her man? She wondered if playing hard to get was the right move. Something snapped her out of the new relationship paranoia; a tension in the air that was heavy. She focused her senses and scanned the bullpen.

Benoit was at his desk appearing to work diligently as usual. Everyone was going about their normal business. Then, Lieutenant Esposito emerged from his office. He made eye contact with Katalina and motioned for her to go see him.

"Andrews, have a seat please," he directed but with a compassionate tone. "I'm afraid I have some bad news."

Her forehead crinkled. She studied the lieutenant's face for clues. "What is it, sir?"

"It's your parents."

Katalina stood fast. The chair beneath her slid back. "What about my parents?"

"I'm afraid there's been a… I just received a phone call from Commander Stevens in district five. Your parents were found murdered in their home."

"What? When? How?" Katalina's hands shook.

Her lieutenant offered her a hug. A single tear fell down her face, but she didn't sob. She held it together. She was in the lion's den with many eyes upon her.

She whispered, "Thank you, sir. But I'll be okay. Can I go to the scene?"

Esposito nodded. "Forensics just finished up there. Kat, remember, it hasn't been cleaned up. Do you have anyone you can call to talk to? Any family or friends to be by your side?"

"Yes, sir."

She phoned the last number Dmitri called her from, but he didn't answer. Katalina arrived at her parents' house in a bit of a daze. Upon approaching the front door, she smelled the metal in the air combined with a hint of decay. Her stomach growled even though her mind couldn't fathom food.

Before opening the door, she turned and scanned the area. There was no feeling of being watched. It was a bright and pretty day except for the glum that awaited behind the doors. When she entered, the living room was in pristine condition. Her mother was a stickler for cleaning.

No signs of a struggle. Nothing ransacked. All electronics were still there. She moved to their bedroom and opened the door. The bed was disheveled; sheets strewn about, completely saturated in blood. There was a pool of blood on the floor that had coagulated to the form of wax. Blood spatter was scattered across the white painted walls. The pattern suggested it was a violent encounter.

Katalina entered the closet and noticed the safe was still there, locked. She entered the combination and opened it. Inside was a stack of cash and a journal. She opened the journal and instantly knew it wasn't her mother or father's handwriting. It appeared to be a female's penmanship, but not recognizable to her. She brought the journal into the living room and sat down. The journal entries were each signed off with, Ivanka.

A tear escaped her eye and ran down her face. She caressed the textured pages and held the book against her chest. Katalina read the journal like a novel, from start to finish. Several times she laughed. Sometimes she cried, and oftentimes she had to re-read what was written out of disbelief. The first entry she wrote was dated in 1991:

Today, a mysterious man whom I'd never seen before came to the café. He was handsome and irresistible. He carried a book with him and ordered hot tea. At first, I tried to ignore him, but his charm was magnetic. I couldn't stop thinking about him. When our eyes met, I knew I was in love. Love at first sight. His name was Erik.

The journal belonged to her biological mother. It seemed to contain every important moment in her life. It described her biological father, her mother, their relationship, their jobs, and where they lived. As Katalina progressed with the journal, her mother's writing grew paranoid, citing things like Erik's change in behavior. She complained about how often he left her alone. Ivanka described the bookstore her husband owned and spent the majority of his time at. When Katalina reached the end of the journal, the last page was ripped out, leaving her with questions; questions now, nobody could answer. The final words read:

I can only hope you never have to read what I'm about to write. I pray you never have to face the—

After reading the journal, she returned to the crime scene with her detective hat on. She gathered the bloody sheets and tossed them in the trash. The mattress was ruined—saturated with blood. She grabbed a pillow and noticed a black hair stuck to a piece of white fabric, not stained with blood. The hair looked familiar. She ran to the pantry and retrieved a Ziploc bag. She turned it inside-out and put it over her hand before grabbing the hair. She reversed the bag and sealed it and then stuck it in her pocket.

Before leaving, Katalina checked her old room out. When she entered, it was undisturbed—still decorated the way it was when she left for college. She wondered what the motive was for the killings. It wasn't a robbery because all of the electronics were left alone. The safe contained cash and her mother's jewelry was proudly displayed in an open jewelry box on top of her dresser.

Katalina departed her childhood home and set off for the forensics lab. Her phone had several missed calls from Benoit, but she ignored them. When she arrived at the lab, she met with the investigator who processed her parents' residence.

"I have to know," she said. "What was the manner of death?"

"I'm sorry, Andrews," the investigator offered. "They were both decapitated."

Instantly, a stabbing pain pierced Katalina's heart followed by gut-wrenching nausea. At that moment she wanted to kill. Something inside of her was awoken; an uncontrollable thirst for violence—revenge, consumed her. As if she was holding an invisible jack hammer, her hands began to shake as the rage coursed through her veins. Katalina's eyes grew large. She furrowed her brow and clenched her jaw, "What? Somebody cut their heads off?"

The investigator shook his head. "No. They appeared to be... torn off." He looked down. "So barbaric."

Her mind immediately went to the Paddio homicide. His neck was sliced so deep, it almost severed. The picture of the person of interest was burned in her mind.

A Hispanic.

Katalina produced the plastic bag that contained the hair and said, "Here. I found this on a pillowcase. First, I want you to try and build a DNA profile on it. Then, I want you to compare it to the hairs collected on my last three suicide cases. In fact, compare it against all suicide cases in the last year."

She returned to her precinct and was welcomed by Benoit, who greeted her with a hug. "Hey, just know that I'm always here for you, Kat."

"Thanks, Duce. Now, stop being a softie and give me some space," she joked.

Katalina lightly punched Benoit in his shoulder. Although a gentle punch, it jolted him and sent him back peddling a couple of steps. He rubbed his shoulder and shot her a curious look.

"Hey, can we talk?" Katalina asked.

"Sure. I have to gather surveillance video from a store downtown. We can talk on the way," Benoit said.

The team headed for the downtown district in Benoit's vehicle.

He turned to Katalina and said, "What's up, Kat?"

"Remember the other night on the docks?"

Benoit nodded and said, "How could I forget?"

"Remember the backpack I found in the boat? The one full of vials of blood?"

Benoit nodded and offered a cautious, "Yes."

"Well, it means something."

"Of course it does, Kat! People don't just have vials of blood stuffed in a bag without some wicked explanation!"

"Last night, I was attacked by two vampires. They wanted the backpack. And, the night just before I killed the vampire on the boat, he said there would be some pissed off friends of his coming for the bag."

"Wait. What? You were attacked by two vampires last night? Kat, what the fuck?"

Katalina snapped her fingers in Benoit's face. "Duce, focus. The blood?"

Benoit pondered for a second. "Well, it is blood, and they are vampires so that kind of makes sense."

Katalina stared at Benoit. "What do you think they want with it? I mean, can't they just feed off of anyone, any time they want to?"

Benoit shrugged his shoulders again.

Katalina grunted, "Ugh. It fucking means something, Duce!"

"Four vampires in a matter of a few weeks? It means we have a serious problem on our hands, Kat."

Chapter Thirty-Two

Growing Impatient

Markus was mid-stroll when something stopped him like an invisible freight train. His eyes lit up and drifted off into a distant place. Amelia and Viktor stopped talking and watched him, each holding their breath. Markus' head vibrated with little shakes as he focused ahead.

"It's her," he said.

Viktor glanced at Amelia, then back at Markus and said, "What did you see?"

Markus turned to Viktor with a look of concern. His normally confident stare was weakened; his eyes jockeying back and forth between Amelia and Viktor's eyes. "It's the redheaded girl."

"The one Dmitri was supposed to dispatch?" Amelia asked.

Markus nodded, "She killed another one of ours…"

"How?" Viktor interrupted.

"She used a gun."

"A gun? That's impossible! Are you sure?" Viktor cried.

Markus squinted his eyes and bore through Viktor's face and said, "I'm growing tired of your insolence. You should do well to mind your tongue, Viktor."

Viktor lowered his head without protest, shaking it in disbelief. "I just don't understand how this is possible."

"Do you think her witch friend has something to do with this?" Amelia asked.

An impatient Viktor chimed in, "That's the only logical explanation! Humans can't kill our kind."

"Can't? We are not invincible," Markus said. "Perhaps we've been too confident over the last few centuries. We've grown complacent with our rule never being challenged, but it's a new day. Just as a virus created us, an antidote could destroy us."

Viktor's face twisted with disgust. His upper lip quivered. "She's not a vaccine. Lucky, maybe. She should be dead!"

Markus turned to Amelia and said, "Dmitri has to answer for this. I expect him here to explain."

Amelia nodded. "It's been more than two days, Markus, and Dmitri still hasn't killed her."

Chapter Thirty-Three

Night to Remember

Katalina's phone displayed UNKNOWN NUMBER. Butterflies tickled her stomach, causing her to smile.

"Hello?"

"Hi there. I've been thinking about you," Dmitri said.

"Oh?"

"I'd love to spend more time with you."

"It's your lucky night. I just so happen to be free tonight and I'm off tomorrow."

"I'll be at the Sazerac bar," Dmitri said.

"In the Roosevelt Hotel?"

"The one and only."

"I'll be there shortly. Bye."

"Bye."

Katalina chose a pair of black lace panties and a matching black bra for her date. She scanned her closet searching for the perfect outfit. Casper rubbed against her shin and cried.

"Tonight just may be the night, Casper!"

She chose a semi-formal black dress that she previously purchased for a funeral that had been tucked away for years. She rubbed vanilla scented lotion over every inch of her body and inhaled with a smile.

"Mmm, good enough to eat," she said with a mischievous grin.

She continued getting dressed and scanned her entire face in her bathroom mirror searching for any blemish. Once satisfied, she shot herself a wink and exited her bathroom. She scanned her bedroom and patted the top of her bed. She adjusted the pillows and sprayed a shot of her perfume above her bed just in case.

Katalina arrived at the Roosevelt Hotel and reverse-parked her Tahoe. She pulled down her visor and checked her lipstick then blew herself a kiss. Her purse was a small clutch-style bag that barely fit her cell phone, so she sat and pondered for a minute. Her Glock was in a bug-out bag sitting on her front passenger seat. She had since refilled her magazine with the bullets her father had gifted her for Christmas. C'mon Murphy, don't show up tonight. My luck, I'm going to need my gun and it'll be tucked away in my car, she thought.

As she approached the entrance to The Roosevelt, a man in uniform opened the door for her. He was dressed in a bellhop's uniform. He wore a tiny hat on his head and greeted her with a smile. The moment the doors opened, Katalina's stomach wretched. It threatened to upheave all contents. She grabbed her stomach with one hand while bracing herself on the bellhop with the other.

"Miss, are you okay?" he said.

She looked at him and recognized the concern in his face but wondered if he was vampire.

His mind eased her concern as he thought, "This poor woman needs help."

"I'm fine," she said, "just a little weak. I need to eat."

The pain in her stomach faded and she stood tall, continuing to walk toward the bar. She heard hundreds of words being said throughout the hotel. She heard the sound of tiny drops escaping glasses and spilling onto the bar. She smelled steak and licked her lips. Her stomach thundered; she looked to her left and right to see if anyone noticed the growl, but nobody paid her any attention. The smell of raw steak made her weak. She wanted badly to order a rare cut of meat. Instead, she pressed forward. She reached the Sazerac and was slapped with more smells; cigar smoke, whiskey, beer, perfume, cologne, vomit, urine, feces, and still raw meat.

As she emerged through the door, she heard a female's voice say, "He better not look at her."

Then another female's voice said, "I hope she sits next to me."

She also heard a man's voice say, "God, I hope she drops something and has to bend over to pick it up."

She easily saw fifty faces and couldn't pinpoint which people were talking. She spun around, her hair fanning in the air as she peered behind her. As she scanned, she observed two different men staring at her butt, but neither appeared to be a threat. Beneath her bra, pressure squeezed her heart. She listened again for any bad thoughts. Nothing.

She felt someone's hand touch her shoulder. She grabbed the hand while spinning around. Her grip-strength was like a vice as she rotated the hand upside down, placing pressure on the wrist. Dmitri fell to one knee and let out a shriek.

"It's me!" he shouted.

Katalina gasped. Her eyes grew large and she immediately apologized, "I'm sorry, Dmitri! I thought—"

He stood and wiggled his wrist. "That's quite a grip you've got there. And so strong!"

"You know what they say," Katalina said.

Dmitri stared at her, his head gently shaking, eyebrows arched upward.

"Dynamite comes in small packages!" Katalina said.

"How are you so strong?" Dmitri asked.

Katalina smiled and offered a quick shrug. "Probably the soup and salad."

Dmitri smiled. "Touché. Or the steak, perhaps?"

"Maybe I'm just a badass."

"Definitely. You look ravishing by the way, Katalina."

She grinned; her face turned red and, in an instant, all of the anxious pain left her stomach as if her knight in shining armor whisked her away.

Katalina and Dmitri's flirty banter lasted a few hours as the two enjoyed one another's company. Dmitri kept undressing her with his eyes yet remaining a gentleman. He touched her hand every chance he got and looked at Katalina like she was the only woman on the planet. She tipped her glass up and swallowed the last sip of bourbon before standing.

She straightened her dress and said, "Would you like to take this elsewhere?"

Dmitri smiled and said, "I'd like nothing better. I happen to have a suite here, at The Roosevelt."

Katalina's eyes narrowed peering into Dmitri's. "You already have a room? You had this planned out?" Her head cocked sideways; one hand on her hip as she shot Dmitri a defying look.

"My house is being renovated so I'm staying here, but if you would rather go somewhere else, by all means…" He sat back in his chair and waved at the bartender. His face was cold and bitter—resentful.

Soon, a pretty woman arrived with a fresh glass filled with Stoli. She smiled at Dmitri and nibbled her bottom lip as he tipped her.

Katalina's heart hurt. The jealousy inside of her burned as the cute little blond appeared to be mesmerized by Dmitri. She didn't just deliver his drink. She stood there ignoring her other duties. She stood there flirting as if she was his date. Katalina seethed and approached the couple, "Excuse me," she barked, but the blond didn't acknowledge her. Katalina stepped in between the two and was nose-to-nose with her and heard her thoughts.

"I get off in about an hour. I'd let him take me home and violate me any way he likes."

The waitress appeared to be in a trance, staring at Dmitri and oblivious to the world around her. She looked star-struck, but Dmitri wasn't a celebrity. Katalina snapped her fingers and stood between the waitress and Dmitri; her eyes fiery and challenging. That seemed to break the spell. The waitress focused on Katalina's face and immediately looked down in shame. She looked confused and tripped over her own feet trying to walk away.

Katalina watched her disappear while she shook her head; her hand still on her hip in a look of defiance. She turned to apologize to Dmitri and was taken in his arms. He grabbed her head with both hands and kissed her like it was their last day on Earth. Katalina's knees grew weak. The force of his grip made her somehow feel safe in his arms. It wasn't painful, but he was definitely present.

Dmitri's hands slid down her shoulders, down the small of her back and gripped her butt before pulling her stomach against his, all while kissing her more deeply.

Katalina pulled back and looked him in the eyes. Her breathing was heavy. Her skin was warm and her eyes lustful. She said, "Let's go." as she walked away from their table holding Dmitri's hand leading him out of the bar.

"Room 2020," Dmitri told the bartender just before exiting, "put it on my tab please."

Katalina and Dmitri walked through the lobby and stopped at the elevators. The metal doors were polished to a perfect mirrored luster. She kept staring at Dmitri's reflection and thought, I'm so lucky.

Dmitri stood there like a patient man with a confident smirk. The elevator chimed and the doors opened. The two stepped in and were the only people nearby. Once inside the elevator, Dmitri produced an electronic keycard and swiped. Katalina looked at the buttons and said, "I thought you were in room 2020? The hotel only has 19 floors." as she pointed at the buttons on the control panel.

Dmitri smiled and waved the keycard. "Penthouse," he said.

The moment he waved the card, Katalina smelled his cologne. She closed her eyes and enjoyed the fragrance while leaning her back against the rear wall. Dmitri seized the moment and turned into her. He grabbed her left leg and pulled it up while kissing her. He simultaneously pushed his hips into hers. Katalina wrapped her arms around his neck and pulled upward, hoisting herself completely in the air; both legs wrapped around his waist. Dmitri gripped her butt and held her up against the wall while they kissed.

The elevator dinged and Katalina opened her eyes. She released her leg-lock from Dmitri's waist and stood tall. She adjusted her dress and preened her hair. The door opened into a vast majestic suite. The room was larger than any home she'd seen and took up the entire top floor. Once inside she marveled in the beauty of the palace. She looked for personal belongings that might provide some insight into her mystery man, but the place appeared to be generic. The pillows lay perfectly arranged on the couch as if undisturbed.

Dmitri entered the kitchen and poured himself a glass of vodka. "Would you like a drink?"

"Bourbon. Neat, please!" Katalina shouted from across the suite. She made her way into the master bedroom which was sprawling. She peeked into the master bathroom and took notice of how tidy it was. She shouted, "Do you mind if I freshen up?"

"Make yourself at home," Dmitri responded.

Katalina inspected the sink and noticed that not a single speck of dust or soap-scum was anywhere to be found. No stubble or hairs left behind. She turned the shower on and watched as the bathroom filled with steam. The closet was full of fresh folded towels. Along the shower racks, she noticed the complimentary hotel soap packets and tiny shampoo and conditioner bottles. None of which had been opened.

She looked at the toilet seat, which was down and thought, this place is really clean for a bachelor. Katalina removed her heels and peeled her dress off. She stepped into the piping hot shower, careful not to wet her hair and exhaled in ecstasy as her pale body soaked up the steam. She peeled the bar of soap out of its package and took in its essence. It smelled like apples and cinnamon. She lathered her entire body up, paying special attention to her neck, breasts, and her bottom.

Soon, she found herself caught up in the moment of never-ending hot water as she sang out loud. She rubbed her legs and looked up. "Thank God I shaved this morning!"

She turned the water off and pushed the foggy glass door open. She couldn't see two feet in front of her through the steam but managed to grab a hanging towel to dry herself off. She wrapped her body in the towel; when she opened the bathroom door, steam escaped like smoke billowing out of a burning building.

Instantly, the smell of blood hit her like a ton of bricks. Her mouth salivated as she licked her lips. Dmitri laid on the bed beneath the covers; his bare chest exposed as he leaned on his side, propped up by his elbow, but that's not what caught Katalina's attention. Suddenly, her burning desire to take advantage of Dmitri paled in comparison to her insatiable hunger for steak.

Dmitri smiled and produced a shiny silver serving tray. He removed the lid and revealed a hot juicy steak. "How's that for service?"

Katalina looked at Dmitri, then at the steak, then back at Dmitri.

"I thought you might be hungry," Dmitri said.

Katalina wanted to devour the steak. She slowly inched toward the tray; her eyes bouncing back and forth between the literal meal and her dark-haired dessert. She felt tingles between her legs and grumbles in her stomach; the sensations bouncing back and forth like an electrode randomly firing electricity. As she looked closer, the steak was already cut into small pieces, each soaking in warm blood.

Dmitri sat up, tossing the covers off of him and revealing his nudity. He was perfectly chiseled; his skin hugged his ripped ab muscles. A perfect trail of thin black hair narrowly split his torso in two symmetrical halves. His chest appeared to be manicured, fully covered with black hair but trimmed to perfection. Dmitri grabbed Katalina's hips and looked up at her as she stood in between his legs. He reached for the corner of her towel that was tucked between her breasts.

As his hand grabbed the towel, Katalina gasped. Dmitri smiled and tugged on the towel; it fell to her feet on the floor. He leaned over, grabbed a fork, and stabbed a piece of steak. His other hand lightly ran down her spine, stopping at her butt. He then squeezed her and stood before her; his stomach pressed against hers.

Dmitri raised the fork and teased her with it. "Don't bite," he said.

He gently brushed the steak across her lips, much like applying lipstick. Her mouth opened and he stopped; he shook his head and said, "Not yet." Dmitri resumed rubbing the warm piece of steak across her lips until he felt one of her hands touch his manhood and begin massaging. Only then did he delight Katalina with her reward.

Katalina opened her mouth and sucked the piece of steak off of the fork. She closed her eyes and savored the taste of warm blood trickling down her throat. She felt energized and refreshed. Katalina pushed Dmitri onto his back and straddled him—still chewing. Her short legs hugged his stomach and her knees barely touched the bed beneath him. She kissed Dmitri and then bit his bottom lip.

Dmitri grabbed Katalina's hips and pulled her body harder against his. She ran her hands across his back. She expected to feel smooth skin with muscular bulges running along both sides of his spine, but instead she felt a rough textured skin. Scarring perhaps.

Katalina quickly grabbed both of his wrists and slammed them against the mattress above his head. She shook her head and began grinding and rotating her hips. She bit Dmitri's lip again, this time a bit harder and heard him grunt. Katalina released his lip and raised her head slightly enough to look at Dmitri's face. His eyes remained closed; a smile painting his face.

She kissed him once more and tasted something different; something sour. Before she could put any thought into the strange flavor, Dmitri let out a moan and thrust his hips upward. She felt something warm rubbing against her back and picked herself up slightly, allowing room for penetration.

Dmitri grabbed Katalina's back with his right hand and sat up while rolling slightly. Katalina fell onto her back and in an instant, Dmitri was towering over her; between her legs. He felt her wrap her legs around his waist and pull him closer by squeezing her leg muscles. Dmitri held himself up by locking his arms out; one on each side of her head. His stomach was pressed firmly against hers as she continued to pull his body into hers.

"Give it to me!" Katalina demanded as she looked up at Dmitri.

She reached down for him, but he pulled his body away. Her short arms couldn't reach him. She sat up and wrapped her arms around his neck, pulling him down with her as she pressed her back against the mattress.

As the two fell, she felt him enter her. She tensed up briefly as the pressure took her by surprise, but Dmitri soon found a rhythm and she quickly remembered the pleasure associated with being with a man. Her eyes rolled back into her head with each thrust as pleasure signals sent shivers throughout her body. She couldn't help the moans that escaped her lips; each push felt like pure euphoria. She heard Dmitri's breathing increase; his pace picked up and he pushed harder and harder.

She grabbed his arms that were planted into the bed and she felt his muscles tense. He rocked back and forth and soon his breathing stopped. She heard him hold his breath and she knew what was about to happen next. His pleasure intensified hers. He pressed harder and harder with each stroke. Dmitri slowed his rhythm and pressed his pubic bone hard against hers.

He plunged deeply inside of her as she reached the point of climax, her breathing rapid. She bit her lower lip and held her breath as her body warned her of the impending explosion that was edging closer. Dmitri's head was beside hers with his face buried in the pillow. He turned to kiss her neck just beneath her ear lobe.

His wet lips and soft breath sent Katalina over the top. As pure elation coursed throughout her entire body, she felt a nip on her neck followed by a stinging sensation. Instantly, Dmitri rolled over off of her body. He laid there as if he was dead—frozen. His eyes were rolled back.

Like a light switch flipped, anger took over. Enraged, she leapt to her feet and looked down at a helpless Dmitri laying on the bed. His fangs still extended. Katalina's eyes frantically darted across the room.

She ran to the closet and jerked the mirrored doors apart, shattering them both when they slammed against the jamb. She looked up and grabbed the clothes rod and yanked it, but it was plastic.

"Fuck!" she yelled.

A quick glance behind her confirmed Dmitri was still paralyzed. Katalina entered the living room searching for something; anything wooden. In the far corner, she noticed a business table with a phone on it and a notepad. She ripped one of the legs from the table and analyzed it.

"This will have to do," she said. Katalina entered the bedroom and found Dmitri stirring. His hands were twitching, and his head was moving slowly back and forth; his eyes still closed. She sprinted toward the bed and jumped on it. Like a golfer she cocked the wooden table leg above her head and swung. When the leg struck Dmitri's face, a loud snap echoed throughout the room. The impact was so powerful that the leg snapped and splintered. Despite the normally fatal blow, Dmitri's eyes opened and focused on Katalina who was straddling him.

In a rapid swoop, Katalina plunged the fractured stake into Dmitri's heart. Immediately his eyes grew large and within milliseconds, he faded. His essence escaped his limp corpse and absorbed into hers.

Katalina's stomach convulsed a couple more times, sick from what just happened. She ran back to the bathroom and turned the water on—only hot water. She grabbed a clean washcloth and lathered it up with soap and scrubbed every inch of her body trying to rid herself of his putrid touch.

Chapter Thirty-Four

Full Circle

Katalina once again emerged from the shower wrapped in only a towel. Her nausea now gone as her detective curiosity took over. The suite appeared vacant except for Dmitri's clothes. There was no evidence that he'd been staying there for any amount of time. The pillows on the couch were perfectly staged, likely from when the cleaning crew last cleaned the room. The refrigerator was empty and at that moment, she knew everything he'd told her was likely a lie. Katalina grabbed his pants that were tossed in the corner of the master bedroom and dug through the pockets. Only a room key and a folded piece of paper occupied them.

Katalina held the paper and stared at it. The familiarity was sickening. The paper shook like a brown leaf blowing in the wind in the fall. It was torn from a notebook; a notebook she'd once held before. She carefully unfolded the page and read the familiar handwriting. As she read line after line her heart felt like it was in a vice being squeezed. A lone teardrop fell to the paper and spread across it. The paper absorbed the salty droplet and smeared the writing. Katalina wiped her face with the back of her hand and sat on the couch.

My beloved was a vampire. His seed impregnated me and together we created a child who now grows rapidly in my belly. The pregnancy is destroying my body. Erik warned me that I likely won't survive and that it would be a miracle if I ever saw our child. Erik also said that if our child survives birth, that it would have powers beyond belief. He said that it would be hunted by his kind because they are a vampire's only true predator. I suspect more information exists in the plethora of books Erik guarded so fiercely in his bookstore. 53.924114, 27.612647

Katalina's world was turned upside down when she read her mother's last journal entry. She knew that he had been the monster who killed her adopted parents. Why else would he have that piece of paper? Then, it all made sense. The black hairs left at every crime scene; the hair found at her parent's house. She stood and looked at Dmitri's disappearing body and felt a hint of depression, now knowing that the driving force behind his pursuit of her was not at all romantic, but rather to kill her. She gathered her belongings and departed the disgusting room that just moments before held her greatest desire.

Katalina drove to the local hardware store and selected four wooden plunger handles, each about two feet long, a skill saw, and a medium-sized hunting knife. She shopped around the store and found a tactical-looking bug-out bag with shoulder straps. The salesman boasted the bag was prepackaged with essential survival tools such as rope, waterproof matches, a fire starter, a knife, compass, miniature flashlight, emergency blanket, and two vacuum sealed freeze-dried meals. Once purchased, Katalina returned home and cut each plunger handle in half, then sharpened one end to a decent point using the hunting knife she'd purchased.

After an hour, she successfully created eight sharpened stakes, each the size of a ruler, and emptied out her bugout bag. She placed seven of the stakes inside the bag and returned some of the original contents and then smiled. She twirled the eighth stake in her hand like a baton and in one fell swoop, she hurled the stake at her wall. The wooden spear almost fully pierced the wall. She cocked one eyebrow, shook her head, and thought, somebody is going to have a bad night.

Katalina poured herself a glass of bourbon and snuggled in her bed with only a bedside lamp illuminating the room. She grabbed her latest vampire-romance novel and prepared for a pleasant reading experience. Soon, Casper wiggled his way beneath the covers and pressed his hot body against hers with a purring so loud that she could barely concentrate.

"Really? Garlic?" she shouted while laughing out loud. "This better get more realistic than crosses and holy water," she said out loud. As Katalina read more, it seemed like every male vampire in her novel was a love god. "I don't know about a god, but at least the author got something somewhat right." Katalina's eyes grew heavy as she broke 100 pages on her new crisp paperback; each blink felt like fifty pounds were weighing them down. They burned and itched as she massaged her eyelids.

Katalina opened her eyes and felt the familiar paralysis. Only her eyes moved as her body lay frozen. She wasn't stiff with fear; she genuinely tried to move but something kept a supernatural hold over her. A deep inhale revealed a stench of body odor. Her breathing was normal; she wasn't scared, instead she patiently awaited the emergence of the monster who had been terrorizing her for months.

A soft-but-firm voice spoke, "Goodbye old friend."

She saw shadows from the floor dancing against her ceiling. There were three shadows of human forms projected onto her ceiling. One stood significantly taller than the other two. The taller shadow raised an arm and swooped down toward the shorter shadows. Both smaller shadows disappeared.

The invisible force released Katalina. She rubbed her eyes and removed the novel that was laying across her chest from the night before. Casper reminded her that the only thing that mattered in his life was food and if she failed to feed him immediately, he would torment her every step by weaving in and out of her feet as she walked.

Chapter Thirty-Five

Benoit's Vision

Benoit exited his vehicle at the precinct and drew in a deep inhale, appreciating the crisp winter weather that New Orleans rarely provided. As he retrieved his bag from his trunk, Benoit noticed a twenty-dollar bill on the ground near the rear of his vehicle. He stared at the money and entertained retrieving it. Benoit remembered the shaman who visited him and warned him against touching currency—something he'd made a conscious effort to avoid ever since. He ignored the hemp rectangle and slung the bag over his shoulders.

Clip-Clop. Clip-Clop. Clip-Clop.

The sound of horse hooves captured his attention. The New Orleans Police Department had a mounted patrol division that often patrolled the French Quarter on horseback. Benoit turned toward the street and observed a lone black stallion trotting down the roadway. None of the police horses were black and this particular horse was naked—without a saddle or reins. It stopped and turned toward Benoit snorting; it stared at him with solid black eyes. Benoit approached the majestic creature and felt a calming sense envelop him. He reached for the steed and rubbed his hand down his muscular neck. As he caressed the silky coat, he felt a sense of comfort laced with intuition.

A sharp stab of electricity jolted Benoit the moment he touched the horse. He heard gunshots and felt a burning pain in his left shoulder. A quick glance offered no bullet holes in his shirt or blood soaking his clothing. Benoit saw a glimpse of a police uniform on the ground and Katalina running away. It was dark outside, and he appeared to be near a bayou. Benoit thanked the horse and turned back toward the precinct.

In the distance the sound of horse hooves clapping drifted. He looked up at the gray afternoon sky and thought, what's tonight going to bring me?

Benoit entered the bullpen armed with an uncomfortable gut-feeling. The mere fact that he had a glimpse of the future placed him in grave danger. The constant paranoia would cause his every decision to be questioned.

"Hey, Benoit," Sergeant Daigle called, "come to my office."

Benoit wearily walked over to the sergeant's glass door. Thoughts of everything he'd done wrong flooded his mind. *Did he catch me improperly parked? Is one of my reports late? Did someone complain about me?* "Yes, sir?"

"There's a detail over at the chief's house. A uniformed officer is assigned to sit out front and monitor his residence."

"Okay?"

"It's a fucking rookie, Benoit, and I want you and Andrews to provide an extra layer of security out there tonight."

"On duty?" Benoit asked.

Daigle's patience appeared to grow thin. His face crinkled and his eyes squinted as he stared at Benoit. "Yes! Fucking vice was supposed to provide an extra layer of support, but you know how Captain Douche is stuck up the chief's ass? Well somehow Drake and his team got reassigned and now it falls on us, so you and Andrews get to be ninjas tonight and lurk in the shadows around the chief's house."

Benoit's eyes grew large at Daigle's tirade, "Why is there a security detail at the chief's house?"

"Fuck if I know, and besides, even if I did, I wouldn't tell you. Any more questions?"

Benoit opened his mouth as if to answer but was immediately interrupted, "Good! Now go!"

"But sir, I have interviews scheduled and—"

"You're about to be wearing a class-a uniform permanently if you don't get out of my face!"

Benoit walked back to his desk shaking his head, "C'mon, Kat, we have a special assignment tonight."

Katalina gave Benoit a curious look, "What the—f"

"Let's go. I'll explain in the car," Benoit said. His eyes were large as if he had something secret to say. The duo entered Benoit's beaten-down Ford Crown Victoria; Benoit felt Katalina staring at him from the passenger seat. "We got reassigned tonight. Our job is to secretly provide extra protection to uniformed patrol. Apparently, there's a detail at the chief's house and we're support."

"Wait. What? We're working an extra-duty detail? On the clock?" Katalina asked.

"Not quite. Patrol is working a detail and our assignment is to provide support to the uniform."

"Um, why is there a detail at the chief's house?"

Benoit shrugged. "Hell if I know." His eyes darted to her feet. "What's that bag?"

Katalina nodded. "Reinforcements."

"Snacks?" Benoit asked.

"Not refreshments, Duce. Tools of the trade." She reached in her bag and retrieved a sharpened stake and admired her beautiful weapon of choice. "When in Rome. Right?"

"I've been doing some research of my own. Preparing, if you will," Benoit said.

"Oh?"

The asphalt turned into gravel and the trees grew thicker with each second. To the left and right all that could be seen was cypress trees and swampland. Gray moss dangled from the branches and made the trees look like curly hair was growing from them. Dusk was upon them as the deep country quickly grew dark. Fog had crept in and hovered over the bayou.

"I've never been to the chief's house before," Katalina said.

"Neither have I, but he sure is way the hell out here in the middle of nowhere." Benoit pulled over and studied a sheet of paper that Sergeant Daigle had given him. "We should be good here," he said, pointing to the map. "This is the only road in. His house is just around the corner."

"Let me see that map," Katalina said. "It looks like the bayou snakes around the back of his house. Shouldn't we have eyes on it?"

"Thank God it's not summer," Benoit said, "or the mosquitoes would feast tonight."

Katalina's face twisted. "What's your problem with mosquitoes?"

"Um, they're annoying little insects that bite!"

"Sissy," Katalina said.

Benoit pulled out a pair of binoculars and peered out the front windshield. "Looks like patrol is posted outside his front gate."

"Is he on foot?" Katalina asked.

"No, just sitting in his unit."

"Lazy fucks! A lot of good that'll do. Are the windows down at least?"

"Nope."

"Son of a bitch. That officer is getting paid thirty-five dollars an hour to protect the chief's house and he wouldn't be able to hear if a bear came crashing in!"

Benoit smiled, "And that's why we're here, my friend."

"Yeah, on-duty and making a fraction of what he is."

The duo went silent for a while, each seemingly in deep thought. Normally Katalina could hear others' thoughts, but not Benoit's.

"Duce, I need to tell you something."

"What's up, Kat?"

"I killed another vampire."

"What. The. Heck. Kat, seriously? What happened this time?"

Katalina went silent as she stared at the floorboard, "So, you know that guy I've been seeing?"

"Yeah, Mr. Tall, Dark, and Mysterious?"

"You mean handsome? Tall, dark, and handsome."

"Nah, I'll stick with mysterious."

"Whatever. Yes, him. So, it turns out he was a vampire. That's not all. I'm certain he was trying to kill me."

"What? Wait a minute, back up."

"I figured it out and killed him first."

"You just said, 'Hi, Mr. Vampire, I'm gonna kill you!'?"

"Not quite."

"Good thing you didn't have sex with him! I mean could you imagine that? Having sex with a vampire?" Benoit laughed and pretended to dry-heave. He turned to see Kat's eyes closed.

Her arms folded across her chest. "You didn't?"

"Well. I didn't know he was a vampire when we did it!"

Benoit looked at Katalina. He remained silent.

"We were. You know." Kat's body began to gyrate. "Doing it, and he was about to—"

Benoit covered his ears. "Kat! No need to give me the play-by-play."

"Anyway, I killed him. There that's it. Please don't judge me."

Benoit and Katalina sat a moment in uncomfortable silence.

"You just fucking killed him? He didn't even put up a fight?" Benoit asked.

"I didn't give him a chance to. He was kind of indisposed."

"You never cease to amaze me, Kat. I'm so glad you're my partner."

"Duce, what did you mean earlier when you said you've also been researching?"

"It's not nearly as Earth-shattering as what you shared but," he opened his door, "check this out." He exited his unit and Katalina followed suit. Benoit sat on his hood and faced the trees to his right. "Ready?"

Katalina first furrowed her brow, then cocked one eyebrow. "Ready for what?"

Benoit raised his hands and closed his eyes. He mumbled something foreign and his body gently shook. The trees whipped violently and the water in the bayou instantly became choppy as if a storm was passing through. He stopped and looked at Katalina, searching for an expression.

"So, you can change the weather now? Can you make it snow? That would be some awesome shit, Duce!"

Benoit's face drooped with disappointment. "No, Kat. This is serious. That was a force field."

"A what?"

"It was a protection spell that placed us in an invisible cone of protection."

Katalina's jaw dropped. "Get the fuck out of here!"

"You should expand your vocabulary, Kat. Do you know that I once read that a person uses profanity because they aren't smart enough to select the most appropriate word to express themselves?"

"No shit? I'm stupid now?"

Benoit's jaw muscles flared out with an irritated exhale, "No shit, Kat. I didn't mean that. I'm just saying…"

"Where did you read that garbage anyway? The internet?"

Benoit looked at the floor. His mocha-colored skin flush and turning a shade pinker, "Maybe."

"Hmm. You know if it came from the internet, it has to be true," Katalina barked, her tone sarcastic. "Well, what else can you do?"

"I think I can—"

Katalina interrupted Benoit. "Shhh. Do you hear that?"

"Huh? I don't hear anything."

"Someone's coming. I hear gravel being crushed. It's a vehicle." Katalina walked to the rear of Benoit's car and waited. She felt an instant headache. Eyes threatened to burst from their sockets as she rubbed her forehead. Headlights illuminated the pitch-black night from a distance. Katalina shot Benoit a suspicious look. "What's the detail shift time?"

Benoit reached in his back pocket and unfolded the briefing sheet. "It's a twelve-hour gig, six at night 'til six in the morning."

Katalina glanced at her watch, "It's nine o'clock."

A white marked police unit approached the team. Benoit stopped the vehicle and approached the driver. He motioned for him to roll his window down. The driver's face appeared confused and nervous.

"Can I help you?" Benoit asked.

The driver was dressed in a New Orleans Police class-a uniform. His radio was blaring communications between an officer and a dispatcher. "I'm here to relieve the officer. Apparently, he has a stomach virus."

Benoit smiled and said, "Go on ahead." and stepped out of the officer's way. The vehicle crept past him and the officer waved. Benoit turned to Katalina and said, "Seems legit."

"Duce. What the fuck?"

Benoit's head jerked back as if he was just slapped. His palms and shoulders rose.

"Who was that?" Katalina asked.

"I don't know. Another patrol officer. Why?"

"He had a full mustache and goatee! That's against uniform standards."

"Seriously, Kat? You're gonna be *that* officer? Don't tell me you're going to report him to internal affairs because he forgot to shave?"

"He didn't forget to shave, Duce! That has been growing for quite some time." Katalina quickly opened the door and strapped her backpack on her shoulders before sprinting down the road. "He's not one of us."

Benoit chased after Katalina. He saw her gun clutched against her side and he drew his. Katalina flanked the unit and disappeared in the darkness. Benoit approached and saw the replacement officer standing outside the driver's side of the original officer's unit. The first officer was still buckled in his seatbelt. The two seemed to be arguing.

A flash of light lit up the sky followed by the report of a gunshot.

Benoit was still jogging when he approached and yelled, "Hands up! Police!"

The officer turned in a flash and fired a round at Benoit, striking him in his left shoulder. A burning pain tore through his shoulder as he fell to the ground. He saw a red blur as Katalina sprinted across his field of view. Benoit rolled into the ditch and clutched his shoulder, placing pressure on the bleeding wound.

After several minutes and no sounds being heard, Benoit rose from the ditch. He jogged to the first officer's unit and grimaced at the blood that sprayed across the windows. He called it in.

"Officer down! Send more units to the chief's house. I have one officer in pursuit and one down! I've been shot!"

Chapter Thirty-Six

Almost Captured

Katalina sprinted after the police impersonator into the dark woods. Although he had a significant lead on her, she raced upon him like a freight train. She tossed him forward. A sharp crack echoed through the forest as tree bark shattered in all directions. His limp body fell to the ground at the base of the tree. His face was smug despite being captured. Katalina delivered a strike to his mouth causing blood to burst into her own face. Her lips tickled and she subconsciously licked them, instantly feeling empowered.

A crackling sound caught her attention behind the killer. She listened and focused her sight ahead. "You're not alone. Who's with you?" she barked.

"Nobody. This is all me, sweet tits."

"Fuck you!" Katalina backhanded the man and leaned to her left, still peering into the woods. "No, we have company." She feverishly removed his handcuffs from his belt.

"Hell yes, that's what I'm talking about!" he said with disgusting joy.

She rolled him onto his stomach and handcuffed him. Next, she hog-tied his cuffs to his feet using his inner belt. She wrenched down on the belt until he cried in pain. "I'll be right back. If you move, trust me, I'll kill you." She stared at the imposter for a quiet second.

"What?" he cried.

"Please move. Please give me an excuse." A single eyebrow arched. "I promise I'll make it hurt."

She stood and cautiously took a few steps further and caught a glimpse of someone she recognized. He had black hair and a deep tan. Then it hit her as she shouted, "Stop! Police!"

The ghost flashed forward and Katalina gave chase. She'd never been outrun in her life before but whatever she was chasing left her. Her hearing confirmed something was still ahead of her as the ground beneath it drummed with each step. She could smell human body odor like a dog following a scent, but suddenly it was gone. No scent. No sounds. Nothing in her sight. She turned and made a full 360 rotation, feeling confused and defeated.

I fucking had him, she thought.

***

Benoit heard footsteps coming from behind the chief's house and knelt beside the front driver-side tire. His head peeked over the hood; his weapon trained ahead of him, bouncing violently as his adrenaline dumped. His left arm dangled by his side. He felt blood running down his arm, but he maintained a steady aim ahead by resting the handle of his handgun on the hood to support his weapon.

"Police! Hands up!" he shouted.

"It's me," Katalina barked back. "I've got him."

Katalina appeared walking the uniformed imposter from behind the chief's house. He was filthy and crying.

"She fucking broke my arm!" he screamed.

"You're lucky that's all I broke," she snapped back. Katalina had the officer's gun belt hanging from her shoulder as she paraded him back to the vehicles. "Did you call it in?"

"Yes. Help is on the way." Benoit grunted with each movement.

"Oh shit! Are you hit?" Katalina asked.

"Yeah, I'll be fine. Shoulder hit."

"Sit down," she barked at the murderer.

He stiffened up and she kicked his legs from beneath him. The imposter fell to the ground, landing on his broken arm. He let out a scream.

"Hang on, buddy. I'll grab a first aid kit." Katalina slung her new bug-out bag from her shoulders and produced a tiny first aid kit. She ignored standard protocol and immediately worked on Benoit's wound without gloves. "Lie down, Duce."

She ripped Benoit's shirt open around his shoulder and exposed the bullet wound, her hands fully covered in her partner's blood. She grabbed a bag and tore it open with her teeth and said, "This is going to burn, Duce. It's quick-clot."

She poured the charcoal-looking gritty substance in Benoit's gaping wound. He groaned; his head and legs shook violently.

The imposter laughed and said, "Damn, just five inches to the left and I woulda killed you."

Katalina stood and told Benoit, "Sit tight. I'll be right back."

Benoit lay staring at the stars. He lost sight of Katalina but heard her.

"Too bad your dumbass isn't smart enough to buy hollow-point rounds. You loaded your gun with full metal jackets, and it went right through him. Rookie."

Next, he heard the imposter scream blood-curdling cries followed by a crack and more painful screams. The tough guy was crying like a child.

"Anything else you want to say?" Katalina asked. "I didn't think so."

Soon a barrage of police vehicles flooded the country cottage. A helicopter hovered overhead with a brilliant spotlight illuminating the crime scene. An unmarked vehicle came barreling down the road and came sliding to a halt. The chief exited the passenger side and saw Benoit laying on the ground. Paramedics were hot on his tail.

"Is he going to make it?"

"I'm fine, chief. Just a flesh wound," Benoit answered.

The chief walked away from Benoit and seconds later let out a litany of expletives.

Paramedics sped to Benoit's side and immediately began tending to his wound.

"You're gonna be okay, Duce. I'll swing by the hospital later to check on you," Katalina said.

She walked over to the chief whose hand was clutching his forehead. Soon, the door to the residence opened and a female and a child emerged on the porch. The chief ran to the woman and embraced her with a hug.

"Are you okay?" he asked.

Katalina approached and said, "He never made it to the house, chief. We got him."

Chapter Thirty-Seven

Karma

Castellano and Cabrera arrived on scene and immediately jumped into fierce detective mode. A strong sense of pride gripped every police officer present. An attack on the chief violated every rule in the book. "We heard the call over the radio. When 'shots fired at the chief's house' pierced the radio waves we high tailed it here as fast as we could. Cabrera and Castellano stopped at the ambulance and checked on Benoit who seemed to be doing just fine.

"We got this buddy, don't you worry about a thing."

When the second team arrived at the murdered officer's police unit, a guttural roar echoed through the forest. "He's just a kid," Castellano cried.

"Did you know him?" Cabrera asked.

"Yes. My cousin's boy. He just got cut loose as a solo officer two months ago."

Cabrera shook his head. His face was folded with anger. "He didn't have a chance. He was still wearing his seatbelt for Christ's sake!" He walked over to the imposter dressed in a police uniform and said, "Why?"

From a seated position on the ground, the suspect spit in Cabrera's face. "Fuck you, pig."

Cabrera looked at Castellano and ripped him up off the ground to his feet. He grimaced, then laughed as they walked him to their unmarked vehicle. "Search him," Cabrera told Castellano.

Castellano patted his waist, his inner thighs, his ankles, and the small of his back before saying, "He's clean."

Cabrera tossed the suspect into the rear seat and slammed the door shut. The entire boat of a vehicle shook from the force of the slam. The angry pair entered the front seats and drove off.

"Who do you work for?" Cabrera asked.

The smug suspect laughed. "Aren't you supposed to read me my rights first?"

"Rights?" Cabrera shook his head. "Rights belong to human beings. Animals don't have rights. Now, tell me, why did you kill that young officer?"

"Young officer? That wasn't the chief?"

Castellano asked, "You were trying to kill the chief?"

Silence cloaked the car as the suspect's face drooped with concern.

"Aww, what's the matter? You killed the wrong cop?"

Cabrera chimed in, "You fucked up big time, you Stronzo! Not only did you not kill the chief, you failed to kill the detective you shot. You must be a fucking rookie."

"You know what? The only organization brazen enough to attempt an assassination on the police chief is the Marcello family," Castellano said. "And I know that organization well. You're gonna pay for your fuck up. Not by us, but by your own people. So, do me a favor. Tell me, who authorized the hit?"

The investigator's vehicle was a Ford Crown Victoria just like Benoit's, only without a cage or partition. Castellano could reach into the back seat at any time and slap the murderer. He was seated in the center of the rear seat in between the two front bucket seats. Cabrera mashed the gas pedal and accelerated. "Buckle up," he told his partner. The two exchanged glances with a silent understanding of what was to come.

Chapter Thirty-Eight

Decision Time

On the following day, Katalina received a phone call from Sergeant Daigle, who told her to wear her class-a uniform to work. Upon arrival, she observed news vans surrounding the police station and thought, *What a shit show.* When she entered the precinct, she was met with a standing ovation. Every officer, including the Salty Sarge was clapping for her. She blushed and looked down, not sure how to handle the praise.

"The chief is presenting you with an award today, Andrews. You've done us proud." Sergeant Daigle said.

"I couldn't have done it without Duce," she said.

"I'm sure he'll get one too when he returns to work."

Katalina nervously approached the podium where the chief and command staff stood preparing for a press conference. She heard a flood of thoughts coming from the packed conference room, but all were positive. She cracked a smile, and her blood pressure dropped a bit.

The chief gave a brilliant, heart-felt speech, condemning the criminal whose name he refused to glorify. He offered condolences for the family of the fallen officer. He stared directly at the television cameras and vowed to dismantle the mafia organization who he felt was responsible for the assassination. The chief ended with the praise and recognition of Detectives Andrews and Benoit. He presented her with a life-saving award, citing how innocent people's lives were spared due to the heroic actions of her and her partner. The crowd erupted in applause as flashes from cameras rattled off like a machine gun.

When Katalina stepped down off the stage, she was met by Lieutenant Esposito who offered a warm handshake. "Congratulations, Andrews. This is quite an honor."

Katalina pursed her lips and held tears back. She felt pride, redemption, and honor, but most of all she felt acceptance—something she's not ever felt before wearing that uniform. "Thank you, sir."

"And that's not all," Esposito said. His head hung low. "I believe Chief is going to be transferring you."

"What? Why?"

"I think he's appointing a new position of special investigator. I think he wants a mixture of a detective and an executive protection position."

"But I don't want to leave homicide."

"Andrews, these kinds of opportunities don't come around very often. Think of what this could do for your resume. One day, if you want to be chief, imagine what this could do for you. Nobody has ever been given this kind of opportunity, Andrews."

Katalina pondered. Her eyes drifted toward the floor. "I've always wanted this. To be accepted. To feel respected. But I can't accept it. I have to take a leave of absence."

"Can it wait? Maybe postpone your plans for a year or so."

She shook her head. "No, sir, it can't wait. Do you remember during my last oral review board, I mentioned my father was murdered?"

Esposito nodded.

"Something's come up and I need to travel to Europe."

"How long will you need?" Esposito asked.

Katalina shrugged. "I'm not sure. I plan to only be gone three weeks or so. I guess it depends on what I uncover."

"Be careful, Andrews. They don't play by our rules across the pond, and we can't go bailing you out of any trouble."

"Thank you, sir. I'll be okay."

"So, let me make sure I understand. You don't want the special assignment from the chief?"

"No, sir, I respectfully decline." Her eyes welled up with tears. Her heart hurt but her mind was steadfast in her decision. "Sir, do you mind if I take the rest of the day off? I'd like to go see Duce at the hospital."

"Go ahead. We've got you covered," Esposito said.

"Oh, is that douche still locked up. I have some choice words for him."

"The killer?" Esposito asked.

"Yes, sir."

"You didn't hear?"

"Hear what?"

"On the way to the station from the scene last night, Castellano and Cabrera were involved in a major vehicle crash. Seems a loose horse bolted across the roadway leaving the chief's house. They swerved to miss it and struck a tree head-on. They forgot to buckle the suspect in, and he got ejected through the front windshield. They tell me his body burst like a balloon upon impact."

Katalina touched the base of her neck. "Oh my God. How are Cabrera and Castellano?"

"A bit banged up. Luckily, they were wearing their seatbelts. Thank heavens for airbags."

***

Katalina arrived at the hospital and knocked on Benoit's door. He was propped up in the bed watching television. He had a tray across his lap with four empty pudding containers. "I thought pudding was for people who just had a tonsillectomy or something."

Benoit laughed and shrugged his shoulders. "I don't know. Maybe? I just asked for pudding and they brought it to me."

"Duce, I was given a life-saving award today and Lieutenant said the chief wants to create a special position for me."

"Congrats!"

She shook her head. "No, Duce. I can't accept it. I have to leave the country."

Benoit looked at Katalina with concern. "Why are you leaving the country?"

"With all the shit that's been happening lately. You know—" She lowered her voice to a whisper. "—vampires. I have to get some answers."

"Answers to what? Why do you have to leave the country for answers? And where are these answers anyway?"

"My dad. My *biological* dad owned a bookstore and if I can find it, I think it'll have some answers to my questions."

"The dad that was murdered in Europe?"

"Yes."

"Why would he have answers to a vampire problem?"

Katalina stared at Benoit; she trembled, and her eyes searched for comfort, but she remained silent.

"Kat, you can tell me."

"Duce, I think my dad was a vampire."

Benoit immediately choked on his pudding. He coughed so hard the spoon flew onto the floor. Katalina stood and grabbed a bottled water beside his bed and handed it to him. "Why do you think that?"

"I found a journal that my mother kept before she died and the last page said that my father, Erik, was a vampire."

Benoit appeared to be in a trance; his eyes stared off into the distance beyond Katalina. He spoke gently, "Does that mean you're a—"

"No! Can't be. I walk around in the sunlight. I love garlic. I'm vulnerable. I'm definitely not a vampire, Duce!"

Benoit nodded in affirmation at Katalina's profession. "Yeah, that's true. So, then you're a hybrid?"

"A what?"

"A hybrid. The technical name is Dhampir. It's a half-vampire, half-human."

"What? You've got to be shitting me, Duce! Are you making fun of me? I'm trying to be serious here!"

Benoit raised his arms and faced his palms at Katalina, a gesture police use to calm people down. "Kat, I'd never make fun of you. It all makes sense now. Hybrids have all the same powers as vampires but are mortal. They aren't fazed by sunlight, garlic, crosses, or any of that theatrical bullshit. They are the vampires' single natural predator. But there is one thing though. Dhampirs have an insatiable thirst for blood." Benoit gave Katalina a look much like an elderly grandfather peers down at his grandchild before he questions her. "But you don't, right?"

Katalina broke eye contact and said, "Well, about that. You see, I do crave the taste of blood. In fact, when I consume blood, my senses and strength increase. I guess that's why my favorite food is raw steak."

"Have you ever tasted human blood?"

Katalina pursed her lips together and gave Benoit a sheepish look. Her face winced as if she tasted a lemon. "Ummm…"

"Kat! Have you ever bitten anyone?"

Katalina's face twisted, "God no, Duce! I've only tasted blood. I don't have fangs and I've never wanted to bite anyone. Ever!"

"I've been wondering about you, Kat."

Katalina's head bobbed back, "Why is that?"

"Since I started really practicing magic, I've begun to develop special talents myself. For example, when I see people's reflections, I see their essence."

"Huh?"

"Okay, so if you're an evil person inside and I look at your reflection, I don't see what everyone else sees on the outside. I see something different. I see your true soul."

She raised her hand; fingers fanned out toward Benoit's face, "Get the fuck outta here!"

"Seriously, Kat. You know Drake? His soul is evil to the core. He's a demon."

"I knew it! Well, I didn't know that, but I knew he was garbage!"

"Kat, he's literally a demon. I saw an actual demon in his reflection. Twice!"

Things went silent for a second. Katalina peered into Benoit's eyes before she spoke, "Duce. What do you see in me?"

"That's the thing, Kat. You don't have a reflection."

"Bullshit! I spend way more time than I need to looking in the mirror!"

"To everyone else, you have a reflection. To me, there's nothing. That's why I had a mini panic attack back in Sheila's apartment."

Katalina gave a dumb look. "Who?"

"Sheila. The cleaning lady who committed suicide."

"About that, Duce. Remember the black hairs we kept finding on all those suicide scenes?"

"I do."

"No need to get those analyzed. I'm pretty sure I know where they came from."

Benoit looked at Katalina with a curious gaze. "Okay? Where?"

"I found the same black hair on my pillow after Dmitri and I…"

"You're kidding? Your vampire lover killed all those women?"

Katalina made a disgusted face. "It sounds awful when you say it like that."

"What?"

"My vampire lover."

"Um, Kat."

"I know. I know. It's just gross now that I think about it."

"Oh my God, Kat! That's freaking brilliant!"

"Eh, it was just okay. I've had better."

"No! His style of killing. Vampires can control humans' minds. It's like hypnosis. They can enter someone's head, read their minds, and control what they do. They basically make humans do whatever they want them to. That's why there was always a personalized suicide note!"

"Why would he do that?"

"Think about it, Kat. He compels humans to write a suicide note, then compels them to slit their own wrists and he feeds on them! Genius!"

"Yeah, but why not just bite them? Like in the movies."

"Kat, what do you think would happen if our 'victims' all had two bite marks on next to their jugular veins?"

"We'd be looking for a vam… Oh, shit! That is brilliant!"

Benoit smiled at Katalina. "So, another thing about Dhampirs. They're immune to a vampire's compulsion and telepathy powers. That's probably why your stud pursued you."

"I like to think it's because I'm a smoking hot scarlet demigoddess."

"Right," Benoit laughed.

Katalina stood up and punched Benoit in his thigh. "Asshole. How do you know so much about vampires and dam, damp… Fucking hybrids?"

"I keep getting visited in my dreams by an African shaman. Ever since the witch doctor invaded my dreams, he's been telling me about evil creatures on Earth and about an inevitable showdown between good and evil. That made me think, if witches exist, then what else exists out there? What could he be talking about? So, I started digging into old books left behind by ancestors and learned about the vampire virus. Oh, and before I forget, if a vampire tastes a Dhampir's blood, it immediately intoxicates it to the point of incoherence and incompetence."

"So, I'm basically a vampire's worst nightmare?"

"Don't get too cocky, Kat. You're not immortal. You could get hit by a bus tomorrow and die. But yes. Vampires fear Dhampirs."

"What else do I need to know about vampires, Duce? I'm about to fly to Europe, where my mom and dad were born, and likely come across more."

Benoit thought for a second. "Oh yes! Silver. Silver is toxic to vampires."

"What do I do with silver?"

"You could melt some down and put a drop inside of a hollow-point bullet. Once it dries inside, you'd have the perfect vampire weapon."

Katalina's eyes almost jumped out of their sockets. "Shit!" She released the magazine from her Glock and analyzed the bullets. She looked at the hollow-point bullets and noticed a shiny speck inside the hollowed-out lead. "Duce! These are the bullets my dad gave me for Christmas! The ones he said a friend gave him from some voodoo shop on the bayou!"

"That's why they killed that vampire on the speed boat that night. Didn't you shoot a vampire before with no apparent effect?"

"Yes! I shot that woman who attacked Pete and she basically laughed at me. Then, when I shot the one on the boat, he dropped like a sack of potatoes. Holy shit, Duce! This is freaking wild!"

"Remember, Kat. You can't bring your gun to Europe. You'll have to find another one there or—"

"I could also find a silver knife and use it like a wooden stake, right?"

Benoit exhaled and crossed his arms against his chest, "You sure could, Kat."

Katalina hugged Benoit and kissed his forehead, "I've got to get packing. My flight leaves in the morning. Oh, I almost forgot. Can you please watch Casper for me while I'm gone?

Benoit squinted at Katalina and leaned back, "That evil-looking shaved cat?"

"He's not shaved! And he's cute!"

"I love animals, Kat. And I love you, so I'll do it, but just know, I think Casper hates me.

"No way! He loves everyone!"

Benoit pursed his lips with a suspicious look stretched across his face, "Mmm Hmm, we'll see. Of course, I'll do it, Kat."

"Thanks! Just once per day, stop in and clean his litter. Fill his food and water and that's it! Feel free to sit with him and give him some loving. Wish me luck!"

"Good luck, partner. Oh, and Kat, be careful. Please come back. New Orleans needs us."

"Don't worry, Duce. I wouldn't leave you out to fight the wolves all alone."

"Oh, before I forget, the asshole who shot you last night? Yeah, he's dead."

Benoit almost jumped out of the bed. "What? How?"

"Turns out, Castellano and Cabrera were transporting him to the station for questioning and got into a violent crash. He wasn't buckled in and got ejected. Talk about some final destination shit huh?"

Benoit pursed his lips, his face screaming bullshit. "Those two are something else! You better believe that shit was planned."

"What? No way? Seriously?"

"Believe what you want, Kat. Those two are old school, eye-for-an-eye cops. I'm just glad they're on our side."

Chapter Thirty-Nine

Stark Warning

Markus was underground in a torture chamber, watching as scientists were analyzing blood samples in microscopes. The bunker was a biology lab with state-of-the-art technology despite the decrepit exterior. Four people were chained to the wall; their arms fully extended and securely cinched against a cement barrier. Their heads, chest, waist, knees, and ankles all were tightly secured, essentially eliminating any chance of movement. IV tubes ran from their veins and slowly dripped into glass beakers. Another IV pierced veins on opposite arms that pumped nutrients into their bodies; enough to keep them alive. As he moved around the room, admiring his lab, he stopped and stared off into the distance.

Amelia and Viktor also stopped. They waited impatiently for him to share what he'd just seen.

"Dmitri is dead," Markus announced.

Amelia and Viktor exchanged glances. "Was it Rainey?" Amelia asked.

Marks shook his head. "No. The redhead killed him, and two others."

"The human? This is preposterous!" Viktor cried. "I shall eliminate this irritation at once!"

Markus shook his head. "Do you really think it's going to be that easy? She has killed five vampires in a matter of a month, and you think that you can single-handedly kill her? You're more of a fool than I thought, Viktor, but go ahead. After all, this is your mess."

Viktor seethed and stormed out of the laboratory, blowing steel doors off of their hinges as he burst through them.

"Amelia, my dear. You'll do well to keep an eye out. I have a feeling we've not seen the last of this, Katalina."

"Of course, your highness, but she can't penetrate the island, can she?"

Markus shook his head and exhaled. "I don't know what to think anymore. And Amelia. Don't go chasing after Viktor. I fear he's waged a war he can't win, and I'd like you here with me. I need my trusted aide by my side at all times."

For the first time in centuries, fear flashed through Amelia's eyes. "Why is this happening?"

"If my suspicion is true, then I believe Katalina is the offspring of Erik, which would mean she's a Dhampir," Markus said.

"Then we just kill her first. Right?"

Markus gave Amelia a look of disappointment. "You sound like Viktor. It's not that easy. You see, vampires nearly became extinct on two separate occasions in our history. Each time, by a lone Dhampir who single-handedly slaughtered scores of us. That's why it's a high crime to procreate with humans, thus creating half-breeds. They are born with an innate hatred for vampires. You see, human children are born without the idea of hatred. They have to be taught to dislike. Human babies are also taught fear. The only fear they are born with is a fear of falling, but not Dhampirs. Dhampirs are born with a gene that remains dormant until the realization that vampires exist. That gene, once activated, burns wildly through their veins, thus causing Dhampirs to engage in murderous rampages targeting vampires."

Amelia looked dumbfounded. "Why haven't I ever known this?"

"For the most part, we have been able to control the minute population of Dhampirs around the world." Markus turned his focus on the human lab rats chained to the wall. "We kill both parents and eliminate the offspring. Sure, some slip through the cracks, but we are normally able to destroy them when they are weak and vulnerable. If we don't get them early however, and their hatred is activated, then they turn into rabid dogs."

"Dogs? I've never heard of such a thing!" Amelia said.

"Not literally. Dhampirs become so determined to kill vampires that all reasoning dies. Their medulla oblongata is rewired, and their anger remains at the forefront of their existence. Another thing that gives them the upper hand is that they can sense vampires whereas we can't sense Dhampirs and as you well know, we can't bite a Dhampir."

Amelia nodded her head. "Intoxicated paralysis. It just doesn't make sense that they're so powerful!"

Markus smiled. "Our creator did an amazing job of balancing the spectrums. For every apex predator, there exists an equalizer—a superior predator. No one species will ever rule the Earth without the threat of neutralization lurking."

"So Dhampirs are the supreme being? The apex predators?" Amelia asked.

"I really don't know. We've done such a good job of keeping them on the verge of extinction, that we haven't studied them much. Katalina is an anomaly—a wild card. Not since the early-1300s has a Dhampir wreaked such havoc on our kind."

"What happened then?"

"You're familiar with the ominous number 13?"

"Yes, as in Friday the 13th?"

"Precisely. You see, on Friday, October 13 in the year of 1307, vampires ruled France under the guise of being Knights who fought for those who were oppressed. Feigning to be protectors of underdogs, they avoided suspicion. The Knights ruled for over 200 years with impunity and without fear of persecution. King Philip IV saw how powerful the Knights of Templar had become and grew suspicious of their true intentions. He feared that the Knights would soon try and overthrow his throne. A general in his army was a Dhampir and had long suspected the Knights of being supernatural. When the general was given a green light to destroy the Knights, he did so single-handedly. The siege on the Knights was deadly and King Philip lost over 100 soldiers to the vampires, but General Andrews destroyed every-single vampire Knight that existed. Our kind almost went extinct because of a single Dhampir."

"General Andrews? Isn't Katalina's surname Andrews?"

"Yes. Coincidence. The point is, if Katalina is indeed a Dhampir, then we mustn't take any chances."

Amelia's face was stretched with surprise. "How do we deal with her then?"

Markus shook his head. "I'm not quite sure. We can't seek guidance from the convocation. The mere fact that a Dhampir exists, puts us in grave danger. If she is the spawn of Erik, then I'm responsible for her existence, which as you know is a high crime."

Chapter Forty

Belarus

Katalina packed a suitcase in preparation of her flight. She stared at the backpack that held hundreds of tiny vials of red liquid and grew curious. She grabbed a vial and held it to her nose, inhaling. Even through the glass pipette, she knew it contained blood. She couldn't tell what species the blood came from; human or animal, but regardless it smelled delightful, so she decided to give it a try.

Katalina broke the end of a vial and placed a single drop on her tongue. Instantly, she felt a surge of power. Her neighbors could be heard talking from across the hall. The smell of a fire made her smile, despite her apartment building not having any fireplaces. After not feeling any adverse effects, Katalina poured the remaining few drops of blood on her tongue.

She packed five vials in a pair of socks that were stuffed deep down inside her suitcase. The remaining vials were kept in the original bag and hidden in her closet. She grinned like a drug fiend hiding her stash of dope, excited at the idea of having a plethora of highs at her fingertips.

Katalina admired her newly whittled tools of destruction and wondered if she could smuggle any of them on a 22-hour flight. Instead, she opted for the safe bet and strategically placed them throughout her apartment. She hid one beneath her pillow on her bed and another in a cereal box in her pantry. She hid one behind the toilet in her bathroom and another in her freezer. One was placed on a top shelf in her closet and the other two were hidden in her living room. One stuffed in her couch cushions, one behind her front door, and the last one was plainly resting on a coffee table.

***

Katalina arrived in Belarus and was shocked at how brutally cold it was. She had never left Louisiana before. The coldest temperature she had ever experienced was thirty degrees. It was ten below zero in Belarus. She wasted no time and stopped at a store located in the airport and purchased a large heavy coat with a fur hoodie. She purchased a pair of heavy boots that were also lined with fur and set off.

After retrieving her luggage from the conveyor belt, she plugged in the latitude and longitude coordinates that were written on the last page of her mother's journal. She was close. Katalina hailed a cab and directed the driver to the address that populated on her phone. The cab pulled along a seemingly abandoned building. The structure appeared to once have several operational businesses occupying the space, now all resembling a ghost town. She looked in the driver's rear-view mirror and caught him staring at her. His eyes were gentle but bored.

"This is the address," he offered with a less-than-amused tone.

"Thank you, I thought this was a restaurant. Can you drive me to The Renaissance Minsk Hotel?"

The driver exhaled and clenched his jaw, seemingly frustrated. He drove a bit faster, seeming to care less about taking turns and curves with grace. The Renaissance Minsk Hotel appeared newly constructed with a postmodernist touch. The windows were a rich blue as it reflected the brilliant sky. The building had a beautiful blend of geometrical shapes that gave it an uncharacteristic look, far from a traditional rectangular building.

Katalina paid the driver and retrieved her suitcase. She pretended to play on her phone after closing the trunk and waited for the cabbie to drive away. Once satisfied that the taxi had departed the area, she called for another cab.

Although she did not get a bad feeling with the cabbie, she immediately grew paranoid after giving him the address of the abandoned building. Within minutes, another cab pulled into the parking lot and picked her up. She directed him to the Crown Plaza Hotel which was much closer to her target destination.

Once checked in, Katalina unpacked and gathered herself. She studied the area using maps and the internet. She stared at her suitcase and rubbed her stomach. Drawn to it, she dove into the pair of socks that concealed her vials of pleasure and held one up to her face—admiring the ruby liquid. The tip was popped off with a simple twist and she turned it up, allowing the blood to drip on her tongue.

Immediately, sounds rushed in. A smorgasbord of not-so-appealing smells infiltrated her nose. She rubbed her arm and made a fist. A slight numbness provided a sense of invincibility as she marveled in the feeling of superiority. She found a shopping center within walking distance and set off on a reconnaissance mission.

Although it was daylight outside, Katalina couldn't help but keep her head on a swivel. She was within walking distance to a big-box hardware store but chose to keep a low profile. She stumbled across a mom-and-pop hole in the wall outfit that seemed promising. It was more like a pawn shop than a hardware store but Katalina had high hopes.

Inside the store was dingy. The colors were basic beiges and olive drab greens. The woman working behind the register appeared to be over two hundred pounds with silver hair and an apron. The place smelled old and dusty with a hint of cabbage soup in the distance—likely being simmered in a back room. The cashier eyeballed Katalina with a suspicious glare.

"Могу я помочь тебе найти что-нибудь?" she said in Russian. (Can I help you find something?)

Katalina answered in the cashier's native tongue, "Yes. I collect vintage dinnerware and am looking for a couple of forks to complete my collection. Would you happen to carry such a thing?"

The cashier seemed to believe Katalina and waddled her way from around the desk. She was taken to the rear of the establishment and produced a wooden box with what appeared to be a family crest carved on it. The plump lady opened the box and proudly displayed its contents to Katalina.

"It is said that this set once belonged to Ivan IV." The contents had a goldish color and indeed had the letter I imprinted on the handles.

"Perhaps a bit too rich for my taste. Do you have anything else?" Katalina asked.

The clerk grunted as she closed the wooden box. She motioned toward a table with her pointer finger. Her hand then waved the petite redhead as if to say, "You can find it on your own."

Katalina located several articles of dinnerware but settled with two items: a silver-looking fork and a utensil that resembled a butter knife. She paid the lady and emerged in the brittle cold. The sun was low in the sky and by Katalina's account, it was rapidly approaching dusk. Just a few blocks away, she came upon the abandoned business strip that she was shown by her first cabbie. She checked her phone and looked around her as if she was being followed but nobody could be seen.

Katalina inspected the front door that appeared to be locked and turned the knob. It was locked. The windows were boarded up on each side of the door in a crisscross pattern. She was small enough to sliver in between the triangle opening outside of the boards so she broke the window and crawled in.

Once inside the place was abandoned. Remnants of a once operational bookstore were prevalent. A feeling of belonging fell over her. Comfort that she hadn't felt since she was a child made her smile. The wall from floor to ceiling had dusty old books still consuming the shelves. Cobwebs stretched from one wall to the next. The wooden floor creaked with every step. Boards threatened to snap beneath her feet in most areas.

Along the back wall an old register was open, long since emptied. Katalina noticed a sofa-style chair neatly tucked against one wall. Someone had taken the time to cover it with plastic; someone who planned to return for it. She removed the plastic cover and sat on the couch.

A deep inhale identified the scent of ancient tobacco smoke and coffee that had absorbed into the cushions from years before. She stared at the hundreds of books that remained in the abandoned bookstore and tried to visualize what it was like when it was thriving. She envisioned her mother working the register while her father pushed a rolling ladder around tidying books.

Chapter Forty-One

Revenge

Darkness fell on New Orleans and Viktor emerged from the shadows. It was a Friday night, and the city was quickly lit with bright neon lights burning from seemingly every window downtown. Chartres Street was no different. It cut right through the French Quarter. Viktor had never left Europe in all his years.

The architecture was a friendly reminder of the old ways in France—a place he had spent many of his younger years. The restored vintage street signs that boasted the street names in English and in French intrigued him. Downtown New Orleans reminded him of Paris in the late nineteenth century except for the droves of diverse people wandering around. He felt confident walking among the humans in New Orleans because most of them looked stranger than he did. Several passed him with painted white faces and black eye makeup, some boasted fangs.

Viktor grew more comfortable as he approached Sylvain's. It was as if he knew his kind were close by. Tourists lined the sidewalk in front of the restaurant—all humans. Viktor crept around to the back of the restaurant and was met by a large guard. The sentry was something straight out of an action movie; he stood over six feet tall and appeared to weigh over two hundred and fifty pounds. His head was clean shaven, and his face was riddled with scars from years of battle.

The guard looked down at Viktor who stood confident with an ice-cold stare. The two gazed at one another with no words spoken and the guard stepped aside. Viktor entered the double doors that descended underground. Once he reached the bottom of the stairs, he advanced through the winding hallway, taking note of the little glass pipettes that littered the tiny rooms around every corner and smiled at the production of Markus' products. Viktor entered the barroom at the end of the walkway and all talking stopped. The place went silent as all heads turned when he entered. He took a seat at the bar and locked eyes with the bartender, Maks.

"I'm looking for an old friend," Viktor said. "Tall, black hair, insatiable thirst for women."

Maks gave Viktor a suspicious look. "You've described just about half the vampires in here. You got a name?"

"Dmitri."

Maks shook his head as he searched Viktor's face. "Haven't seen him in a while. What did he do now?"

Viktor shrugged his shoulders. "Let's just say I have some unfinished business to attend to and I think he can help."

"Does Rainey know you're here?" Maks asked.

Viktor bore deeply into Maks' eyes. "So, you know who I am?"

In a flash, he grabbed Maks from across the bar and hurled him across the barroom; his body struck the wall and crumpled to the floor. Viktor leapt onto the bar and prepared to battle droves of vampires advancing on him. They all stopped just short of converging on him. "I will kill every last one of you," Viktor professed.

The first brave vampire jumped on the bar with Viktor. He flashed toward him and was met with the force of a train as Viktor grabbed him by his throat and launched him in the same direction as Maks.

One by one, vampires descended on Viktor, each taking a shot at the seasoned executioner, but he operated with surgical precision and deadly delivery, striking each taker down. The advancing crowd dwindled. Each vampire stepped forward with hesitation as limbs from their comrades lay scattered throughout the barroom.

Viktor showed no signs of mercy or fatigue as he crushed the younger vampires like an alley cat toying with a baby mouse. The last remaining vampire armed himself with a pool cue and broke it in half, wielding a splintered stake in each hand.

Viktor smiled. "Perhaps the smartest in the entire place. Finally, someone realizes he can't beat me unless armed." He smiled at the lone standing soldier. "I'm going to take that stake from you—" He pointed to his left hand. "—and jam it through your throat. Then, I'm going to take that one—" He pointed to his right hand. "—and impale your heart. Tonight, is the night you die."

The vampire was committed. He pushed forward and hurled one of the cue halves at Viktor. The spear cut through the air like a hot knife cutting through butter. Viktor snatched the flying instrument from the air and hurled it across the room, striking Maks in the heart.

He looked at the last vampire standing and said with a smile. "Time's up."

Viktor hopped down from the bar and asked, "Fast or slow?"

The sole vampire remained quiet as he stared at Viktor. Before he could formulate a word, Viktor tore his head off and said, "Fast. I've got business to attend to."

He walked to the far end of the bar on his way out and knocked a flickering candle off the wall. As he exited and began his departure, flames exploded behind him, burning the remaining corpses of dead vampires. Viktor continued through the winding hall and observed intoxicated vampires on the verge of death as they enjoyed their comatose high, oblivious to the impending inferno that was soon to end their undead addicted lives. Once outside, the large sentry who stood guard earlier, was no longer there.

Wisely, he fled.

Viktor retreated to the shadows and watched as the restaurant went up in flames. The ancient building was no match for the hungry fire that ravaged every weakened board that held the place up. Screams could be heard as humans from the restaurant failed at their attempt to escape. Within minutes, red flashing lights and an annoying siren converged on the blaze. Dutiful men worked diligently like worker ants trying to extinguish the flames, but the building was damned. Viktor waited for his target to arrive, but even hours after the fire was put out, Katalina did not appear.

Chapter Forty-Two

History

When Katalina arrived at the bookstore, she saw it the way her parents had, because nothing about the building seemed like it could have changed much over the years. The store sat along a busy street that had plenty of other shops running down both ends of it. Like the other spaces, the bottom floor sat as a business and up above sat four stories of apartment living.

The first three floors were made of large industrial bricks, giving the architect a modern, almost Western appeal. The top two floors were traditional in design: white painted stucco with French-style doors that led out to tiny private balconies that sat enclosed behind wrought iron railing.

The difference with the bookshop is that it was the only building that sat abandoned. Whereas all of the other shops had glass windows that were polished and had attractive displays behind them to lure customers, the glass windows of the bookshop looked as if they hadn't been cleaned for many years and the painted name of the shop had faded in some areas.

Katalina searched the books that lined the wall from floor to ceiling for clues. She was hoping to find a smoking gun. "Would it be too hard to have a book titled *A Complete History of Vampires*?"

As she scanned the litany of dusty books, one stood out. It was larger than the others along the same shelf. She felt drawn to that particular book and reached for it. She removed the book that was titled *America*. She thumbed through the pages and found nothing out of the ordinary. She hoped to find a cryptic message or code somewhere in the book, but nothing of such materialized. She placed the book back in its slot and noticed something that stood out. It appeared to be a button of some sort. She pressed it and the entire bookshelf moved about an inch as if a latch was released.

The storage area led to a tiny hall that had several small offices that had all of their doors open. She peeked inside them imagining her father using these offices while he had been alive. Nothing looked out of the ordinary. The same furniture she imagined that her father had used years ago still sat in place and frozen in time with cobwebs and dust that gave proof that no one had been inside this part of the building for some time.

The actual bookshop sat similar; a large open space filled with large bookshelves that still had books arranged on them. The shelves were arranged by topics. Because she didn't have a title to refer to there was no way to find what she was looking for. But as a detective, she knew that what she needed to find wouldn't just be sitting out in the open. Her mother's last journal entry had made that evident. Whatever her mother wanted her to find would be hidden and to find it Katalina knew she needed to rely on her investigative skills.

The floorplan is where she needed to start. A vampire owning a bookstore had to be for a cover. A vampire would have to live a double life, one for the public and one that was kept secret.

The area was equally abandoned and had plenty of cobwebs. A desk, with a hefty layer of dust, was inside that had several papers strewn about as well as a sketch. The sketch was of two men.

Katalina's hand shook as she gazed at the drawing. Her heart raced and threatened to burst from her ribcage. One man held a close resemblance to Katalina, but she did not know who he was. The other made her heart skip a beat. He was a taller male with black hair who had a command presence. His appearance screamed authority. He was the man who kept haunting her nightmares. *Who the hell are you?*

Katalina sat at the desk and perused through the papers. She took note of a hierarchy of some sort. It resembled the organizational chart used at her agency. In the center of the chart was something called the Vampire Convocation. Surrounding the nucleus were smaller charts with the names of continents on them: Europe, America, Africa, and Asia.

Each chart had three names on them: America had Rainey (elder), Atticus (enforcer), & Cyrus (diplomat). Europe had Markus (elder), Viktor (enforcer), & Amelia (diplomat). Asia had Takeshi (elder), Virole (enforcer), & Jiang (diplomat), and finally Africa had Adisa (elder), Janga (enforcer), and Nini (diplomat). Each faction-elder had notes jotted alongside their chart. Markus of Europe—can see through the eyes of vampires just before their deaths, thus seeing who their killer is. Takeshi of Asia—can change the weather in her territory. Adisa of Africa— had the ability to deliver fire with the point of a finger. Rainey of America—cannot be lied to.

She continued looking through the files and came across a file that was titled, Vampire Convocation Charter of Rules. The first four rules were emphasized with hand-written asterisks and squiggly lines.

It shall be a high crime for any vampire to commit the following violations. Any such violation will result in execution:

1. *No vampire shall leave his or her territory.*
2. *No vampire shall kill another vampire without just cause and permission from said vampire's territorial elder.*
3. *No vampire shall procreate with humans, thus creating Dhampirs.*
4. *No vampire shall feed on the blood of Dhampirs.*
5. *No vampire shall infect children under the age of 15 with the virus.*

As Katalina continued to read through the treasure trove of notes, she realized her father, Erik, was being groomed as an alternate diplomat for the European faction of vampires. He kept a detailed journal outlining his innermost thoughts.

I fear Markus has gone rogue. He has inhabited an island where vampire scientists are searching for a cure to the virus. Tests were conducted using hybrid blood and a most interesting discovery was made. The search for a cure has taken a back seat to his obsession with Dhampirs. He lures Dhampirs there under the guise of protection from angry vampires. A family member gets murdered and Viktor, with a fully quenched palate, promises protection to the Dhampir and his family. If the Dhampir agrees, they accompany Viktor to Voz Island, and they're kept prisoner until they die all the while Markus' team of scientists extract the Dhampir's blood and package it for distribution. Markus is smart though; he provides them with just enough nutrition to keep them alive yet lethargic. Markus is committing a high crime by all accounts by providing Dhampir's blood to reckless vampires across the world. The other factions suspect Markus is still actively searching for a cure.

Katalina thought back to when she was attacked in the parking garage. The male vampire who bit her neck had an immediate reaction—a reaction similar to someone sedated. She wondered if that rule had been enacted to protect vampires from being vulnerable. She located another note titled, American Faction. Her father wrote:

The American Faction of vampires is the least vicious. The elder, Rainey, is a female who was turned as a young native on the continent of North America. I believe she is the oldest living vampire but by far the strongest. Her reign over America is with an iron fist. Although her views on killing humans are considered weak by vampire standards, she makes up for it in violence

Katalina opened the desk drawer and found a picture. She thought she was looking at herself in the photograph. The woman had fiery red hair and milky white skin. Her facial features were identical to Katalina's. Her face was small and round. Her nose was thin and tiny. A man stood next to her, holding her waist; the same man pictured in the sketch.

The couple was her parents. They looked happy in the picture. Vibrant and full of life. Her mother had a radiant glow around her body. Her face screamed happiness. A tear fell down Katalina's face. She shared features from both of her parents. She'd never seen pictures of them before and until that moment, only had a made-up mental picture of them. She pressed the photo against her chest then slid it in her back pocket. A book hadn't been found, but what she had found was good enough for now.

Chapter Forty-Three

Impatient

Viktor departed the shadows beyond the fire in haste. He walked along the sidewalk and blended in with the crowd. He studied the bodies that moved around him, searching for someone with orange hair. A man dressed in all-black clothing and a long black jacket bumped into Viktor as he walked. The clumsy walker shot Viktor a disrespectful look as if expressing his discontent.

"Pardon me," Viktor said.

"Fuck off!"

The walker was snatched from the sidewalk and dragged into the darkness between buildings. Viktor held him up against a brick wall; his feet dangled. "You should have better manners. Why the black paint on your face?"

The gothic-looking male spoke, exposing his artificial fangs, "I'm sorry!"

Viktor noticed elongated incisors protruding from his mouth. "What's wrong with your teeth? Do you want to be a vampire?"

The dangler tried to nod as best he could while being held up by his throat. He couldn't speak. Viktor lowered him to his feet. "What do you know about vampires?"

Mr. Gothic rubbed his throat and said, "They're cool as shit. Immortal, they drink blood, they do what the fuck they want to."

"Are you afraid of vampires?" Viktor asked.

"No."

Viktor shook his head. "You should be," and bit into his neck, puncturing his jugular vein.

The Goth couldn't scream. He just stood, his life fading before his eyes as Viktor fed. Once satisfied, Viktor dropped the corpse to the ground, wiped his mouth with his sleeve, and disappeared into the darkness. He found himself perched atop a building peering down at the busy bodies moving about. It didn't take long for someone to notice a pair of black boots pointing up toward the sky from within the alley.

Within twenty minutes, police officers converged on the area and began roping the area off with yellow tape. Viktor observed from above and waited for the redhead detective to arrive on scene to no avail. A man approached the busy scene below that caught Viktor's attention. He zeroed in on the dark-skinned newcomer.

Viktor's black heart skipped a beat. "It can't be," he mumbled to himself. He heard his own breathing increase, sounding like the wind blowing from a powerful fan. Subconsciously, Viktor rubbed the side of his neck as he drifted.

***

Belarus, 945 AD

Blistering snow blanketed the soldiers traversing across Kievan Rus'. Viktor watched as his soldiers engaged in a barbaric battle with the Byzantines. His men were well-trained and appeared to have the upper hand. Horses could be heard screaming as large ice-cold swords aimed at soldiers, missed their marks, and pierced their furry flesh. Heavy thuds followed as men were thrown to the iced ground below. His men were valiant, many of which had been soldiers since the tender age of ten. Some had been so good at battle, they managed to reach the ripe old age of thirty-five. Viktor the Old was an anomaly; ancient by all accounts for he had weathered many storms and had grown old and wise.

As most Kings do, Viktor was following behind his troops. He was surrounded by a personal protective force, fearless men who laughed in the face of danger and had fantasies of battling to their honorable deaths. He felt something change; the tension in the air shifted and although just moments before his men were advancing, they suddenly retreated. Viktor searched the facial expressions of the gladiators beside him and they all appeared just as confused. Soldiers don't run.

"Advance forward!" he shouted to his protective team.

The four men kicked their horses and moved forward to investigate. Viktor continued at a slow pace through the blizzard. He couldn't see five feet in front of him as the snow blew sideways. Each foot forward, bodies were stacked, all saturated in blood. Many decapitated. His horse abruptly stopped. Viktor kicked the horse but instead of moving forward, it stood on its hind legs and neighed his front legs kicking violently.

He held the reins close to his chest, trying not to fall out of the saddle. His strong arms failed him and he released the rains, falling to his back. The horse turned and ran away from him, leaving him in the blinding white blizzard. He heard no voices. No horses exhaling. No hooves crushing the ice. He heard no men screaming and no swords crashing against one another. Instinctively, Viktor drew his long sword and readied it for an attack. He had not experienced fear since he was a boy and wasn't anxious, despite the strange feeling surrounding him.

He called out to his most trusted soldier, "Igor?"

Silence.

"Vladimir?"

Silence.

A brown-skinned man appeared through the snow. His uniform didn't match Viktor's or the soldiers who opposed him. The man stood with minimal dressing; something that belonged in a hot climate. He stood stoic and unafraid.

"Who goes there?" Viktor shouted, but the man didn't answer. Instead, he just offered a sadistic smile. "I am Viktor the Old, King of Kievan Rus', ruler of the Varangians."

The strange man spoke in Viktor's native tongue, "I know not who you are, nor do I care. It is most unfortunate that you've interrupted me.

"You do not frighten me!" Viktor professed as he advanced forward.

The mystery man shook his head and in a flash was standing behind Viktor. He held his head and rotated it to the side before piercing his fangs into the king's neck. Viktor felt as if fire was ignited through the veins in his neck, yet he couldn't resist. He felt strangely helpless. He simply allowed the attack without resistance. Viktor fell facedown into the snow and watched as the ice became saturated with crimson.

***

Viktor stared down from the building's rooftop at the figure who haunted his dreams for over a millennium. "What are you doing? Why are you pretending to be human?" Viktor glanced at his right hand that shook, overcome with nerves. "Is this a trap? Has Rainey sent my maker to kill me?"

Chapter Forty-Four

Baited

Benoit stretched his arms across his chest and rubbed his shoulder. Immediately, he regretted touching the tender injury as he flinched. "Today is the day," he announced to himself as he prepared to return to full duty after being shot at the chief's house. "What kind of insane drama will New Orleans throw at me today?"

Before setting off for the graveyard shift, Benoit opened a drawer that held the few articles of jewelry he owned. His father's wedding band, his senior ring, a cheap watch given to his graduating academy class, and a necklace he'd owned since high school, a gift a significant other had given him for a one-year anniversary years before. Each article was silver in color, but he wasn't sure which, if any, were really silver. Inside the two rings he observed the inscription .925 and presumed that was the silver content. The necklace was too small to tell.

Benoit grabbed a loose coat hanger from his closet and gathered up the loose jewelry, except for the watch, and brought it to his workshop. He sprawled it out across a bench and retrieved a porcelain crucible. The crucible resembled a half coconut shell. He set it in a tray and dumped the two rings and the necklace inside of it.

Benoit produced a box of hollow point 9mm rounds and slid the tray out. Each round perfectly pointed upward with the hollowed-out lead facing the ceiling. The bullets were cheap rounds purchased from the local gun store and were not department issued. He found a set of heavy gloves and a propane torch that he'd used on a few rare occasions. The coat hanger was untwisted and straightened, then placed beside the bullets.

Benoit fired up the torch, looked up toward the ceiling and said, "I'm sorry, father. I hope you can understand why I'm doing this." and placed the flame directly on the pile of jewelry in the crucible. It took just six minutes to fully melt the items into a shiny hot liquid. Quickly, Benoit dipped the tip of the coat hanger into the liquid and hovered it over the first bullet. A tiny droplet of silver fell into the hollowed-out bullet and immediately hardened. The silver in the crucible was resistant and threatened to harden if not under constant heat, so after each dip and drop, he had to reheat the silver to keep it fluid.

The process took about an hour to fill only fifty bullets. After, he had a small coin-like chunk of silver that remained. After it cooled, he dropped it in his pocket as a good luck charm.

"Dad, I will keep this with me as long as I'm alive."

Benoit retrieved three spare magazines for his Glock 17; each held seventeen rounds. He emptied the department-issued bullets and replaced them with all fifty newly upgraded bullets.

Benoit was a bit more seasoned than Katalina and knew better than to completely replace all bullets in his service weapon. He had been in a few on-duty shootings and knew the consequences of using bullets or a weapon that was not department-issued, so he kept a fourth magazine loaded in his weapon with Golden Saber bonded rounds. The other three magazines were tucked away in a backpack he wore to work.

He had to be on duty at 9pm. He worked the graveyard shift for eight hours and if New Orleans didn't want to punish him, he'd get off on time at 5am. It didn't take long when he settled in at his desk before he had to hit the streets. He looked at the empty space next to his and smiled. He scribbled on his notepad while his mind drifted to the rollercoaster of a ride his life had taken recently.

"Benoit, we got a body in the French Quarter," Sergeant Daigle barked. "Patrol already has the scene roped off."

"I haven't even been on the clock for thirty minutes, Sarge." Benoit laughed. He stood and hoisted his backpack onto his shoulders.

"What the fuck is that?" Daigle asked as he pointed at Benoit's legal pad. "Katalina's back? With some half-moons on either side?"

Benoit snatched the pad up on his way out of the door as he yelled, "It's nothing, Sarge!"

He heard Daigle mumbling as he trotted down the hall, "I got a homicide detective who thinks he's fucking Van Goh."

"I wonder if he realized those were fangs?" Benoit asked himself as he snaked through the halls. "Half-moons work though," he laughed. Benoit, in his absent mind, bumped into Drake as he barreled down the hall. "I'm sorry, Drake!"

"Where's that evil bitch of a partner at, Benoit?"

"C'mon, Drake. She's not evil. What's the deal with you two anyway?"

"She's the one with the problem! Not me!"

Benoit shook his head. "Gotta go!"

Benoit approached his unit in the gated parking lot and took note of how eerily quiet it was outside. He looked up and saw the bright yellow moon showering light down on the busy city. While staring up, a bat bounced through the air, making whipping sounds as its wings fluttered. Bats didn't bother Benoit, but lately when random animals graced him with their presence, he took that to be either an omen or a blessing.

The problem was not knowing which one was lurking. When he sat in his vehicle, he saw a glimpse of something. The vision was of him kneeling over a body as if he was looking down from above. As quickly as it flashed through his vision, the glimpse was gone. He shook it off and cranked his vehicle up.

Benoit arrived on the scene and observed a white male corpse crumpled on the dirty alleyway. The light makeup made his skin appear pale. Black makeup circled his eyes. Benoit signed the crime scene log before crossing beneath the yellow tape marked POLICE LINE DON'T CROSS.

"What do we have," he asked the supervisor on scene.

"Looks like something took a bite out of his neck. The fucking irony, huh? A guy dressed as a vampire gets killed like in vampire movies. This town never ceases to amaze me."

Benoit studied the patrol sergeant's face, hoping to see sarcasm, disbelief, or humor, but the officers' gestures were normal. He couldn't read him. "Okay, have we identified him?"

"Yes, sir." He handed Benoit a driver's license that read Anthony Labauve. "He's a local. There's an emergency contact attached. Want me to contact them?"

Benoit shook his head. "Not yet. We'll need the medical examiner to pronounce him dead first."

"He's already in route."

Benoit knelt beside the body and said, "Good work." as he analyzed the neck wound. The skin was torn; almost shredded. He expected to see two perfectly round puncture wounds, but instead he saw a chunk of flesh missing with veins and tendons hanging. "God, I need you here, Kat," Benoit said to himself. His phone buzzed. A reminder scrolled across his screen:

"Get Katalina from airport at 3 a.m."

The medical examiner arrived and met Benoit who was still studying the body. Benoit asked, "You ever see something like this before?"

The examiner studied the wound and said, "This is fresh. I'm calling the time of death at ten p.m." He rubbed the gaping neck. "This is definitely a human bite. Investigating is your job, but it seems to me someone from his 'vampire' circle decided to prove a point."

"What's that mean?" Benoit asked.

"The cause of death is hemorrhage as a result of his artery being severed. Somebody obviously bit his neck, acting like a vampire—" His fingers made air quotes. "—and pierced his jugular. You'll notice the pool of blood surrounding his body. He likely bled out in two minutes."

Benoit breathed a sigh of relief after hearing the medical examiner's theory of death. *The last thing I need is for the public to know there are legit vampires running around this city.*

"Thanks, I'll reach out to his next of kin and make a death notification," Benoit said.

The hair stood on his arms. The familiar sound of wings slapping the air made Benoit rub his forehead. He remembered his glimpse and instinctively looked up. The sky was no longer illuminated by the moon. Instead, clouds had drifted in and hid in the moonlight. He only saw darkness but couldn't help but to feel as if he was being watched.

Chapter Forty-Five

Viktor the Old

Katalina read over every note that was sprawled across her father's abandoned desk. The picture of her parents remained tucked tightly in her back pocket. She realized the old bookstore likely delivered its purpose. Katalina noticed the condensation escaping from her nose with each exhale. The temperature had dropped considerably.

The lighting in the bookstore had all but vanished—an indication that daylight was long gone, but she didn't need it. Much like a cat, Katalina could see in the dark. Her entire life she assumed that everyone else around her had poor eyesight, but recent revelations suggested she was gifted with superior senses.

Before exiting, she took one last glance at the plethora of ancient books that lined the walls. She ran her finger across the spine of each book as she walked by. Dust flared up with each touch. She came upon a book that had her partner's last name down the spine, BENOIT. She pulled the book out and opened it. It was written entirely in French, but she knew instantly that it was a book on witchcraft. Limited on time, she tucked the book in her bag and set off. She carefully snaked out of the boarded-up window and escaped into the frigid night.

The street was empty after dark. No signs of life threatened to bother her on her stroll back to the hotel. Streetlights illuminated the substandard roadway along the route. Katalina knew her destination was about five miles away but wasn't fearful of being alone. A loud guttural sound emanated from her stomach.

She stopped and rubbed her belly while looking all around her, double-checking to see if anyone was nearby who could have heard her stomach growl. Habit. She was all alone, and she knew it. Katalina knew she had four more vials of blood in her pocket. The thought of savory drops of blood drove her mad. All she could think about was dropping more blood on her tongue. *All you need is a little taste. That'll quench your thirst; besides we leave tomorrow*, she thought, *plenty more where that came from back home.*

Katalina never broke stride as she reached for another vial. Like a professional, she snapped the end off of a vial, threw her head back and emptied the contents of the pipette onto her tongue. She closed her eyes and savored the taste.

"Oh. My. God."

As she continued to walk, the road improved slightly. An old cement fence lined the roadway and encompassed a cemetery. Intrigued, Katalina dipped under the fence and marveled at the ancient tombstones that seemed to line the land for miles. The cemetery was empty. No people. The only sounds a normal human being would have heard was the wind cutting through the gravesites, but Katalina heard everything. She heard trees rustling in the distance. She heard a rodent scurrying but couldn't see it.

As she walked in total darkness, she came upon a mausoleum. Just outside the mausoleum stood a large statue carved in marble of a soldier on a horse wielding a sword. The artist depicted the soldier as muscular with a determined look, but something was peculiar about the statue. The facial features of the soldier held an uncanny resemblance to the phantom in her dreams. A chill raced down Katalina's spine as she tried to make the connection.

The plaque read: Viktor the Old. Valiant ruler of Kiev. Son of Rurik.

Katalina snapped a photo of the statue before continuing on her trek back to the hotel. She snaked through the cemetery and admired the numerous tombstones with dates back to the ninth century. Soon a fog crept onto the grounds, hovering just at ankle-level making the vacant grounds an eerie place to wander alone. She decided to ease her way back to the sidewalk that paralleled the road. The sound of rubber on the roadway humming from a distance behind, perked Katalina's ears up. Ahead, she could see the sky lit up from the lights on the busier road where her hotel was.

Two miles, Kat, she thought as she picked up pace.

The road noise grew louder and as it approached, Katalina knew it was a vehicle. A white van without windows came to a stop just ahead of Katalina. The side door slid open at the same time as the two rear doors. Two men simultaneously exited the van and approached Katalina with a determined pace. Each wore thick winter clothing that covered their faces, except for their eyes. She could see their eye lids and knew they were white males. The men looked as if they were walking through a smoke screen as each exhale produced a thick white condensation that engulfed them.

Katalina retrieved the silver butter knife from her inside jacket pocket. Neither of the men bolted in her direction with lightning speed; instead, they simply walked briskly. The first person reached for her, but she took quick steps backward.

The second produced a switchblade knife and said in Russian, "If you don't resist, we won't hurt you."

She kicked the closest assailant in the groin, dropping him to his knees. He let out a shriek as he clutched his crotch. The second assailant was swinging the knife wildly. The heavy coat restricted each swing of his arm. Katalina dodged each swipe with ease. The knifer was within two feet of Katalina; they were face-to-face. His right hand rose, clutching the switchblade. His breath smelled like vodka and cigarette smoke.

Katalina raised her left arm and blocked the assailant's right arm as it was plunging downward. She lost her butter knife upon contact. She quickly transitioned into a wristlock and the switchblade fell to the ground. A quick jerk snapped his right wrist. He let out a visceral scream that was interrupted by an elbow strike to the mouth. He fell to the ground clutching his mouth with his left hand while his right dangled helplessly by his side.

The first attacker had regained his composure and was behind Katalina. She was too preoccupied with the knifer to notice. She had done a quick priority assessment and wisely decided the edged weapon was a greater threat. Strong arms snatched her from behind and pinned her own against her torso.

She jumped and flailed her legs about, trying to break the bear hug grip that was squeezing the breath out of her. Whoever had her was strong and large enough to control her movements. Reverting to her martial arts training, Katalina plunged her head back and connected with the attacker's face. She heard a growl and felt her feet leaving the ground as she was flipped over his shoulders. She crashed into the grass but remained conscious. The initial impact took the wind out of her.

If she was injured, she didn't realize it. She surely didn't feel it. Katalina laid on her back looking up toward the sky. The giant of a man fell to his knees with his right fist raised above his head. As he fell forward, his fist came plowing down. Katalina moved her head to the side and the fist crashed into the grass beside her head. She heard bones crunching as the force of his punch backfired. He was strong though, he barely hesitated and cocked his arm back again, preparing for another blow.

Katalina was in a jiu jitsu position with the attacker between her legs; a position she'd trained in for countless hours. Her feet were planted on the ground on each side of the attacker with her knees bent as if in a sit-up position. His posture straightened as he prepared to deliver more blows. She grabbed the fork that was still in her jacket pocket and stabbed the attacker in his thigh. It had no effect.

Katalina knew at that moment that either the attacker wasn't a vampire, or the utensil wasn't real silver. His forward momentum continued, and he struck Katalina in the face. She suffered two blows as her head struck the ground after he punched her. She raised her hands in an attempt to block the barrage of punches that kept connecting. No pain was felt despite being hammered.

Perhaps it was from the cold weather numbing her face. She kept resisting and pulled the fork from his thigh, seeking any sort of weapon she could find. Another meaty fist smashed into her face. That time she saw black and heard ringing. She clutched the fork in her left hand and brought it to her face hoping to stab the attacker again but dropped it. The fork bounced off her face and onto the ground beside her.

She thrusted her hips upward in an attempt to hurl the assailant over her head. It threw him off balance and he had to brace himself with both hands by her head in order not to fall forward. Katalina licked her lips and tasted his blood giving her a boost of energy. He had mounted her and was straddling her stomach, kneeling over her waist.

Her hip thrust had hurled him forward. The goal was to send him flying over her head, but he caught himself. He was holding himself up while straddling her stomach. His face was inches from hers. The veins in his eyes bulged a bright red. His pupils were fully constricted as she listened to his thoughts.

"Feisty bitch. I'm gonna fuck you, alive or dead."

All pain left Katalina's body. Acute clarity enveloped her mind and her strength returned. With the would-be rapist still straddling her, she grew angry. Her emotions had temporarily left her as her body prepared to die. She went to an automatic defense zone as she fought for her life.

"Wait. Wait. Wait. Okay, I surrender. Please don't hurt me!" she begged. "I'll do whatever you want me to. Just stop hitting me."

The attacker briefly paused which is all that she wanted. Katalina reached her arms above her head and pinned his right arm. At the same time, she launched her hips as high as she could, sending the attacker forward.

As he fell forward, she jerked his trapped arm toward her body, causing him to roll forward onto his shoulder. The attacker was sent tumbling. His heavy body crashed into the ground. With lightning speed, Katalina was on top of the attacker. She delivered punch after punch to his face. His nose exploded like a watermelon, painting Katalina's face with his blood. She didn't skip a beat and continued striking him until his body went limp.

She stood and licked her lips again, consuming his vile blood and grew angrier. She stepped back and took a running stride before delivering a forceful kick to his groin. The kick should have sent his genitals inside of his body, but he didn't even flinch.

She kicked again and again ensuring his manhood was rendered permanently useless. After regaining her composure, she remembered the knife wielding suspect and scanned the area. He wasn't on the ground anymore. He had crawled into the driver's seat of the van.

"Oh, no you don't!" Katalina screamed as she broke into a full sprint toward him.

When she reached the van, he was sitting in the driver's seat looking pitiful as his right arm hung like a limp noodle. The van had a manual transmission, and his broken arm wouldn't even function enough to operate the stick shift. Katalina grabbed him by his ear and dragged him into the street, screaming, "You like to rape girls? You like to take advantage of women? Huh? Answer me!" With each scream, spit flew from her lips. Her eyes were filled with tears of anger as she shouted.

Katalina's tirade was interrupted by whimpering. One armed Willy was petrified and wasn't making any sounds. Sasquatch was lifeless with a concave bloody face.

"What the fuck is that?" she screamed.

With a hand full of ear, Katalina pulled the lone rapist toward the rear of the van.

"Open it!" she shouted at him.

The sound of her voice startled him as he flinched. The doors opened displaying two pet cages, each with an adolescent girl inside. One girl had duct tape fastened across her mouth with her hands bound behind her back. She wore a white nightgown that was stained with blood. The second girl had a strip of duct tape hanging from her cheek; her wrists also bound behind her back.

In Russian, Katalina said, "Everything is going to be okay. Help is on the way." She shut the van door and peered down at the lone survivor. "Did you rape her?"

His eyes grew large. He instinctively shook his head.

"Liar!" she screamed. She aggressively patted his pockets down. "Where's your phone?"

With his good arm, he grabbed his phone. It shook violently in his hand.

"Call the police," Katalina directed.

He punched some numbers on the phone. Katalina heard it ringing as she stood next to him. She heard a dispatcher answer the phone and she knew he had actually called the police. Katalina stared at him with threatening eyes. She didn't have to say a word.

He spoke into the phone. "There are two girls in a van. They were abducted."

The dispatcher asked a multitude of questions and he answered them. Katalina heard sirens in the distance and smiled. She kicked the lone rapist in his shin and snapped his ankle. He fell to the ground screaming.

Katalina stood over him and said, "You're lucky I didn't kill you."

Satisfied he wouldn't be able to run away, she slunk back into the darkness of the cemetery to observe the arrest from a distance. A police vehicle arrived, and two uniformed officers exited. The first looked at the man lying on the ground and laughed. The second opened the van and saw the two kids. The officer who discovered the girls retrieved his gun and pointed it at the attacker on the street.

He was screaming, "You piece of shit!"

The other officer interrupted, "Wait, Tovarisch. He will receive a much worse punishment in prison."

Katalina patted her jacket pocket in search for another vial. She pulled pieces of broken glass from her inner pocket that were covered in blood.

"Shit!" she screamed.

She kept digging and pulled another vial out; still intact and popped the tip off. Tiny droplets of blood drizzled her tongue as her eyelids closed in ecstasy. After the Russian police departed, Katalina made her way back to her hotel.

As she approached, she looked at her reflection in the shiny polished door frame and expected to see a prized fighter's swollen face after a twelve-round match. Surprisingly, she looked just as pretty as when she left hours earlier.

She drew a bath and waited for the tub to fill as she thought to herself, *If it isn't fucking vampires, it's child rapists.*

Chapter Forty-Six

Unfinished Business

"What's up, fuck stick? Miss me?" Katalina punched Benoit in his shoulder as he met her at the luggage return.

"Shoot, It's been nice not having to carry your extra weight around," Benoit answered.

"Screw you, ass! You know you missed being berated daily."

Benoit smiled and nodded. "I did actually. So, what are you now? A gypsy? Who goes roaming around Europe like a freaking vagabond anyway?"

"A vampire slayer." Katalina nodded, her face scrunched as if rock music was playing in the background. "That's who."

"Did you come across any vampires there?"

"No. But I did almost get abducted."

"For real? Do tell."

"Don't worry, Duce. I'm fine."

Benoit looked at Katalina with suspicious eyes. "Do I even want to know what happened to them?"

"Let's just say that neither will ever touch another female again."

"You taught them a lesson I presume?"

"You could say that. A rather painful one."

"At least they lived," Benoit said.

Katalina shrugged her shoulders and grunted, "Well…"

"Kat! You're a freaking cop! You can't! Please tell me you're not on a worldwide wanted bulletin?"

"Duce, I'm just joking. Europe was fine. I found my dad's old bookstore and learned all kinds of cool shit. I'll tell you all about it on the ride home."

"Have I ever told you that you have a potty mouth?" Benoit asked.

Katalina laughed out loud. "A potty mouth? The fact that a grown man, who doesn't have children mind you, uses the word potty, fucking baffles me, Duce! What was that you were saying? Oh, yes, my selection of words. Go on?"

Benoit pouted his lips. His brow hung over his eyes. "You know, that's not very lady-like. That's all I'm saying."

Katalina's face lit up as if she had an epiphany. "Duce, tell me, how many 'ladies' do you know who investigate homicides? Oh, or how many slay fucking vampires?" Katalina was yelling by that point.

"God, I've missed you!" Benoit laughed.

"Aww, Duce." She slapped his shoulder. "I've missed you too! Hey, can you stop at the convenience store by my apartment. I need some caffeine. Oh, I almost forgot! I brought you something." She dug around in her backpack and produced the book with Benoit's name across the spine. "I found this gem in my father's bookstore. It's written in French, but it's a book on witchcraft!"

Benoit's face lit up. "I don't know what to say, Kat. I don't speak French, so it'll take me some time to decipher what it says, but thanks!"

Katalina smiled and in a botched attempt at an Italian accent, she said, "I know a girl." The two laughed at the terrible accent. "What did I miss while away?"

"Same old shit. Former murder capital of the world. You know. Natural selection," Benoit joked.

Katalina looked at Benoit as if there was a story to follow. "What does that mean? English, Duce."

"Would you believe I only worked one homicide while you were gone?"

"Oh? Don't tell me it was a staged suicide?"

"Haha, nope. I think those are long gone, thanks to you. It was rather peculiar though. Poor guy was bitten. On the neck."

"Seriously? By a vampire?"

Benoit shrugged. "I'm not sure. It was an ugly bite; it looked like a wild animal attack, but it was along his jugular. Medical examiner was oblivious; claimed it was a prank gone wrong. He chalked it up to a human pretending to be a vampire."

"But you know better?" Katalina asked with suspicion.

Benoit nodded. The two exchanged a silent understanding.

The store was on the same block as her apartment building. It was a twenty-four-hour joint that never closed; not even on major holidays. Benoit waited in his vehicle while Katalina entered the store. She went straight to the cooler and grabbed a cold drink. She reached for something inside her pocket and fiddled with it in her fingers before pouring something in her mouth.

Katalina sat in the passenger seat glowing with excitement. "Man, it feels good to be home!"

A pressurized release of carbonation spewed as she twisted the cap off her diet Coke and tilted it upward. Benoit drove across a parking lot and parked at Katalina's apartment complex. He slid the shifter in park and pressed the trunk release button. Katalina exited with her backpack in one hand and her diet soda in the other. He met her at his trunk and reached for her luggage.

"I got this, Duce," she barked.

Benoit looked her up and down and said, "You have a third hand I don't know about?"

Katalina wanted to contest, but realized he was right.

"Look, it's not like I'm opening your car door or anything," Benoit said as he pulled her suitcase out.

Katalina sniffed a deep breath in and looked at Benoit. "Do you smell that?" she asked. "It smells like ass and armpits."

Benoit shook his head. "I don't smell anything." He observed Katalina rub her stomach; her face grimaced. "You okay, Kat? That Diet Coke not agreeing with you?"

"I'll be fine."

***

Viktor entered the empty lobby just after 4 a.m. and scanned the room. On one side there were mailboxes spanning the entire wall. On the opposite wall were two elevators and a bench along with two small trash cans. The elevators did not have buttons; instead, there was a card scanner.

"Hey, buddy, can I help you?" a stranger asked.

Viktor looked at him and said, "I'm looking for a friend. I believe she lives here." He had a thick Russian accent. He saw the stranger's face change; his eyes squinted, and his head shook.

"You should go. Only those with an access card can enter the elevators," the stranger reached for his phone and began punching numbers on it. "I'm calling security."

"No need," Viktor said as he launched toward the unsuspecting man.

In a single snatch, the stranger's head snapped forward; Viktor's hand clutched his throat. His head fell like a bowling ball rolling off a table. Viktor pulled the limp body close to his and sunk his teeth into the dead man's neck before discarding the body in the corner. He heard a vehicle pull into the parking lot followed by two voices, so he decided to take a seat on one of the benches near the elevator. His face stretched with a smile as the doors slid open.

First the object of his pursuit; a redheaded spitting image of Ivanka and Erik entered. Immediately behind her was the same brown man who he had seen from atop the building. The same man who had bitten him so many years before, waltzed in with a smile across his face. The girl's face was twisted with disgust the instant she caught a glimpse of him. The moment their eyes met, she reached for her waist. Her eyes darted to the body slumped on the floor, then back to his.

"Old friend," Viktor said, "do you remember me?"

Benoit looked at Katalina then back at Viktor. He placed his hand over his chest. "Who? Me? I don't believe we've ever met. Have I arrested you before?"

Viktor laughed. "It's been over a thousand years. I am sure you've turned hundreds if not thousands since then. I understand if you've forgotten, but I haven't."

Benoit's eyes grew large.

Katalina interrupted, "Duce, stand behind me." She cracked each knuckle on both hands. "This is going to get ugly." Her eyes never left Viktor's.

"You've been a pain in my ass, Katalina. I'm going to enjoy killing you, just like I did your dad."

Fire boiled Katalina's blood. "You're the one who's been invading my dreams," she said.

Viktor smirked and said, "I wonder if you'll die as easily as your father did? He was sharp. He fled with one of his vampires who resembled your mother. I'll admit, he fooled me. I thought I killed both of your parents." Viktor smiled as he shook his head. "I digress. I caught them at the docks. He didn't even resist. Instead, he just stood there like an obedient little puppy as I tore his head off. The little redhead pretending to be your mother also met the same fate." Viktor paused and basked in his superiority, searching Katalina's face for weakness. "Then I burned them both."

"I know who you are, *Viktor the Old*," Katalina growled, "and I think it's time you got sent home."

"You've done your homework, I see," Viktor said as he nodded then looked past her at Benoit. "Don't worry old friend. You can stop pretending now, but I must kill her. I am surprised she has not tried to kill you. She has already killed five of us. She's a feisty one."

Benoit closed his eyes and mumbled. His hands rose in front of his face; his body swayed back and forth before Viktor.

A piercing battle cry burst through Katalina's lips. Her eyes watered and her feet trembled as she sprinted toward Viktor. He smiled and planted his feet firmly on the floor with his arms covering his face like a boxer. Blow after blow, Katalina delivered punches in a perfect cadence. Each hit was blocked with precision.

Her left arm swung widely; her fist, fast approaching Viktor's right ear, but he lifted his right arm, bent at the elbow. His hand behind his own head. A thousand years of barbaric battling, poised Viktor for an epic battle. Her fist smashed against his arm. Immediately, she reloaded and launched an uppercut with her right hand, but Viktor side-stepped, sending her fist flying wildly into the air.

Viktor smiled, secretly impressed with Katalina's fighting skills.

She stepped forward and swung her left arm again. Her fist tucked against her chest as her pointed elbow cut through the air and struck Viktor beneath his right eye. The impact sounded like a roast falling off of a counter and slapping the floor. She was relentless. No sooner than she connected her elbow to Viktor's eye, she stepped forward. Viktor paused for a second, caught by surprise with her elbow-strike. Katalina rocketed her right knee upward and struck Viktor in his groin. She screamed like a powerlifter pumping out her heaviest rep as her knee drove into Viktor's pelvis. He let out a roar. His eyes burned with hatred.

Viktor grabbed Katalina and threw her like a rag doll as if she was weightless. She flew across the lobby and slammed against the mounted mailboxes. Upon impacting the wall, she grunted and exhaled all the air in her lungs. Viktor wasted no time and advanced on her. He picked her up by her red hair and exposed his fangs. A hissing sound blew through his teeth along with tendrils of saliva.

Katalina regained her composure. Her feet dangled in the air. Pain radiated from her throat as Viktor's grip tightened. While Viktor was mid-hiss, he released Katalina and fell to his knees, releasing Katalina's neck. Behind Viktor, Benoit continued his chant; his fingers pointed toward Viktor.

Katalina quickly patted each of her pockets, searching for any type of weapon to leverage Viktor's strength. Instead, she leapt behind Viktor and grabbed his head. Her arms tightened around his neck as she prepared to twist his head off like a diet Coke cap, but Viktor stood with Katalina gripping his back like a monkey. He reached behind him and grabbed another fistful of hair while simultaneously leaning forward, launching Katalina into the air, then crashing into the floor on her back. The impact cracked the ceramic tile beneath her.

Viktor, breathing heavily, turned to Benoit and said, "The resemblance is uncanny. You had me fooled, but you're no vampire. You're the witch that Dmitri spoke of who cast a weak spell!"

Another unsuspecting stranger entered the lobby and froze with confusion. The first body still lay slowly stiffening in his own blood as rigor set in. Katalina was also sprawled out but slowly moving about. The new stranger, a female, covered her screams with both hands over her mouth. Her eyes almost jumped from their sockets.

Viktor proudly announced, "Wrong place. Wrong time." and sped behind the girl. He held her head and cocked it slightly, exposing a juicy carotid artery. "Do you hear that?" he asked. "Her heart is about to explode. It's pumping ever-so-fast. Just look at her veins."

Benoit stopped his chanting and turned his attention to Viktor. "Stop! Don't hurt her, please! She's got nothing to do with this."

"Would you look at this? A regular hero. Since when do witches want to help humans? Since when do witches do anything good?" Viktor tore into the young girl's neck.

As his incisors pierced her bulging jugular vein, blood spewed and painted his face and Benoit's face. Instantly, the girl's knees buckled, and her eyes turned gray as her life faded away. Viktor wiped his mouth with the back of his hand and flung excess blood on the floor as his hand fell toward the ground, much like shaking water from wet hands.

He looked at Benoit. "Tell your friend goodbye. You're just a victim of coincidence—collateral damage."

Benoit pleaded, "Why did you have to kill her? She was innocent!"

Viktor laughed. "Nobody's innocent! The longer this drags on, the more blood will pour. The next person who enters will die just like she did. Just like you both will."

Benoit closed his eyes again; arms extended toward Viktor. His concentration was deliberate. His focus laser sharp as he mumbled. Shadows shimmered with each pulsating flash of light. A sharp crack startled Viktor as light bulbs burst in several different fixtures. He smiled at Benoit and shook his head. A deep laugh grumbled from Viktor's gut.

He took two steps toward Benoit and said, "I've always wanted to taste witch blood." then dove into him. Viktor's teeth sunk into Benoit's neck.

Benoit screamed; his chant failed; his body crumpled to the floor, with blood spewing everywhere.

Viktor stood and looked at Katalina who by now was sitting upright with her back against the wall and met his gaze. He noticed her attention was stolen. Katalina's eyes widened; her head tilted slightly to look beyond Viktor.

Viktor turned and took two steps backward. His eyes now about to burst from their sockets. His heart raced, breathing now rapid. A towering man entered the lobby. His skin was dark brown; almost black and was paper-thin. The veins in his arms appeared to be on the outside of his skin and throbbed. He looked down at Viktor as he stepped through the entrance. Behind him, a Native-American man entered. Red and white painted lines snaked across his face. His skin was the color of chestnuts.

Numerous scars tattered his chest; some long, some short. His eyes locked onto Viktor's eyes as he entered and stepped to the other side of the entrance. Both men stood like guards; erect and angry. Finally, a third person entered; a female with high cheekbones and jet-black hair. The handle of a samurai sword extended above her shoulders; her fists clenched.

"Janga, Atticus, Virole, why are you here?" Viktor asked, his voice trembling.

Atticus, the Native American responded, "I could ask you the same. Are you lost?"

Viktor's normally smooth tone was shaken. His chest rose and fell in rapid succession. "I... I was—"

Atticus interrupted him, "Did you seek approval to leave your territory?"

"Markus knows. Yes." Viktor's head nodded as he spoke.

"That's not how it works, Viktor. Did you get permission from Rainey? After all, you're in her territory."

Viktor's eyes darted across the three executioners; all once close allies who shared the same role in their respective territories. "A simple misunderstanding, Atticus, that's all." Viktor's hands rose in defeat.

"I do recall an American vampire defecting to Europe without seeking Markus' permission. Several actually, and I also know what happened to each of them. If I remember correctly, you dispatched each of them. Tell me, Viktor, did you allow them an opportunity to plead their case?"

"I did! Each one explained their story to me!"

"Did any of them live?"

Viktor fell silent. He searched reactions on each of the three faces who towered before him. None faltered; each expressionless.

"Viktor," Atticus called. "You also have to answer for the vampires you killed here in America. Two high crimes by the convocation's account."

Viktor stared at Atticus with a confused look. "I was attacked. I was simply defending myself."

"Your mere presence here was unsanctioned. Then, you killed thirty-seven vampires at Sylvain's, and then burned the place to the ground, Viktor!"

Katalina watched as the ancient enforcers exchanged sarcastic witty banter back and forth like long lost friends. She hated Viktor but found herself angry with each glance at each of the other three. Janga had vicious eyes that begged to kill. His jaw muscles extended like a set of wings. His nose, broad with flaring nostrils. Janga's skin appeared to have a silky sheen to it. He stood there looking angry at the world; salivating to devour anything in his path. Although furious at the presence of vampires, Katalina's trepidation was beginning to surface. She took note of her hand shaking and looked up to see if anyone else noticed.

Virole shot a smile at Katalina accompanied by a wink.

Katalina studied the Native American who Viktor called Atticus. Suddenly, everything around her faded as her focus sharpened on his face. Like an old flickering film, glimpses of the man fleeing behind the apartment scrolled through her mind, followed by the wanted person's picture from the jungle homicide. Finally, her eyes enlarged as she understood. The Native American before her was the same man who fled behind the chief's house. The same phantom that eluded her on three previous occasions.

Soon, the sounds of the world returned. Her epiphany had drifted, and anger returned as the sound of Viktor's voice brought her back to a place of revenge.

Katalina rolled onto her knees and crawled to Benoit on the floor beside her. She held his head in her arms and shook her head. D*on't you worry, Duce, I'll make him pay for this*, she thought to herself. His neck was swollen and bloody as she wiped the excess off to get a better view of his wound. Two perfectly round puncture wounds gaped beneath his jawbone; her hands fully covered in crimson. She stood behind Viktor, poised to destroy the monster who killed her father. She had a score to settle.

She knew it.

He knew it.

When she stood erect, Viktor and Atticus stopped speaking. Viktor turned to face her and spoke loudly, "My friends, she's a Dhampir. That's why I'm here. To kill her. You should be praising me for bringing this kind of threat to your attention!" He smirked at Katalina; pompous and arrogant as if he had just won an argument.

Katalina extended her hand to Viktor; her middle finger extended toward the sky and winked back at him then slid her tongue up the underside of it. Benoit's blood gathered on her tongue briefly before absorbing in her body.

Immediately she heard Viktor's thoughts for the first time, "I'll snap her neck before they even have a chance to react."

She wasted no time and lunged at him, feeling invincible. Even if she died while attacking Viktor, as long as he died with her, she would have avenged her father's murder. As Katalina advanced on Viktor, she stared into his dark eyes. Time seemed to have slowed down. She saw his eyes widen. Surprise? Fear? Excitement? She did not care.

They collided like two freight trains. Grunts and screams poured from their mouths as they maneuvered to secure the superior position. Viktor was far stronger than Katalina, but he was ignorant to her modern combat tactical training.

Viktor grabbed Katalina by her shoulders and picked her up into the air. He rotated her body and slammed her onto the ground. The impact jolted her to the brink of unconsciousness. She blinked a couple of times. Upon focusing, Viktor stood towering over her looking down. He had the positional advantage. Katalina laid in a defeated posture with nowhere to go. An ancient vampire stood over her marveling in his feat.

He looked over at his three friends and said, "Thank you for letting this happen." and closed his eyes as if he knew he was about to die. Viktor fell to his knees, almost crushing Katalina as he sat on her torso. He grabbed her two wrists and pinned them to the ground above her head. His strength threatened to shatter her wrists.

He felt like a thousand pounds crushing her as she struggled to breathe. "Tell your father I said hello," Viktor roared. His fangs fully extended.

Katalina was helpless. Despite her superhuman strength, she couldn't budge from beneath Viktor. She spat in his face in a last deliverance of defiance before everything went black.

Chapter Forty-Seven

The Convocation

The grand elder of each territory took their assigned seat at the table for their annual meeting. Markus sat with his diplomat, Amelia, standing behind him. Across from Markus sat Rainey. Cyrus stood behind her. Beside Markus, Takeshi sat with Jiang standing behind her and on his other side sat Adisa with Nini flanking him. Each represented a territory that encompassed several countries on a continent: Markus of Europe, Rainey of America, Takeshi of Asia, and Adisa of Africa.

Rainey spoke first, "My friends, it is no secret that I don't allow vampires to kill humans in my territory unless said humans have committed some sort of atrocity. This has served me well for centuries. As you all know, I don't allow humans to be turned into vampires without just cause either."

Markus interrupted, "But Rainey, if you don't allow your kind to kill humans, how does our species survive in America?"

Rainey squinted her eyes at the disrespect. "Markus, have you ever wondered why I'm more powerful than you are? Why the American vampires are superior to European vampires?" She arched a single eyebrow.

Without giving Markus a chance to answer, she continued, "I'll tell you. You see, the more we restrict our kind, the more power we maintain. Each time a vampire infects a human, our life force is diminished slightly."

Markus' face crinkled. "I've never heard of such a thing." He looked at Takeshi who nodded, then at Adisa who also nodded. "Do you practice the same restraint?"

Takeshi and Adisa nodded again.

"That's preposterous!"

"Markus, there is a delicate balance in my territory. A sort of natural selection, if you will. We only feed on those damned by society."

"They're all damned!" Markus laughed.

"Fellow elders," Rainey's voice was matter of fact, "Our first order of business involves several of my vampires being killed recently." She scanned the table and took note of Adisa's shock. Takeshi's head rocked back; eyebrows raised. When she got to Markus, he appeared bored. She continued, "I wondered if any of you knew who could be responsible or why?"

Markus' face was defiant. "Perhaps if you'd allow your kind to do as they please, something like that wouldn't have happened?"

"The second order of business involves the production of D-blood being distributed. I learned that several of my vampires who died, did so while under the influence of Dhampir blood."

Takeshi spoke, "How is that possible? No Dhampirs should be permitted to live. Are you sure?"

Rainey nodded her head. "I'm afraid so. Markus, perhaps you could enlighten us?"

***

Markus drifted to another place. He stared off into the distance as if dreaming. His lips parted in awe as glimpses burned his eyes. He saw Atticus, Virole, and Janga's faces converging, blood bursting in the air, then dark.

His eyes blinked rapidly as if trying to focus before he refocused on the convocation. His head feverishly swung from side to side hoping to gain intelligence from his co-elders seated before him. Eyes wide, breathing on the verge of hyperventilation, and his hands shook.

***

"Welcome back, Markus. I presume you had a vision. Care to share?" Rainey asked.

Markus glared at Rainey, then Adisa, and finally at Takeshi. "How could you?" he shouted, "You will pay for this!" Markus stood from his seat, waving his trembling hand, his mouth spewing saliva.

The three elders stood before Markus as Rainey spoke, "Markus, you are hereby charged with violating the convocation's high crime laws. The first of which is allowing a Dhampir to live. The second is distributing Dhampir blood to other vampires, and the third is allowing your enforcer to leave your territory without securing permission. How do you plead?"

"What is this?" he cried, searching the faces of his fellow elders. "I will come for each of you, one by one. I will slaughter your—"

Markus froze in mid-sentence as he faced the elders before him. A large wooden stake burst through his chest, tearing through his shirt. His hands instinctively clutched the weapon of destruction as Amelia whispered in his ear from behind.

"I'm sorry, old friend."

Markus fell to his knees and immediately shrunk. His perfect skin wrinkled. His body shriveled and collapsed.

Rainey gave Amelia a nod and spoke, "Amelia, I hereby name you as the grand elder of Europe. You are now charged with upholding the convocation's laws and are responsible for the actions of your vampires. Ignorance is no exception. You are to report here, annually, to convene with your fellow elders."

Amelia knelt before the troika, her head bowing to the floor, "I graciously accept, and will make each of you proud."

Rainey said, "You now must appoint a diplomat and an enforcer. Do so with caution and wisdom. I expect the D-blood production will cease?"

Amelia nodded. "At once."

Chapter Forty-Eight

Stay With Me

Katalina opened her eyes and scanned her surroundings. Benoit was laying on the ground, barely alive. His eyelids fought the urge to close with every fleeting second. Thick coagulated blood caked his neck, but he was alive. Beside her, the remnants of Viktor lay scattered across the floor. His head severed from his body, was missing. Both of his arms were ripped from his trunk that was shriveled before her.

Katalina gently cradled Benoit. "We've got to get you some help, Duce." She hoisted him to his feet and walked him outside to his car.

"How much time do we have?" Katalina asked.

"These are just flesh wounds. Luckily he didn't puncture any arteries."

"No, Duce. How much time until you turn into a full-fledged vampire?" Katalina opened Benoit's car door and eased him into the front passenger seat, then buckled his seatbelt. She walked around to the driver's side and cranked his car. "Stay with me, Duce."

Benoit moaned and said, "Kat, I vant to drink your blood." Then he laughed in a terrible Germanic accent. "Kat, seriously, I'm fine. I do think it's bullshit that you chose to ruin *my* upholstery though. I mean, you legitimately walked past your Tahoe to get to my car."

"Duce, no offense, but your car is a piece of shit."

Benoit nodded. "It is kinda crappy. All joking aside, I'm fine. Just drive me home. I have some ointment that will fix these wounds right up. Hey, Kat, who were those other three people in the lobby?"

"I have an idea. I'll tell you all about it when you're all healed up. They looked like something straight out of a movie though. Did you see that one black guy? He looked like a giant Mandingo warrior! And the Indian? What the hell?"

"Whoever they were, they didn't seem to care about us."

"Obviously!" Katalina said.

"You know, Kat, I'm thinking about moving to Alaska."

"What the fuck? It's freezing there. Why in the world would you want to do that?"

"It's daylight around the clock. You know what that means, right?"

Katalina nodded. Her right eyebrow arched, "That's fucking genius, Duce, but that only happens at certain times, I thought. Plus, you hate the cold!"

"I know, but I like my life more, soooo…"

"No way, Duce. We have some serious vampire ass to kick!" Her eyes trailed from his blood-soaked pants to his wounds. "You're still with me, right?"

Benoit shook his head with a shit-eating grin and gave Katalina a thumbs up. "Who else is going to watch your six?"

"You think that special position is still available? Maybe we could do it together? Like a vampire slaying squad."

Benoit shook his head again, "No, Kat. That ship has sailed. In fact, the chief was kind of pissed that you turned it down. Besides, how would that look? 'Hey chief, Andrews and I want to start up a new division that kills vampires.' Yeah, we would get sent straight to the psychiatrist."

THANK YOU TO THE READERS

Thank you so much for reading Scarlet Day Walker, I hope you enjoyed the story. If you did, I invite you to take a few moments of your time to leave a review. As an independent author, exposure is everything, and positive reviews help a great deal. I much appreciate your support should you choose to do so.

I love interacting with readers. Please feel free to email me at info@christophergalvez.com. I'd love to thank you personally. I am grateful for all your support, and I hope you will share the books with your friends, family, book clubs and anyone else who you think might also enjoy it.

Please join my mailing list for free giveaways and to be notified of new releases before anyone else. www.christophergalvez.com. I assure you, no spam mails will be sent as a result. Thank you again.